DEEP
WATER
DEATH

by
Glynn Marsh Alam

MEMENTO MORI MYSTERIES

Memento Mori Mysteries
Published by
Avocet Press Inc
19 Paul Court
Pearl River, NY 10965
http://www.avocetpress.com
mysteries@avocetpress.com

AVOCET PRESS

Library of Congress Cataloging-in-Publication Data
Alam, Glynn Marsh, 1943-
Deep water death / Glynn Marsh Alam.— 1st ed.
p. cm.
ISBN 0-9705049-1-8
1. Women detectives—Florida—Tallahassee Region—Fiction. 2. Tallahassee Region (Fla.)—Fiction. 3. Women divers—Fiction. 4. Scuba diving—Fiction. I. Title.
PS3551.L213 D44 2001
813'.54—dc21
2001002639

Cover Photographs:
  Cave Diving - copyright © 1999 Ken McDonald and Pat Kennedy
  House - copyright © 1999 Glynn Marsh Alam
  Author - copyright © 1999 Melodie Earickson

Printed in the USA
First Edition

To Dianne Marsh Clark

A late evening rain patters against the picture window, but the sounds are uneven, like some rain god spitting against the glass, then gathering momentum and spitting again. When the spatters stop altogether, the silence wakes me and I realize there has been no rain at all. On a humid night, the haze dances among the cypress knees. Swamp fauna arise in warm wetness. Moths and night gnats aim for light, beating their minute bodies against window glass that blocks them from fiery ruin. That's when frogs take over the food chain. Tiny, black-green pieces of jellied flesh with sucker feet fly to the window, hitting it like rubber darts, then pulling free and hopping to the next insect. Had I a magnifying glass, I would surely see a sticky tongue dart and grab.

I live in this swamp, alongside the frogs and their more lethal neighbors of the reptilian world. We get along with the help of instinct, a bit of knowledge, and a large dose of fear. But Darwin was right. The fittest survive here. And cunning is decidedly an advantage in ultimate survival.

CHAPTER ONE

Funny how creatures grow dead quiet when someone screams in the forest. Heeding the approach of the Angel of Death, their silence serves them like the blood of the first-born over the doorway. I am one of the swamp creatures. I know because I stopped in my tracks, dead still and silent as a tomb, just like the others. I heard the screams, a wrenching struggle to deal with pain, a long stretch of high-pitched sound, then silence, followed by shorter screeches. I heard them in the distance, ahead of me through the dense cypress growth across one end of Lake Palmetto. The sound came from one of my own species. I didn't stay still for long.

I thought I knew all who lived inside my swamp. My cottage, renovated from a falling-down family home, gave me as much solace and protection as did the anhinga bird's aerie atop a dead cypress tree. Right now, that bird had taken to the air in alarm. I wasn't in my sanctuary, either. I stood in a heavy swamp area next to a river-lake formed from an offshoot of Palmetto Springs, where underwater caverns run so deep and winding no one has ever discovered where they came from or where they went.

Until now. With my former lover, Harry MacAllister, I was attempting to map these offshoot spring caves. I had joined him when I couldn't face returning to teaching college classes in Tallahassee. We had finished the area on state-owned land. Now we had to have permission from private land owners to set up diving equipment and mapping camps along their shores. My search for an operating site had taken me deep into the swamp that day, and the screaming guided me to one stretch of water we wanted to map.

"Stop!" The voice rose to decibel heights. As I approached a wood-frame cabin, muffled voices in the background joined the scream.

"Watch her," was all I could make out.

In the distance, a muscular, male figure in a boat rowed around the river bend.

I stood outside a window that had no screen. The front porch and roof sagged in parallel dips. Two frayed reed chairs sat like aging sentinels on the gray boards. Molded black wicker had rotted through the seats. I hesitated to go inside. The porch might not hold my weight. When I heard the last cry, one that began at top pitch and suddenly lowered to a choking baritone, I risked the rotting boards.

There was no front door, not even rusted hinges. This was a cabin used years ago, probably by some swamp hermit who bathed in the same water where he fished for his supper. Unfit for human inhabitants now, it would house colonies of wasps on the ceilings and swamp spiders in the floor corners. I followed the voices, the muffled ones. The screaming had stopped.

"She's quiet at last." The voice was female and elderly.

"And this one..." A similar voice drifted away.

This was a shotgun house, one where you could stand at the front door, look directly down the hall and out the back door. Rooms ran along either side. I followed the voices to a middle room on the right. The door here was missing, too. As soon as I

7

stepped under its jamb, the smell of warm blood flooded my nostrils, and I felt my stomach leap. Backing out, I took a whiff of fresh air, then turned around and faced two women. Dressed in flower-print house dresses with blood-splashed plastic aprons, they busied themselves at the far wall. On a rusted iron bedstead, double size, lay a single dingy and torn mattress—and a woman drenched in sweat. She wore no clothes, but clasped a stained towel between her legs.

"What the hell?" I said, and the two aproned women, startled, turned toward me.

"You can't come in here," said one and rushed me, hands outstretched with palms open. "This is a private place."

"I heard someone screaming. What happened in here?"

The other woman stared like a frightened doe in headlights at me a moment, then turned her back. "Leave her, Sadie."

Sadie was the one coming toward me I presumed. She stopped, dropped her arms to her sides, turned around and picked up bloody rags from the floor.

"Who is she?" I pointed to the woman on the bed, who opened her eyes, looked my way, then shut them again.

The second woman stopped. Her cropped gray hair lay in humid tendrils around her hawk-nosed face. She turned her eyes upward towards me and I had the sudden thought of Medusa about to turn me to stone. "She just gave birth. That was the screaming you heard. It's all over now."

"Well, shouldn't I call someone? I mean she doesn't look so good." I reached for the cellular phone in my backpack.

"Don't think she wants any help, other than us," said the woman.

Sadie glanced at me when she took hold of some towels, pressed them into a pan of bloody water and headed for a window. One hand grabbed the rags as she leaned the pan on the sill. She tossed the water on the ground outside with the other hand. She wiped the pan with one of the bloody rags, then bundled them all together. She looked a lot like her companion, but meeker. When she finished with the rags, she folded and unfolded her hands, finally removing the plastic apron. Her eyes darted from me to the other woman.

"Where's the baby?" I moved further into the room and pretended to search the corners. The only other piece of furniture was a folding plastic beach chair. It looked new; I assumed one of the women brought it. Upturned crates served as a table.

Both women stood still. The Medusa woman turned round to face me. Her large face sat neckless on heavy shoulders. She had about her a grayness that matched the gray cabin down to its aged boards. She cradled a bundle of white cloths in one arm.

"Who are you?" she demanded, adjusting the top of the cloth bundle. Her frightened stare belied the snake woman image.

"Luanne Fogarty. And you?"

"What is your business here?"

"I'm a diver and I need to locate the owner of this place." I looked around, realizing no owner had lived in this house for years. "What is your business here?" I refused to back down.

"Midwife. She," the woman nodded toward the bed, "called me when she felt the kid coming. I birth lots of babies in these parts." She walked to the bed, and with one hand removed the bloody towel from between the woman's legs, and tossed it onto the pile in the pan. She nodded toward Sadie who handed over a clean cloth; her companion tucked it between the woman's legs. Blood soaked through and saturated the mattress.

"That woman is hemorrhaging. I'm not going to let her die here." I pulled off my backpack, jerked out the phone, and dialed 911. The women suddenly burst into energy; Sadie grabbed the bloody cloths, the pan and the chair, and ran for the back door. The bundle in the other woman's arm whimpered slightly as she held it close to her chest and hurried after her partner.

"Wait!" I yelled after them. "Who is this woman?"

"Theresa Grassfield," said the Medusa who didn't look back.

I watched them make quick time through mud and marsh grass. They headed for a turn in the river where a thicket of oaks bent toward the water. The boat must have waited for them there, and I started to run after them, maybe to grab the child, when I heard a pitiful groan from inside the cabin.

I returned to Theresa.

"Please," she said, and reached out a hand across the bed. She held it in the air a few seconds, then let it drop to the bloody mattress. She began to rock her head back and forth, her eyes closed. I could tell from the sweat pouring off her face that she was feverish. The cloth between her legs neared the solid red state. If the paramedics didn't make it into the swamp in time, she would bleed to death.

"Why would they do this and run?" I said to myself. But I had no time to think about them now. I needed to stop the bleeding, and since it was internal, I didn't know how I was going to do that. The women left no other rags or towels in the room, and I saw no sign of Theresa's clothes. I stepped into the open-ended hall, then darted in and out of the other rooms. The place was a ghost house, nothing remaining from its occupants but the crude boards that defied swamp humidity. The open windows assured the place of a breeze every afternoon; there was little dust. In its place, mildew, sometimes solid black, grew around the base boards.

10

The only thing to do was to go back and hold the woman's hand. If she died, at least she wouldn't be alone. Taking a look out the window, I thought I heard a scream from around the bend in the river, but decided it must have been the boat siren coming across the lake. I patted Theresa's limp hand and slid my fingers from hers. She didn't respond.

Traipsing through muddy grass, I ended up ankle deep at the shore where I waved both arms in the air. The paramedics steered as close as possible, then waded knee deep toward me, their medical gear held above their heads.

"We'll have to get the raft out if somebody needs to go to the hospital," said the lead medic. "Helicopter can't land around here, and the sea plane is on another job." He turned to aid his two colleagues on shore.

"Well you better start blowing it up because this lady needs a hospital bad," I said as I led the way inside the house.

We stood around the bed, our feet making mud prints on the old boards. Blood dripped from the edge of the mattress now and mixed with the river dirt from outside. Theresa lay still, her face no longer sweating.

"She's gone into shock," said one medic as he pulled out a hypodermic. "We've got to get her out of here quick."

One of the medics ran outside. In a few seconds we heard the air raft filling its innards, then a voice, "Ready!"

From one end of the room I watched the two medics lift the woman onto a fold-up stretcher, an intravenous bottle hanging on the side. They had placed cold packs between her legs and on her stomach. I wondered if this had stopped the bleeding or maybe there was just no more blood in her. The saturated mattress and floor seemed to have taken all of it.

"Get hold of the sheriff, Luanne," said the lead medic as they pushed the woman to the back door. "This may be a criminal case."

I followed and watched them stand in the mud, pass the woman onto the raft, then pull it over the grass and into the shallow water. One man climbed into the boat and pulled while the other two pushed the raft. They lifted her into the boat, shoved the raft away, then climbed aboard. In five minutes, they headed full speed, with siren blasting, toward Palmetto Springs. If Theresa were lucky, the clinic there would stabilize her until she could reach the hospital in Tallahassee. As they moved out of sight, I stood next to the stretcher they left behind and watched the stained raft, red on yellow, bob against tall river reeds.

In the silent, ruined cabin, its drama out of the way now, I could still smell the blood as it aged rapidly in the humidity. I pulled out the cellular and phoned the sheriff's office in Tallahassee.

It would take the officers a while to reach this place. They probably wouldn't come by boat, and the only other way was to walk through the swamp from a rutted dirt road off the Palmetto Springs paved road. I leaned against the rough, gray boards of the hallway and suddenly remembered my earlier question.

Where is the baby?

I plodded through the marshy reeds. The path the women had taken had all but folded over on itself. The swamp does not love a road. I sloshed around in ankle-deep water, skirting the edge of the river, my eyes surveying every marsh hen nest, every cluster of rotting limbs, even a slithering water snake. When I hit a thick grove of oaks, I climbed into the low branches of one and gazed around like radar trying to latch onto something valuable. I

12

was sure the women ran this way, but when I spied not even a piece of a bloody towel, I headed for the side of the shack. It was full of eel grass, shallow water, and a tall white crane. I returned to the house and sat on the muddy back step. The swamp had swallowed the whole business, women, baby, all.

"Tony, they took the kid with them," I said as I stood in the hallway to feel the breezes against my soaked skin. Clouds had begun to gather in the afternoon heat, forcing the humidity even higher. I could feel the flush in my face. Sheriff's Detective Tony Amado had rolled up his white shirt sleeves, his wing tip shoes ruined from soaking up mud on the walk through the swamp. His sergeant, Loman, managed to keep on his jacket, but his thin blond hair stuck to his head like a marooned octopus.

"Did they say the kid was stillborn?" Tony's irritation came through and landed right on me.

"No, and I'm sure I heard it whimper." I tried to stare down this man who questioned every statement ever made by anyone. I suddenly shivered. A baby, dead or not, would be gator meat in seconds if it landed in this part of the lake. The cold spring water was deep in the middle, but along the shore line, there were breeding grounds for alligators. Water moccasins had their place here, too.

"I'm going to call the crime scene boys out here to get some blood samples. If this woman dies, two midwives are in deep shit." Tony moved back into the birth room. I followed and immediately backed out again. The odor was sickening now, the stench of blood powerful enough to draw swarms of flies. I nearly retched when I saw a host of them on top of a red puddle.

"Place will be crawling with maggots tomorrow," said Loman

13

as he looked over my shoulder, his heavy lidded eyes showing no revulsion. "Mosquitoes moving in, too." He pointed to a few buzzers near one window.

"Funny how something foul smelling attracts so many creatures," I said.

"How old do you think the mother is?" Loman pulled out a small notebook when he asked the question.

"Old enough to be called a woman and not a girl," I said. I felt a small surprise inside. Why hadn't I noticed from the beginning that she was older than her teens, even twenties? Maybe because I was in my forties and saw anyone giving birth as younger?

"She was old enough to know better than to give birth out here in a shack." Tony turned away from the room, then gulped a deep breath in the hall.

"That woman said Theresa had called her to deliver this baby. There's no phone anywhere. Not a cell phone or a line in this place." I gave the room another search with my eyes.

"Probably the delivery had been arranged with the midwife months ago. Why they'd do it here, I can't imagine."

"Maybe it came before the due time," I said. Being the only female in the room, I felt I should know about these things. But I had never given birth, never even been pregnant. I probably knew less than the men who had training for emergency deliveries.

"Anyone here?" We turned to the voice shouting from the front of the cabin. "Scene tech has arrived!"

CHAPTER TWO

"Only you?" I said as I stepped cautiously onto the sagging porch boards. Below me, ankle deep in swamp mud stood Marshall Long, crime scene genius and all round big guy—literally. He had been on vacation, and from the size of his gut overlapping his snug pants, he had spent most of it consuming every oyster in Apalachicola Bay.

"And why not only me?" He would have shook a fat fist at me except he was hanging onto two cases of equipment. "Here, do something besides criticize." He lifted one case to the porch edge. A deep gut grunt sounded for a moment like a giant bull frog.

"I thought I heard Amado call for the unit, and big as you are, Marshall, you are not the entire unit." I reached with one hand for the case, while holding onto a creaky support post with the other.

"Can't afford to send all those people when we don't even know if it's a crime, and definitely not a murder." He stared at the rickety steps and even worse porch, tapping the boards with his toe before taking a step. "From the looks of this place, I may be the first victim." He walked around a rotted spot and grabbed hold of the door jamb when he entered the hallway.

"You been eating well, Luanne? Butt looks puny from back

15

here."

I flipped him a finger and led him toward the room where Tony stood with his hands on his hips. "Take photos and blood samples," he said to Marshall.

Marshall placed the cases on the floor near the door, a spot likely void of stains and prints. Snapping on gloves, he walked toward the bed, then bent over it and stared for several moments. "And tissue, it seems. You want that, too?"

"What tissue?" Tony moved to the bed. I followed.

"There." Marshall placed his finger as closely to the mattress as he could without touching it. "Probably from the afterbirth. You find it anywhere?"

Tony pursed his lips and looked at me. I said, "One of the women tossed bloody water outside. I looked out there, but it got mixed in with marsh water; I didn't think it would be evidence."

"Show me," said Marshall.

"You'll have to come out the back door, then round to the side. Unless you want to crawl through that window." I smiled, patted my butt, and crooked my finger for him to follow.

"This is one precarious place," he said as he stepped from the back door onto a board that had been placed over a muddy spot.

We walked to the side of the house where dense swamp grass grew in the soggy dirt. I pointed to the spot. Marshall leaned his heavy body over and stared for long moments. He never got down on his knees.

"You're right. Too much swamp water. I can't see any flesh or afterbirth material here." He stood up, hiked at his nearly invisible belt, and turned toward me. "Okay, Luanne, where is this baby?"

"With the midwives, I guess."

Back inside the cabin, Marshall took photos of the scene, then opened the cases to collect the samples. "Don't know why we're doing this. No murder, and you know whose blood this is." He looked at Amado. "You do know who the girl is, right?"

"Theresa Grassfield is the name they gave Luanne. I'm having her checked now. And she is no girl. A woman, possibly in her late thirties."

"They, who?"

"The midwives—or the two women who were here when I caught them cleaning up," I said.

"Not Josie Wilburn?" Marshall rested his body on one hip as he scraped blood off the floor.

"You know her?"

"Of her. Her mother had a reputation for helping out pregnant ladies in these parts—if you know what I mean." He flipped his hand toward two flies. "Bet this swatch is going to have a few maggot eggs on it."

"What do you mean?" Amado moved toward the man, then turned his face away, revulsion of flies and blood in his expression. He glanced at both his rolled-up sleeves as if daring any bloody fly to find a landing spot.

"The mother delivered lots of swamp babies once upon a time. Folks don't speak as highly of the daughters." He dropped the swatch into a paper bag, then retrieved another from the case. "How come you don't know this, Amado?"

"Never had a baby in the swamps, I guess."

Tony left the room, and I could hear him exhale in the hallway. Marshall smiled.

"Hey," he said as he shifted his attention to the iron bedstead. "Got something here."

I moved closer. Marshall took a long pair of tweezers from

his pocket and stuck them between the iron rail and the foot of the mattress. Carefully pulling out a clot of tissue and blood, he dropped it in a bag. "Afterbirth, like I said."

I felt sick. The smell, the tissue, the flies. It smacked of Faulkner's description of birth as "liquid putrefaction." I stepped back toward the door. With closed eyes, I told myself a woman was in dire states over this, and a tiny life was off somewhere in the swamp with two aging midwives. I couldn't dwell on the scents that bombarded me now.

"Better look this mattress over good." Marshall stood now, gazing at the rusty ticking. The place where Theresa's body had been was outlined in blood. "Looks like some...yeah, okay." He spoke to himself as he scraped something off the mattress into a vial. "Not just drool around her head area." He went to his knees again, following a vomit stain down the side of the bed.

"How did those women get out of here with a newborn?" I asked the room, turning my face away from Marshall's activities.

"Easy. Kid is tiny. Just wrap it up in a towel. Same for the afterbirth, although that might drip some. Probably need two towels at least."

"Marshall!"

"You asked, Luanne." He held onto the iron bedstead and pulled himself to a standing position. I heard his knees snap like rubber bands. Taking his equipment to the wooden crates, he scraped more blood samples and placed them in bags. On his face, a series of folded skin flaps, sweat droplets ran down in undulating waves.

"You said they worked in this area?" He looked over the crates. "Okay, I'll dust for prints. See if you can find any footprints that might not be yours or Amado's."

"Loman was here, too, and the deputy, not to mention the

18

paramedics."

"Yeah? Find footprints. They'd likely be in places where ya'll didn't step." He nodded toward the side of the bed.

I found foot tracks everywhere. The muddy water outside had come right inside with us all. I wore high swamp boots. Tony had wing tips. Loman and the deputy did, too. I looked down at Marshall's feet. Extra large running shoes, no laces.

"You wear those things to work?"

He looked toward the floor. "What things? Haven't seen my feet in years. Yeah, got any complaints? My feet don't, and that's the idea."

I shrugged and moved near the window where Sadie had tossed the water outside. A small footprint in dried mud was barely visible.

"Yep, could be one of them." Marshall took a picture, then began to shine a light around it. "Here, hold this for me." He handed me a black cloth and told me to stand in various locations, always with the edge of the cloth near the print. "Okay, I got to set up the tripod. Get that deputy in here." The man heard him and took over for me. I watched Marshall for a while as he shot photos, getting the three dimensional effect of the back light.

When I'd had enough of the stench, I joined Tony in the hallway. He knelt near the back door, searching the floor. "There's a print here made by some kind of tennis shoe. Get Marshall out here."

"Marshall! Out here," I yelled. Tony frowned.

We stood aside as the big man stretched his pants to their thread limits to see the print.

"Why would a girl give birth the hard way in this day and age?" I said, knowing the obvious answer was money, and maybe family or church pressure.

19

"It may be the twenty-first century, but there are still places where an unwanted pregnancy is a shame to the community."

"Especially if the father is unacceptable," I said.

"Yeah. Another race, or a member of the family. People around here aren't going to accept that. Probably beat the girl senseless." Tony wrinkled his brow, then turned to me. "You got a friend who knows these swamps, Luanne. You want to get in touch with him?"

He meant Pasquin, my pal, surrogate granddad, front-porch rocking partner. In his eighties, he still roamed the river where he had worked as a young Cajun whose Catholic family married into Protestantism. His swamp house was within walking distance of mine, and I counted on him for everything from motor boat chauffeur to dining companion.

"Tell you what, I'll go find him right now." I wanted out of the stuffy, malodorous heat of this cabin. "You'll let me know about Theresa?"

"Before you find Pasquin, why not see the woman yourself. Maybe she'll wake up and recognize you. She's more likely to talk to a woman than to one of us." Tony searched his pockets, then gave up and scraped the sweat off his face with a white sleeve.

"It'll take a while to get there, through the swamp and all." Even fecund swamp mud would be a relief from this cabin.

"And, Luanne," Tony followed me toward the front door. "You're an agent as of now. Find anything, even if it's underwater, I have to know."

Tony was referring to my status as a reserve diver for the sheriff's department. He also meant that anything suspicious I might discover in my cave mapping would be police evidence, and I'd be obligated to turn it over to him. He felt he had to tell me this in every case, like I was some dimwit woman who couldn't remember my purpose in life.

"Right, and what about Harry?" Even though I'd proved myself on several cases, Amado preferred to work with a male diver. He had always given deference to Harry, another reserve diver, but since I discovered the scene, he would have to work with me.

"Just tell him to stand by in case you need help."

I didn't like trekking through the swamp in an afternoon thunder storm. Instead, I phoned Pasquin to pick me up at the Palmetto Lake landing, a deep end not far from the cabin. The place would be suitable to set up diving gear for mapping the caves in the lake. From the depth and clarity of the water, I estimated a cave opening maybe six to ten feet down. A current of fresh water gushed up from some unknown depth.

The clouds moved slowly in from the Gulf, their thunderheads growing darker and fiercer. We had maybe thirty minutes to move off the lake and the river before risking lightning strikes. I sighed relief when I heard the steady putt-putt of Pasquin's boat. He kept it in tip-top condition sort of like he did himself. Neither he nor the boat moved very fast.

"You get stuck in the oddest places, Luanne," he said as he held out a wrinkled hand to steady me. "What's them cop cars doing down on the rut road?" Pasquin's slow, musical cadence blended with the flow of the forest and the river. It never changed, just drifted into the wind.

"Midwifery in the cabin back there," I said as I took a checkered plastic cushion and steadied it near the rear of the boat. "Let's get out of this weather, okay?"

"You mean a baby's been born?" Pasquin squinted his eyes in mild curiosity as he steered the boat into open water, dodging clumps of grass and broken tree limbs. He raised his lined face to the sky as he had done years before, and, for a moment, I saw him young, the strong cheek bones under tight, tanned skin.

"We didn't exactly see a baby. Can you make this thing go any faster. It's thundering." I had once seen lightning strike a cypress tree in the middle of the Palmetto River, and I didn't want the forces to take me for one of those trees.

"Hold on." Pasquin made a motion near the motor which gave a revving sound. We moved maybe five miles an hour faster.

"I know some women doing that birthing business. At least I used to. Swamp people don't have any insurance sometimes. They call in these women to do it for them at home. Good women who don't mind getting paid in chickens, maybe fish. One woman got a whole bucket of pecans one winter." He stopped and chuckled to himself. "Now ain't that something, a baby for a bucket of pecans. Matter of fact Luanne, if my memory serves me well, you were birthed by a swamp midwife."

My mother died before I was old enough to ask her those questions and I wasn't about to talk with Pasquin about them now.

"Who do you know does this midwifing?" I concentrated on Pasquin, trying to keep my attention off the distant flashes in the sky. The boat moved so slowly, the breeze barely whipped my short-cropped curls.

"Oh, there's the sisters Wilburn, and…"

"Wait! Wilburn, that's the name Marshall Long gave me. Do you know where they live?"

Pasquin's eyes smiled as I winced at a clap of thunder. "Now I'll get you there without frying you, Luanne." He took a deep breath. "Wilburns got a farm house about two, three miles down the river from Fogarty Spring. Back in the woods, though. You might get a little car back there on a dirt road. Their daddy grew

22

some cotton and tobacco, but never made much out of it. The old lady Wilburn was the real bread winner. She did the midwifing and brought home bacon and eggs. When they died, I think the sisters sold off some acreage. Far as I know, they do just a bit of midwifing and a little gardening. Haven't actually seen the place in maybe thirty years—hell, maybe more."

"Do they have a river landing?"

"Nope, too far inland. There is one about a mile from their house, or used to be. You want to go there?"

"Yes, but not now. Get us home, Pasquin!" I jumped when a sharp light flashed nearly directly above us.

"Better put in here, instead," he said as he moved around a grove of cypress and headed for Palmetto Springs. I could see the glass bottom boats tied to the dock. The life guards had cleared all the swimmers from the cool waters and the diving tower. Heavy drops of rain pelted the clear spring. By the time we exited the motor boat, they pelted us, too. I helped Pasquin cover the seats, then both of us took off for the hotel.

We made it as far as the bath house and crowded among the dripping swimmers. They would wait the half hour it would take for the storm to move on toward Tallahassee, then run down to the springs again. A wave of nostalgia hit me. I had done the same as a teenager.

I remembered dripping with sweat, covered with gnats and jumping into the deep spring water, colder than air conditioning and shocking to the system. Then the adjustment, and sheer joy of clear water swimming. By the time I got home, my well-iced body had welcomed the Florida heat.

The noise of a baby's cry shook me into the present. A mother bounced her bored toddler in her arms. It wore a tiny bathing suit ruffled down the bottom. Would Theresa be awake now, longing for her child? Light streaked across the sky and the crowd screamed. The toddler's face grimaced into a howl.

Among the noise of thunder and lightning, I heard the faint ring of the cellular in my back pack. The crowd heard it, too, and turned toward me as I rummaged through mapping notes.

"Tony here. Where are you?"

I explained, then he said to stay put. "We got evidence of a row boat here."

"Tony, I searched that shore. There was no row boat when I was there."

"Not on the shore. Out in the water, down from the cabin. Upside down. It looks like somebody turned it over, maybe drowned. Soon as you can, I want you and MacAllister out here to look for bodies."

I looked at Pasquin who had cornered a young swimmer and rattled on about his adventures. He fanned himself with his battered straw hat in rhythm with his tale. The swimmer stared as though mesmerized by the gaze of some ancient mariner.

"You're going to have to take me by the mapping camp, then back to the cabin," I said.

He shrugged, never breaking the rhythm with his straw hat. He had seen it all on this river.

CHAPTER THREE

Harry MacAllister, archeologist and diver, had set up his research camp in a cove not far from the main spring. It had become one of the sights the boat tour guides pointed out as they made their rounds of the spring and part of the river. From the open spaces on the boat, the tourists could see two tin roofs and the top of a pick-up truck camper. If they were lucky, they might spot a diver go into the water at the shallow edge. More than likely, they would see an alligator sunning itself on that same edge. It was no place for an amateur.

I had reluctantly joined Harry in his mapping because I couldn't bear to return to full-time teaching. The linguistics department allowed me the time off if I taught two night classes a week. During the fall, winter, and spring quarters, I made the trek into Tallahassee every Tuesday and Thursday evening to unload my knowledge of transformational grammar and the history of the English language. Summer session meant only one class, Tuesday nights.

Harry and I still skirted around each other, our former affair off bounds for conversation. We stuck to limestone structures and underwater currents.

"Here 'tis, ma'am," said Pasquin as he pulled the boat as close as he could to the muddy shore. I heard water splash nearby and knew a gator had sensed our presence. He would scurry underwater until all was quiet, then return to soak up the sun. In spite of their reputations and thick hides, gators were rather sluggish and mostly nonaggressive, forgoing anything as large as a full-size human—most of the time.

"I'll wait right here." Pasquin adjusted a ragged cushion under his bottom, shoved his hat across his eyes and leaned back in the plastic seat.

I stepped into clear water then immediately sank into a foot of mud. With heavy sucking noises, I trudged to shore. Turning around, I reached over and threw river water over my boots. Most of the dirt cleared away.

At the camp, two graduate students sat under a tent where they had set up a card table. Pouring over some crude map drawings, they ignored my approach.

"Is Harry around?"

Without looking up, one said, "He's gone back down. Had to help Tibby."

The other grad student snorted.

I wondered whether Harry was romantically involved with Tibby, the only female grad student in the group. Strange, as much as he had disappointed me, it hadn't even occurred to me that he might be interested in someone as young — and incompetent — as Tibby.

I was surprised when the second one addressed my unspoken question. Why was he reassuring me? Did rumors about our affair circulate among Harry's students?

"She's got a boyfriend."

The first student snorted once more. "Big, muscle-bound cretin. Arnie thinks he can dive. But if Harry ever catches him around here…"

I got the picture — the two scrawny grad students were jealous of Tibby's suitor. I didn't have time for this.

I knew the problem. Tibby, an ocean diver, had signed onto this project because it sounded like a new adventure, a chance to see what fresh water diving was like. But it was defeating her.

Nothing like the warm currents in open seas, the depths here were cold, and the currents changed with seasons. The worst part was her increasing fright within the cave structures. She had panicked in the beginning, becoming disoriented. She went too deep, building narcosis in her blood, impairing her judgment. Harry managed to pull her to safety. Later, she learned to have confidence in the life lines we tacked onto the cave walls. Without them, she groped about nervously, unaware of the turns and bends.

"She maps well," Harry said in her defense. But I knew he worried. He feared losing a diver on this project.

"He's needed. Sheriff's request," I said.

One student shrugged and moved to the camper. We had set up an underwater communication system. At least one diver had a full mask with a speaker at all times. The student used the system to let Harry know he was needed topside.

I didn't wait long. On the other side of the wooded peninsula, two creatures emerged from the water. Both sat on the shore, removing fins, masks and tanks as they metamorphosed into humans. Their conversation struck a chord of unfriendliness.

"Damn! Tibby, you can't do that down there." Harry's voice rang tired.

"I'm sorry, Harry, it's just freaky when it gets dark and the passage is narrow. Let me do the big caves, please." Tibby, her short crop of black hair plastered to her head, whined. It was a grating sound, one I could barely tolerate. I tried to do my work when she wasn't around.

27

"If you keep this up, you're going back to the Gulf. You're too much of a risk." He grabbed his gear and left her on the bank. "Well, did you find a place?" Harry snapped when he spied me.

I could tell he didn't want bad news now. Some little knot of sadistic pleasure rose inside me.

"Sheriff needs both of us at that lake. Don't put your gear away. Pasquin is waiting." I turned around and pulled my own gear from the shed.

"I can't go down again. I've been down twice and my veins are feeding on nitrogen." He tossed the fins on the ground.

"Okay, if anybody has to go down, I'll do it."

"Yeah, Luanne, like you'll go down alone."

He grabbed hold of his equipment and took off in front of me. We ended up on the muddy bank, staring at Pasquin who snored underneath his straw hat.

"Now, Pasquin," I said. He jerked upward.

"Not going to be much space for that stuff in here." He always said that, but his little motor boat had often found ways to accommodate diving equipment. As we tucked it in, then crawled in ourselves, he said, "I ought to get paid for this, Luanne."

"Talk to Amado," I said as I touched Harry's tanned arm. Close physical proximity still reminded me of another kind of physicality we once had, and it disturbed me. My relationship with Deputy Vernon Drake was going well, and I disliked dealing with two chemistries.

"How come Amado didn't call Drake?" said Harry as though he'd read my mind.

"He's on vacation. Visiting his mother in Jacksonville." I turned my attention to the sky. Inside, my stomach tightened. Jacksonville was also where Vernon's ex-wife lived with her new husband. I shook the uneasy feeling, telling myself I was too old for teenage turmoil.

"What's Amado got this time?" His voice had a lilt that told me anything was better than dealing with Tibby.

I spent the rest of Pasquin's slow boat ride explaining the event with the midwives, then Amado's discovery of the over-turned row boat. He took a deep breath, and said, "Guess we're not going to be mapping in that area after all."

"Hang on, Harry. I might be able to make a deal with Amado."

Pasquin stopped the boat before the eel grass got thick enough to stall the motor. Someone on the shore near the cabin waved his arms, then gestured in the direction of a bend in the shoreline. Pasquin revved the motor and headed around a heavy clump of cypress, coming into a small cove with a car-size beach of white sand. Tony and Loman stood in the shallows, their suit pants rolled up and their shoes and socks on the bank. Tony waved us to the side.

"Keep your boat there," he yelled. "The overturned boat is to your right."

Pasquin shut down the engine and let the boat drift in the current until we could see an object a few feet below the surface. Nearly raw wooden boards formed the outline of a row boat. The color barely showed among the green-black of the thick grass below it.

"It couldn't be too deep here," I said.

"There's a spring somewhere. Look how clear the water is." Harry leaned over the side and dipped his fingers into the water.

"I'm going in without the tank," I said as I stripped off my shirt and jeans to the suit I habitually wore these days. I slipped on the face mask and rolled backward off the edge of the boat.

Swimming in the direction of the overturned boat, I felt the rush of current and tensed my muscles. The boat rested above the long eel grass and for some reason didn't move. The grass always gave me an eerie feeling. It could hide snakes, even gators. I didn't think either would attack unless I surprised it, but the grass made it difficult to see what was there. I parted the long thick blades just underneath the boat and found the anchor. An oar had lodged itself in the seat slat. Its paddle end jammed into the grass and brushed the top of the sand, just enough to keep the boat from drifting away. Holding my breath, I made a quick look around me. The eel grass stopped suddenly, exposing a down-turn of the river floor. The sand, white here, led to a shadowy opening. A cave was close by. Something waved near the entrance.

"I'm going down again," I shouted to Harry as I came up for air. I cleared my mask and dove toward the dark area.

Some cypress branches had fallen into the water and buried themselves in the silt. On a protrusion, a piece of cloth, torn and discolored, did a wave dance in the current. Had the branch not been there, it would have taken off down the cave entrance. I unhooked it from its watery shackle and headed to open air.

"It's a bloody cloth," I said as I handed it to Amado. Pasquin had moved the boat close enough for Harry and me to join them on shore.

"Wouldn't blood wash off in there?" said Loman, his sleepy eyes following the stains as it lay on the sand.

"Not if the blood had dried enough first. The water is cold; it would wash off surface or fresh blood. But it might leave a stain, especially if it hadn't been in there too long," added Marshall who had lumbered from the cabin to the shore. He pulled out an evidence bag and lifted the cloth into it. "These rips are fresh, too." He pointed to jagged edges that appeared whiter than the rest of the material.

"We've got to get that boat out," said Amado.

"I'll do it," Harry said, then waded part way into the lake. He seemed to have no compunction about the eel grass. Disappearing underwater, he resurfaced with the oar in his hand. He floated it on the water; I waded to retrieve it. Behind me, I heard a low chuckle from Pasquin who knew how I felt about walking in the grass. Harry then took hold of the upturned boat and pulled it as far as he could to shore. When he could stand, he told me to grab one end. We placed it right side up on the water. Amado waded out and helped us drag it onto the sand.

"Homemade," said Pasquin who had pulled his own boat close enough to see it. "Slats look like old boards from a crate. See that?" He pointed to one that appeared to have printing on it.

"Something…," said Amado as he twisted his head around to make out the writing.

"…Oyst…Ste…*Homegrown Oyster Stew*, I'll bet!" I said as I remembered the stuff from my father's shelves. He had owned some bait and tackle shops that also carried food staples for weekend fishermen.

"Wonder where they got this crate board?" said Loman.

"Any place that stocks this stuff and tosses out the delivery crates. Or maybe the owners buy the stuff. Get on it, Loman." Amado's expression didn't change. In spite of the humidity, his wet, sandy feet, and the excitement of a clue, he looked pristine, like his shirt had just been ironed and the hairdresser had recently finished shaping his dark locks. Only the grayish damp smudge on his sleeve gave away his sweat wiping spot.

"You think those women used this boat to get away, right?" I said as I watched Loman grab his shoes and head for the cabin.

"Don't you?" Tony never looked at me when he spoke. Instead, he began swiping his feet on the grass. He frowned when the river sand stayed put.

"Could be. They disappeared quickly. Maybe they had this boat waiting, then something happened. Turned over and…"

"And drowned as they were pulled into a cave?" Harry looked weary, his hands on his hips.

"Well, this cloth *was* near the opening," I said. I knew what this meant. Not only were we going to map this cave, we were going to search it for bodies—two women and an infant. They probably would never be found unless they snagged on something.

"We can't be sure," said Tony. "We're going to look for them above ground, too. When can you two be ready?"

Harry and I shrugged. He couldn't go down again today. I wouldn't go without a swimming buddy. We'd have to wait until morning.

"Good," said Amado. "Gives me time to notify Mr. St. Claire that we've got a police operation on his property."

"St. Claire?" said Harry. "Not August St. Claire, the attorney?"

"The very one," said Tony. "And he's not going to like this much."

After dropping Harry off at the dive camp, Pasquin turned his slow boat toward our part of the forest. I leaned back to look at the clouds, soft fluffs now, that made figures in a blue sky. "Like fat cherubs," I said. Pasquin didn't hear, or chose not to, as he guided the boat into the currents. His straw hat rested on the boat bottom. River breezes blew steadily through his white hair, like a peace flag on top of an old warrior's head. His skin mapped out his life in deep lines.

Pasquin had known my mother, had been her companion when my father was away in the military. Friendship with both parents continued after I was born.

Did those gnarled hands once cuddle me in clean towels?

"Pasquin," I spoke over the engine noise. "It's not going to be dark for a while yet. Take me by the Wilburn land."

CHAPTER FOUR

"This is the place, through those trees," Pasquin said as we sat in his boat on a narrow offshoot of the river. "If you get out here, you can walk straight to the side of the old Wilburn homestead."

"And what will I see?" In spite of the reason for heading down this stream, I felt a pleasant sensation. The water, deep and clear, flowed through a grove of oak trees that overlapped and intertwined like a canopy. Tallahassee is noted for its canopy roads. Tiny Fogarty Spring had a canopy stream. Sunlight darted through the leaves and played sparkling games on the surface. The occasional bird or croaking frog were the only sounds until Pasquin and I broke in with human voices.

"Last time I was there, let's see. Probably the garden was on this side of the house. I remember that one," he chuckled softly. "They grew strawberries once. Full of worms. People got pretty darn mad when they bought pints and had to toss them to the hogs. 'Course hogs wouldn't eat them, either."

"I thought hogs ate everything," I recognized another old tale surfacing.

"Some hogs got sense. These did." He grinned and placed his hat over his face. "You planning on getting out?"

"Don't go to sleep yet, you old coot. You've got to hold the boat." I shoved on boots that reached to mid-calf.

Pasquin sat up and grabbed hold of some low-growing oak branches, steadying the boat as I stepped to the bank. The water, deep here, would have covered my head by several feet had I tried to wade ashore.

"Holler if you need help." He leaned back, replacing the hat. "I mean if you need me to whollop a snake or something."

"Yeah, and if I do, you'll come running, right?" I flashed my cellular phone, but I don't think he saw it.

The narrow footpath consisted of mashed-down grass in a muddy rut, but it did indeed lead to the side of a house. I kept my eyes to my feet as I walked past heavy thickets of palmetto and ivy. My thick books would probably repel a snake bite, but if one struck, I'd be a mental case for nights on end. Fortunately, the only reptiles who crossed my path were rubbery frogs the color of dark earth. Moss flourished here, hanging nearly to the forest floor from the grand old oaks. The terrain, unlike the swampy scrub areas around parts of Palmetto Springs, wreaked of Old South. I expected to see crumbling columns as I made my way through the tangle of vegetation. Instead, I saw crumbling wood frame.

I pushed through some low-hanging moss and ran smack into a rusted wire fence. The garden it surrounded looked more like a cemetery for cucumbers. A few scrawny watermelons lay rotting in the sun next to some unidentifiable leaves. I had visions of Pasquin's worms inside sun-bleached fruit.

I felt my way around the fence. The vegetation that covered it acted like a curtain. I couldn't tell where it ended. When it did end, I stood under an seedy scuppernong grapevine and spied the boards of a box house a few yards away.

The Wilburn homestead made it clear they did not descend

from Southern gentry. In the front, I saw the same shotgun arrangement as the cabin in the woods. This one, however, had a section of rooms added to one side. On the other, a roof supported by thin boards acted as a carport, or more likely an outdoor storage and sitting place—junk yard might have been an accurate term. They hadn't bothered to brick over the ground. Around two plastic chairs, grass shot up in uneven sprigs.

Paint peeled off the old boards, the add-on less so than the shotgun center. The sisters had painted in sections separated by years. The overall effect became a color palate of gray graduating to dirty white.

The front door, locked behind a torn screen door, had a small diamond-shaped window, under which lay a rusting knocker. I lifted it, then pounded it against the metal base. It had been used so infrequently that I needed both hands to force it to resound inside the house. No response. After two more tries, I stood on tiptoe and peeped through the window. Dust made for a hazy view, but I could see down the hall and a mirror effect from the back door. Trudging through ankle-high grass, I reached the rear of the house.

The window on the back door was larger and afforded a wider view. The doors of the rooms, all shut, stood as guardians against generations of secrets. Pounding on the back door brought the same silence from inside. Pressing one ear against the door, I held my breath and listened for a sound, hoping it would be the cry of a child. I heard only the distant cry of a mocking bird.

I gave up and made a circle of the house. The added-on section was two story. Looking up at the windows, I could see no evidence of anyone gazing down at me. But a sound nudged at my ears, a kind of whimpering and stirring from beneath the house. I moved to a corner where the lattice had been broken. Bending over, I came face to face with the mangiest dog I'd ever seen. His wiry brown hair appeared glued on in tufts, raw bare skin showing on the rest of his bony body. He sat half up, his energy sapped from disease, but his eyes begged and his head turned in that cute way puppies have of seducing humans. Reaching into the sack I had been carrying ever since I started trekking through swamps, I pulled out a bag of cheese cubes and tossed them to the mutt. It didn't have the energy to gulp them as a healthy dog would, but it ate until they were all gone. I found an old pail and filled it with water from an outside tap. When I placed it in front of the animal, it lapped slowly, unsteady on its feet.

"Don't worry, fellow. I'll get a vet on your case in short time." I wanted to pet its still pert ears, but I dared not touch it.

Under the carport, I found some old canvas that had been ripped into large squares. Pulling out the least dusty one, I headed back to the dog.

"Okay, little guy, I just want to help you out," I spoke gently, hoping the mutt wouldn't turn savage on me. Enclosing his pocked body inside the canvas, I pulled him from under the house. He never resisted, but whimpered at tinges of pain.

"What you got there, ma'am?" I could hear the caution in Pasquin's *ma'am*, his usual affectionate address. "Hope you ain't planning on transporting a dead body in this here boat."

"Not dead, but dying. I found him half-starved, half-eaten away," I said and pulled aside the canvas to give him a better view.

He winced. "You sit down at the other end with that thing."

The dog trembled all the way to Fogarty Spring, the boat landing and little town that had been named for my ancestors. As we pulled next to the dock, I could see Mama, the proprietress of Mama's Table, standing at her picture window. She, along with everyone else on the dock, would know we were coming. I had phoned ahead to the local veterinarian to meet me there.

"Don't get much call to come down here, Luanne," said Kendall, the vet whose usual clientele were broken-wing anhinga birds or a snake-bitten calf. He had been around for years, not as long as Pasquin, but enough to be trusted by everyone in the county.

"Can you save it?" I sat the dog on the dock and knelt beside it. Still trembling, it looked from one human face to the other.

"In bad shape, but I think I can pull it through. You got an interest in this pup?"

"Sheriff may have," I said, and with that I guaranteed the dog's survival.

"I'll get right on it." Kendall pushed the dog into a cage door, latched it, and headed toward his truck.

Pasquin tied up his boat. Standing in front of Mama's Table with its appetizing odors of fried fish and lime pie meant patronizing the place. I decided not to argue, but to phone Tony from here. He got to me first.

"Wait for us there, Luanne," Tony spoke from his own cellular across the swamp. "What made you...never mind."

"I think his nose is out of joint because I went to the Wilburn house," I said as I headed for the lady's room to wash up.

Pasquin chuckled and mumbled something about moving men's noses around could be the purpose for women's existence. He grabbed a table and slapped his straw hat onto the seat beside him.

"You found a dying mutt and nobody at home?" Tony played with his plate of fried oysters.

Loman, sitting next to him, ate his with globs of ketchup

stirred up in tartar sauce. His half-closed eyelids hid the gusto with which he took in the seafood laced with spoons of cheese grits and slaw. When he did come up for breath, his belly heaved against the table edge.

"If anyone was inside that house, they weren't going to let me know it. And that poor dog. Obviously, it was somebody's pet, but it hadn't been fed in days. Not to mention dipped for mange." I couldn't take my eyes off Loman. My appetite for the freshly batter-fried shrimp sitting in front of me disappeared.

"Well, we might have to get a search warrant, but I've got to make a case before a judge. You are willing to tell him what you saw in that cabin?" Tony looked at me. I bristled inside. I had been through gun shots, risky dives, and surveillance missions for this man, and he still had that edge of not trusting me. I stared back, refusing to answer.

"What are we gonna do about St. Claire?" Loman said, his mouth stuffed with hush puppies.

"See him at his country home," Tony said, emphasizing the snobbishness of the idea.

"You don't have permission yet?"

"Man wasn't in his office," said Loman. "Secretary said he was doing some work out here."

"And where is that?"

"Not too far from the Wilburn place," piped up Pasquin who dumped hot sauce onto fried fish.

Both detectives looked at him in surprise.

"St. Claire done bought up that property where you found the boat and the old plantation home next to the Wilburn place. I hear he's employed some swamp people to refurbish the old boards."

"I swear, Pasquin, the snakes tell you tales," I held back a smile.

"Could be, ma'am."

"How do we get there?" Tony had placed his fork to the side of his plate. Loman eyed the uneaten oysters.

"Imagine you could go round the paved road, then onto his paved drive. He finished it a week or two ago." Pasquin pretended disinterest as he sipped strong coffee. "Of course, he does have a nice boat landing."

Silence prevailed as Mama stood at the table, refilling the iced tea glasses. Her hips spread wide beyond the apron she wore. Pasquin smiled up at her and waved his coffee cup for a refill.

"Don't know how you drink that hot stuff in this weather," said Loman. He turned to Amado, "You gonna eat those oysters?"

Four of us rode in Pasquin's boat as he guided it slowly down the river, past the Wilburn place, and around a swift moving current to a new wooden dock. He tied up next to a late model speed boat. "Lawyers do live nice," he said as he ran his fingers over the shiny fiberglass rim.

From the dock, we climbed a steep bank where we came upon workers painting a gazebo. From the fresh lumber and tools, we could tell it had recently been built, not renovated.

"Mr. St. Claire around?" Tony flashed his badge as he spoke to one of the workers.

The man stared for a moment, then nodded in the direction of the big house. At the edge of the forest, a dog had taken up barking as though we had invaded its master's kingdom.

"Damn strays," murmured the man.

We walked on carefully tended lawn, flanked with strategically planted azalea and crepe myrtle bushes. The myrtle, still in bloom, showed off large purple and pink blooms. Passing a graceful oak, its moss tickling the ground in a gentle breeze, we stood at the edge of a once magnificent staircase. Workers, in the process of sanding off the old paint, stopped and moved aside for us to climb to the antebellum porch.

In spots, new, unstained wooden boards replaced rotted porch flooring. At one end, two men worked with a chisel on decorative molding.

"Mr. St. Claire?" said Tony to a man who brought out a box of tools. The man nodded inside just as a diapered toddler waddled to the porch. A woman's voice cooed after it. "No, no, sweetums. You'll get hurt out there."

A woman with recently beauty-parlored gray hair and a baby blue pantsuit stood in the doorway. She nodded and moved aside and grabbed the child. Still cooing baby talk, she walked into the yard.

"I need molding out here today, you hear." A man's voice spoke into a phone. It was a Jimmy Carter Southern accent that expressed anger without crudeness. He poked the *off* button when he saw us.

"May I help you?" The handsome face froze for a second when Tony and Loman showed their badges.

"With some information, yes, sir," said Amado. St. Claire's face relaxed. He bowed slightly and showed us to a small room that had been set up as an office.

"Soda or beer is all we've got at the moment," he said as he motioned to a half-size refrigerator. "I sometimes keep milk for my grandbaby, who thinks she's got the run of the place." He craned his neck to look out the front door.

"Nothing, sir," Tony turned up the Southern politeness,

catching the man off guard.

"Then what is it I can do for you?" He smiled at me rather than look at the two men. I found myself with a little butterfly fluttering in my gut. The man, probably fifty-plus, had neatly combed thick black hair, with graying temples. He wore expensive safari clothes. Well-manicured nails revealed hands not involved with any of the reconstruction work here. His eyes sparkled. This was one kind of ladies' man, I told myself.

Tony explained the problem with the overturned boat. St. Claire sat behind his desk, the tips of his fingers together and touching his chin. He frowned as though concerned, even alarmed at such action on his land. "By all means," he finally said, "set up an investigative unit over there. I don't plan to do anything with that land right now anyhow."

"Mr. St. Claire," I said, and the man turned to me, smiling, placing his hands on the desk in front of him. "Do you know anything about the old Wilburn place?"

"You mean that place just down from here?" He winked at me, and I wanted to kick myself for liking that.

"Yes, down the river from here."

"The one with the put-together, shotgun house?" He patronized me, and Tony noticed.

"Sir," he said, "that's the one. Do you know where the sisters are?"

"Sisters?" He stopped smiling.

"The Wilburn sisters—Josie and Sadie," added Loman.

"Now, I don't know any sisters, but then I don't know a lot of my neighbors. I guess I will when this place is done, and I can move in." He waved his hand around the air space above his head.

"Then you don't know why the sisters are not at home?" I said.

"Well," he relaxed again, leaning on his forearms and looking my way. "I hope you don't think they live there."

"Don't they own that house?"

"No, ma'am," he said with childlike defiance. "I do."

He rose with a polite, "excuse me for a moment," and headed out the front door. I watched him talk to the woman and give the toddler a kiss on a fat cheek. He grinned broadly when he returned.

"My wife brings the grandbaby down here. The kid loves romping out there, but we've got some dog problems. Strays. These swamp people don't seem to know about spaying."

CHAPTER FIVE

"If you bought the land, then the sisters had to move. So, you might know where they moved," said Tony, his tight jaw warning impending irritation with the man.

"No, sir," St. Claire shook his head, "that's not how it happened. A real estate agent let me know the land was available. I took a look around the place—nobody was living there—and said I'd buy it. That was that. No sisters, nobody. Agent took care of the paper work." St. Claire held up one hand as if to fend off any more accusations.

"When do you plan to work on it?" I asked.

"Oh, not for a long time. It's investment right now." He winked again. I prayed not to blush.

"Then would you mind if we looked around there?" Amado caught him off guard. The man turned his head away from me and frowned at the two males. He thought for a minute.

"When would you want to do this?"

"Is there a problem with right now?" Tony answered.

"Well, I don't exactly have insurance." He twisted in his chair. "I mean if one of you gets hurt on the property…"

"Look, let's call it an extension of police work, okay? If you want, I'll get a search warrant, because as far as we know, that's the last place the Wilburn sisters lived around here."

St. Claire frowned deeper, again placing his fingertips to his chin. "Have these women done something illegal?"

"Possibly," said Amado, leaning forward now, assuming the upper hand.

St. Claire breathed deeply, and stood up. "Then, sir, you must by all means get a search warrant." He started to move away, then turned back. "But I want this on the record. I don't know the women, nor did I ever meet them in the land transaction."

"You can give us the name of the real estate agent, right?" Tony said just as another man entered the room. He stopped and stared at us. From his three-piece suit, I figured he was one of St. Claire's law partners.

St. Claire nodded to the man, then said to Tony, "It's in my car. Follow me."

The workers had built an open-sided shed at one end of the house not far from the newly paved drive. It served as a carport for St. Claire's four wheel, army-camouflaged vehicle.

"Good swamp van," said Loman.

"The best." St. Claire opened the glove compartment and pulled out a black notebook. "Charlene Brennan. Here, you can have this card. I think I have several more somewhere. Best agent in town." He held the card between two fingers toward Tony who pulled it from them.

"Thank you," Tony said and immediately turned his back on the man.

"Must be nice to have the *best* car and the *best* agent," said Loman as we walked away.

Not to mention a perpetual wink, I thought and smiled in spite of myself.

Pasquin leaned over the boat edge and stared at the water as we returned to the landing. "Got some large mouth bass here," he said as he held the boat for us.

"Yeah, probably stolen from a fish hatchery," said Loman.

"Man like that has lots to hide," said Tony, "but it may not have anything to do with this case."

I sat in silence, fighting my feelings for this handsome man with great hair, one who could probably turn a witness to jelly on the stand. At the moment, my stomach felt like jelly.

Pasquin revved the engine, and we headed to Fogarty Spring.

As we pulled up to the dock, two people turned to watch Loman tie the boat. I looked up the staircase where Harry held the door of Mama's Place for a young woman. He met my glance for a moment, his thick salt and pepper hair glistening in the afternoon sun.

Kind of like St. Claire's hair without the stylist.

His tan diver's body, covered in khaki pants and a yellow polo shirt, stood on display for my hormones' undivided attention. I tried to think of Vernon, his body not much different from Harry's, a little taller but just as tan and lean muscled. And bald. "He smiles better than you, Harry," I whispered under my breath. "Damn! Comb all that hair right and you'd look just like St. Claire."

"What's that, Luanne?" said Pasquin as he followed my gaze up the stairs. "Oh, I see." And he did. Pasquin knew me better than most anyone, and he delighted in the turmoil my romantic life often churned up with these two men.

"You see nothing, old man," I said as I let him take my hand and gallantly help me off the boat.

"I see a pretty young ma'amselle with that MacAllister."

"Yeah, well Vernon is due in next week." I sat back down in the boat. "Why am I getting out? You need to take me home."

"Flustered you, didn't he?" Pasquin hit every emotional nerve and brought it out where he could stomp on it. I was relieved he didn't see me with St. Claire.

"Pasquin, did you ever have sisters?"

"Not a one."

"Well, good thing. They'd all be in therapy by now." I leaned back in my seat and pulled his sleeping stunt. I could feel the warm river sun on my face and the damp breeze against my cheeks as we headed to my landing. Troublesome divers, winking lawyers, and mangy dogs couldn't take away my part of the forest. I comforted in the sounds of distant crows and the incessant singing katydids. In a few minutes, I would stand before the house which I had lived in as a child, since renovated into a modern wonder in the swampy woods.

"Gon' to rock on your porch for a while?" Pasquin pulled close to the landing, not long ago a few dangerously rotting boards and rusty nails for a foot ladder. I had redone it—new boards and a real wooden ladder built from the water level to the walking deck.

"Come on in." He had been my evening companion for all the time I had spent in this house, rocking well past dark on the screened porch, listening to the swamp creatures wake up in twilight.

I brought out lemonade and set it on the round table between the two rockers. Pasquin reached behind him. "Thought you'd like to help me nibble on these," he said.

"Boiled peanuts!" One of the favorites of Southerners in these parts, they were less well known outside the area than grits. When confronted with them, most Northerners winced. I delighted in them, another treat from my childhood. Peanut farmers from the area would fill chest-high cauldrons with unshelled peanuts, water and salt, then boil them for hours, making the nut inside a tender meat-like substance. When I grew up, young boys would often sell baskets of bagged nuts on the streets, yelling at passers by, "Fresh boiled peanuts!" I grabbed paper sacks for both of us, and we sat, shelling, eating, tossing the hulls into the bags.

"Make good mulching, these shells," said Pasquin.

"And good stomachaches if we don't stop." I pushed the bag to the other side of the table.

He continued to eat while I sat in silence. The South is like that, lazy, in no hurry to say things as shadows circle the porch on a summer's evening. When the frogs struck up their choir, darkness surrounded us. I wouldn't turn on a light as it tended to draw more bugs than we could handle.

"Ah, enough," said Pasquin as he leaned back and began to rock slowly. The runners on his chair made soft click-clacks as he swayed to and fro.

"Pasquin, tell me about the Wilburn sisters. I mean what you know about their midwife activities." I let my chair join his so that we made harmonic rhythms across the wooden porch.

"Luanne, if you and one of them fellows ever decide to produce a little one, and you get stuck out here, you don't want to ask Sadie or Josie for help. Their record ain't nowhere near their mama's."

I closed my eyes and tried to see myself with a child. Would I teach her to dive like my daddy taught me? But my head wouldn't make an image like that. All I could see was that bundle the Wilburn woman clasped tightly to her bosom.

"Do they take money payments?"

"Sure. That's what they want. Only sometimes neither the mama nor the papa has the cash. They have to settle for barter. That Miss Grassfield probably didn't have much to give."

I sat up quickly. "Damn! Theresa Grassfield. Tony said I should try to see her." I hit the arm of the rocker. "Oh, damn!"

"Stop your cussing, ma'am. You can drive to Tallahassee in the morning."

"She may not last till morning." I stood up. "I'm calling right now."

The hospital information desk gave me the data they send out on all patients. "She's still in intensive care, ma'am. No change in condition for now."

I didn't rest well. Around midnight, I awoke from a dream about hearing a baby cry in the dark swamp. Panic gripped my throat until I realized the sound was a screech owl chasing after some helpless prey. Guilt wasn't something I liked to carry as baggage.

Before the ICU nurse would allow me in, she wanted notice from the sheriff's office. After calling someone, she pointed to a cubicle across the counter. From the short distance, Theresa's face, bathed in the hospital light, took on the hue of a corpse in the morgue. She lay with tubes in her nose and mouth, her eyes closed. The monitor on the wall sounded out her life in intervals.

I approached the bed and leaned close to her ear. "Theresa, I'm Luanne Fogarty, the woman who found you in the cabin. Do you remember?"

After asking several times with no response, I gave up and started for the door. Tony met me with the doctor.

"We did some metal toxin tests before we transfused her." The man eyed me, then looked at Tony who nodded my legitimacy. "Normally, we don't do those tests at all, but your crime tech alerted us to something he found at the scene."

"Loss of blood wasn't her only problem?" said Tony.

"No, a trace of something else appeared in her system." The doctor stopped talking and looked at me again.

"Luanne," Tony greeted me, then turned to the doctor. "Go on, please."

"I can't be sure why she had this stuff in her system. It wasn't enough to kill her, probably not enough to kill a full-term child."

"What was it?" Tony's jaw clenched. He hated it when people talked all around the issue.

"*Cardiac glycoside*—Oleander poison."

"Oleander?" I said. "Most people in these swamps would know not to ingest that. It's one of the best known poisons around."

"Yes, but she didn't ingest enough to kill her, only to make her sick. And…"

"Doctor, go on." Amado placed his hands on his hips.

"This is conjecture only, you see. Oleander in the right amounts can act as an abortifacient—cause a spontaneous abortion—and quite a distressful one. It's not used often, but maybe in cases of desperation."

"You mean like swamp people who can't afford an abortion clinic?" I said.

"That, yes, but more like some kid who didn't want the world to know she was pregnant and used a coat hanger in the days when abortion was illegal. Only, this is no kid, and our tests indicate she was near term. I don't understand an abortion attempt so late in the gestation period—unless they were using it to hasten labor." The doctor rubbed his chin and frowned at some faraway thought.

"Could someone have given it to her, in a drink or something?" said Amado. He looked toward Theresa's face as he asked.

"It can be disguised fairly easily. But whoever did it—and she may have done it herself, you know—either didn't know how much could kill or they didn't want to kill her, just make her distressed." The doctor checked something on Theresa's chart. "Or she may not have known how much to take to kill herself."

"Or maybe somebody wanted to abort the baby—make sure it was stillborn," I said. Both men turned to face me.

"Terrible way to do it," said the doctor.

"And we don't know what happened to the baby, do we?" Tony faced me, but I looked away. I could feel his criticism, blaming me for letting the sisters run off with a towel full of newborn.

"No sir, but if you find the baby's body, I can tell you if this stuff killed it."

"The baby might still be alive," I said without conviction.

Tony looked from me to the doctor, then said, "Okay, Luanne, let's go find a baby."

Theresa still hadn't moved, her eyes stayed closed, and the machine on the wall continued to bleep off the rhythm of her life. In the hall, I turned to Tony.

"I'm sorry I didn't get in here sooner. I got so caught up in all that other stuff…"

"The woman wouldn't have known if you were here or not." He poked his finger at the down button on the elevator.

We rode in silence until Tony changed the subject.

"Drake's coming back Sunday, right?" He said as he walked me to my car.

"You know he is."

"You and Harry all right these days?"

"Tony, the thing with Harry has been over for nearly two years, okay? It hasn't rekindled if that's what you're asking."

"Not because of Harry, I'll bet. See you at the site." He didn't give me time to respond, just saluted and left.

I rested my head on the back of the car seat. "Why did you say that, Tony?" I asked aloud. He did that to me, planted little hints then ran. He had to know it would shake me inside, and I couldn't understand why he would want a diver to be rattled.

Harry hauled in diving gear and mapping equipment on two boats piloted by graduate students. Tibby had been grounded at the Palmetto Springs camp to work on maps and catalog the various silts we collected from the caves. Not trusting her alone, he sent one graduate student back as soon as he had unloaded his boat.

"If we get St. Claire's permission, we'll move to the old cabin. At least we'll have a roof, and that old tin keeps the rain out fairly well," he said as he erected a canvas tent on the shore several feet from the sand.

"I'm not crazy about going in there and smelling that blood again," I said as I lifted tanks and placed them under the tent.

"We'll get these guys to scrub it down if we use it," he nodded and smiled at the students.

One mumbled something derogatory about the price of an advanced degree. The other one said, "Why not hire Tibby's friend Arnie?"

Harry ignored them.

"When will you be ready to go down?" I said.

"Soon as I have some lunch and finish here. We have to wait for the law, too, you know."

I shrugged, took a seat on the grassy bank and watched the three men struggle to haul gear, tents, and supplies from boats to shore. Harry finally left it to the students and joined me. He lay back, his arms behind his head.

"Kind of like the Keys, isn't it, Luanne?" He referred to our dive near Key West where his project was to investigate some peculiar stone formations. It was the summer of bliss and abandonment for me. Then came the fall. That turned out to be Harry's abandonment of me in favor of another archeologist. It didn't work, and he came back, but my trust had disappeared. Our affection, at least mine, had turned sour. Vernon Drake appeared to restore my faith in male divers.

"No, Harry," I said, "it's not like the Keys. I was naive then. I'm not anymore. And we're looking for a baby now."

Why did I say that? Harry and I never talked about babies. Getting pregnant then would have been about the biggest disaster in my life. Would I have sought an abortion clinic? Harry absent-mindedly ruffled his hair, something I had done to him many times in the Keys.

A quick gust of wind blew across the river, forming parallel ripples that scooted beneath a mama duck and four babies. She darted out of the water surge, leaving her ducklings to paddle off in all directions. The last duckling got caught up in the breezy current and swept toward the depths. Only the mad paddling of his webbed feet and the dying of the wind got him back on course in line behind his siblings. Mother duck never looked back.

CHAPTER SIX

"Tony," I sat in shallow water and pulled on my fins, "has anyone spoken to Theresa Grassfield's family?"

"We've found an uncle, but he says he hasn't seen her in years."

"Well, somebody ought to talk to Pasquin. He'll know about the family name." I began to rinse my mask in the water when the roar of an engine sounded in the woods behind us. Through the trees and over the brush, an off-terrain vehicle came to a sudden stop on the rim of the bank. It was a four-seater, and three men in suits sat in the passenger seats, while a striking woman in safari clothes pulled on the emergency brake. Shoving oversized sunglasses through bleach-streaked hair, she darted towards us.

"Excuse me," she said as she hurried toward Tony, "this is private property. You can't swim here."

Tony said nothing, his expression cold, his olive skin free of sweat. He held up his badge.

"Oh," the woman said as she slowed to a stop. "I'm sorry." She handed over a card, which Tony gazed at then turned to me.

"Charlene Brennan?" I said as though we had mental telepathy. He nodded.

"Didn't Mr. St. Claire tell you we have a police action going on here?" He stood tall, visibly intimidating the woman who looked like someone used to turning the tables on clients. She glanced toward the men in the buggy, then thrust her fingers through the blond tresses.

"No, but then I haven't seen him lately." She hesitated, bent down and brushed some sand off her loafers. "Look, I've got some developers here. They need to look at this location now. We could roam around a bit, right?"

"Wrong," Tony said as he placed the woman's card in his pocket. "This area is secured for police work. I suggest you leave. If you move around here too much, we'll be forced to take your fingerprints—all four of you—to eliminate you as suspects."

Ms. Brennan twitched her face and placed her hands on her hips. "Did someone commit a crime here?" She looked toward me, then at Harry who stood in the sand, waiting to don his fins. "Or drown?"

"I'm not at liberty to say, ma'am," Tony said, his *ma'am* nothing like the affectionate tease Pasquin had used with me all my life.

Ms. Brennan then leaned toward Tony, and in a whisper that I could hear, but clearly meant to hide things from her suited men, said, "Just what am I going to do with these guys? They've come from Miami and have tickets to return tonight."

Tony said nothing, but passed her and approached the men. Charlene Brennan came running behind him.

"Gentlemen," he said, "you'll have to leave. We have a police action at this site; you won't be able to see it today. Nor tomorrow. In fact," he turned toward Charlene, "call my office and I'll let you know when the coast is clear." He handed the woman one of his cards.

Charlene threw her hands to her sides in exasperation. Turning to the men, she said, "I'm sorry. I didn't know this was going on. Could you look at some property farther south, then perhaps I can work out something with the sheriff's office?"

Three frowns greeted her. The one in the front seat shrugged. "Can't do much else, can we?"

Ms. Brennan turned to Amado as she jumped into the driver's seat. "You'll hear from me soon. Please be in your office." She started the engine and roared back into the oaks.

Tony's jaw gripped in a snarl. He turned to us. "I won't be in my office much at all, but I don't know how long I'll be able to hold her off. Get going, will you?" He nodded toward the water.

"Tony," I said, "you don't suppose St. Claire is planning to develop this area?"

"Wouldn't doubt it, but he's going to have trouble. Laws don't like wetlands paved over with concrete."

Harry pulled the full mask over his face. He would speak underwater, recording the soil, grass, niches, and offshoots we encountered for the graduate student who had set up the recording equipment on the bank. Tony agreed to this since any discovery of criminal evidence would be recorded, too.

I took the buoys with flags that would mark our territory and waded into the water. Not more than two feet out, the bank dropped off ten feet, deep enough for a motor boat. I secured one buoy here, tying it to some eel grass on the bottom. I headed downward to the cave opening, then secured another flag by tacking its rope to the limestone outside the entrance. When Harry joined me, we waved and rolled under the water, adjusting our belt weights.

I reached the cave first, where I felt the rush of current cross my face. Without touching the walls, I pushed into the opening where I could see only a few feet ahead. I made way for Harry, then turned on the underwater torch. Catfish scurried in all directions, but stayed near the sloping floor. There had to be something that attracted them, and in the back of my mind, I thought *body*. I dreaded that it might be an old woman, or worse, a baby.

It wasn't human flesh they nibbled on, but a partial deer carcass that had lodged on the slope. I tried to imagine what had happened. An alligator grabbed the small animal as it came for a drink in the shallows. Taking it to the bottom and holding it there, the gator drowned the deer then returned to the surface where he placed it in the grassy shallows to rot—or tenderize in gator terms. When the reptile pushed the softened meat to shore to gulp it down, part of the body broke off and fell into the currents. They swept it into the cave where catfish cleaned house. All perfectly legal, and normal, in the animal kingdom.

After pointing to the carcass, Harry motioned for me to follow him deeper into the cave. It was not a friendly cave. Instead of a vast open space with white limestone walls, it housed several rooms with large openings and dark innards. The walls tended toward crumbly dirt, dangerous when stirred because a diver could be temporarily blinded, then disoriented, and drown in the process. I kept Harry's light in sight at all times.

We made a circle as best we could. I could see Harry's throat muscles moving as he described the location of each opening, knowing he would be back to explore the inside of each cave. I also knew each cave could house more openings, even dangerous underwater sloughs from one cave to another or to an outside sinkhole opening. These sloughs, no more than tunnels of water, tended to push water both ways. A diver caught in one of these currents could be pounded back and forth as he tried to swim through.

From the outset, I tacked lifelines to the walls. When we reached a large opening, Harry motioned that we would explore this one. Larger than the others, the currents whirled about force-fully. I felt the cold rush as I followed him inside.

Things rested on the sloping sandy bottom inside this cave. Water-soaked tree branches, tires, remnants of a wooden boat—all pushed into the hole by a strong current and stored in their watery graves. A few fist-sized holes shot cold spring water into the cave, but we could find no more large openings. The walls, covered with current-gouged niches also had their share of de-bris—leaf clumps, fish bones, and oak bark. We had gone about as deep as law enforcement allowed. Even if we expected a body to be in a cave, we wouldn't go after it like cave divers in a scien-tific exploration. It would be too dangerous.

Then we saw it, both of us at once. In our lights it glowed a bluish-pink. Caught between jagged outings, the towel waved back and forth in the currents, one end forming a hand-like shape. Its silent back and forth movements made a Captain Ahab call to death.

I saw Harry's jaw move and knew he had reported to Tony. He took the evidence bag from his waist. I held it for him as he gently, almost as if the cloth were the baby, grasped it in both hands and pushed it into the bag.

We made a quick search of the walls. No body attached it-self to the rocky limestone. We headed topside.

"No sign of any adults down there?" Tony asked as he leaned over to retrieve the towel.

"None so far," I said, "but it's full of caves. Nasty ones. It'll take weeks to explore them all."

"I've got the medical examiner," yelled Loman from the bank. "He'll come out in a motor boat."

I tried to distract my mind from the possibility of an inno-cent baby flowing through dark tunnels on its way to the Gulf by imagining Marshall Long's tonnage inside a motor boat. He wouldn't like being on top of water. Swimming was not his talent. Sure he would be sent on this mission because he had been inside the cabin, I drank mineral water and wondered how he would make it up the steep bank.

"We've got lifelines down there, Tony," said Harry as he peeled his wet suit off his chest and let it rest on his hips. "I've got plenty of excuses to go back down and map this place while I do police work."

"Yeah, but don't let anyone know you're doing that, too. In fact," said Tony as he placed the bag with towel on the grass, "I'm going to have to tell that grad student up there that he's acting as an agent of the law. Think you can keep him quiet?"

"He'll be quiet if he wants a degree," said Harry and marched up the bank.

Humid air sat atop us like an electric blanket in a sauna. I sat on the sand, my feet in water that no longer felt cool. I waited here instead of the upper bank where the baby's birthing cloth lay stuffed inside a large bag. *Like garbage,* I thought.

Finally, in the distance, a siren screamed from down the river. Tony waved from the bank. A deputy guided the boat to the shallow edge. Marshall Long filled one end, grasping the sides with both hands. His pale face had lost all signs of his usual cockiness.

"You'll have to take the case, Luanne," said Marshall as he leaned over the boat and handed me his evidence kit. "I don't like this." Both of us could see the sharp drop-off and knew if he made one slip, nearly three hundred pounds of medical examiner's assistant would tumble into the deep.

"Just take it easy. I don't want to have to rescue you," I said as I passed the black case to Tony. I held out both hands to give him a feeling of balance. He thumped into the shallow water, nearly tumbling backwards. When he righted himself, he held onto my arm and waded to the sandy beach.

"Damn! I hate wet shoes."

"You should have taken them off," I said.

"And step barefoot in that grass? No way."

He grunted up the hill, then leaned over to remove the towel. He lay it over the bag as gently as a new father scared of fracturing tiny limbs. What had been Marshall's expression of horror over eel grass and deep water turned to one of curiosity, even fascination.

"Workable evidence from the deep." He placed his chubby fists on his ample hips and circled the cloth like a vulture. "Thing stayed wadded up enough to keep blood from totally washing away."

"What's that?" I asked as I pointed to something that looked like blue cartilage.

"Looks like part of the umbilical cord. Probably torn in the currents. Crudely snipped, I'd say." He had pulled on gloves and moved the knobby object back and forth. "I'd better get this thing out of the sun. You didn't happen to find the baby that goes with the blanket, did you?"

"Wish we had," I said. "Probably in some bottomless pit by now." I shook inside and spoke what I didn't believe. "Or, it could be alive somewhere."

"Hold the bag," he said, and with both hands replaced the towel. He held the evidence in his palms, like a daddy handling a broken doll.

"Let's get this to the lab." He looked toward the water. "I'm not going back in that boat. Bring the cooler!" He yelled at the officer in the motor boat.

Placed in a cooler that looked like it should contain Saturday's picnic beer, the baby's towel would ride in the rear of a deputy's patrol car, Marshall sitting next to it. Before that, just to get to the car, Marshall and the deputy would have to trek through the swampy woods to the paved road.

"Luanne," said Tony, his gaze still on the woods long after the two men and the evidence had disappeared, "call Pasquin. We need to find some Grassfields. And I have a search warrant for the Wilburn house. I want you present for both."

"I have a class to teach tomorrow night."

"Then we'd better get rolling, right?"

We decided to take the sheriff's boat to the Fogarty Spring landing. We spent the next hour packing tanks. The tent, surrounded with police tape, would remain at the site. I stood on the bank for one last look before joining the others on the river. Behind me, a flock of swamp birds suddenly hit the sky together. Standing very still, I tried to see what disturbed them. The woods returned my gaze in silence, refusing to declare its secrets. Maybe the disturbance was a deer, a fawn perhaps, running from the rare Florida panther.

"You have searched the swamp over there for signs of the women and the baby, right?"

"Got a search crew out the same day, Luanne." Tony glanced into the woods. "Not a sign of anything."

CHAPTER SEVEN

At six o'clock, I hit the road to meet my seven o'clock class in History of the English Language. A required course for linguistics majors, it attracted large numbers. The department chair saw fit to offer it only once per year. Students fought for a spot. The first night, forty people showed up. It had since dwindled to twenty-nine.

Six-thirty and I finally found a parking space at the far end of the lot. Taking off on a fast trek to the anthropology building, I wound through tall pines that cast long shadows in the setting sun. In spite of shrub lights placed around campus, this place basked eerie after dark in the glow of Tallahassee's yellow street lights. Tripping over lovers rolling in the bushes had once been common. But after two robberies and one rape on campus grounds during the winter quarter, I didn't need to worry about the embarrassment of lovers.

Plopping my notes on the scratched surface of the desk that had been used for thirty years, I found myself facing strong fingers clasping a white paper.

"I'm changing to audit," said the young man, his too-small tee shirt rippling atop gym-developed muscles. Tall, well-formed, the number of hairs on his shaved head probably matched the number of brain cells inside his head.

"Sorry, I don't take audits," I said as I handed the slip back to him. "You'll have to drop the class."

I ached at the thought of another argument with a lazy student. I'd had too many these past years, too many papers ripped off the Internet or written with enough grammatical errors to wonder how they ever entered college. The push now was to audit when you started to fail, then take the course again.

He placed his hands on his hips, refusing the paper. I shrugged and dropped it on the desk in front of him.

"The department chair okayed this." His finger pointed to the signature area on the paper. His pleading eyes reminded me of the mangy puppy under the Wilburn house.

"Mr. Summers, this class is jammed full of linguistics majors. Why should you audit this—to take it later for credit? Besides, the class is half over."

He grinned. "I'm just not sure I want to work on this major. Kind of trial and error, I guess." He smiled and passed the paper onto the desk. "I would appreciate it."

Nick Summers, the muscular young man, plopped in his seat near the rear of the room. He tossed a small note pad on the desk in front of him, pulled out a pen and rested it on the spiral binding. The rest of the class drifted in with coffee cups and sweet rolls.

On a wall map, I began to trace the movement of the early Germanic tribes out of the European continent and into the British Isles. Giving a short history lecture, I moved about the room. Nick scratched notes on his paper, his eyes darting and frowning in confusion, his muscles nearly bursting the seams of his shirt. He looked up and grinned at me each time I neared his seat. That grin, nearly imbecilic at times, unnerved me.

At nine-thirty, I dismissed the class with their reading assignments for the next session. After dark, I tried to walk with the crowd to the parking lot. Nick Summers waited for me at the door, nodded and said, "Good class." I ignored him and pushed ahead to a group of students I had taught in a previous year, joining them in conversation about Low German dialect. This didn't deter him. He followed close enough to hear the chatter.

I separated from the students when we reached the cars. Faculty parked on one side of the lot.

"I'll walk with you," said Nick. "Not too safe out here for women alone." He took my elbow like an old time gentleman.

We walked under the lights; I unlocked my '84 Honda, and tossed my notes into the back seat.

"Thank you," I said and pulled my elbow away. I held the door, half expecting to slam it against him and feeling like an ingrate for not trusting him.

Nick nodded, waited until I had locked the door, then moved into the shadows.

I sat still. In the rear view mirror, I saw him pull a crash helmet onto his shaved head and straddle a motorcycle like a metal bronco.

An eeriness enveloped me as I headed out of town. Lights followed me. I fought with my head, telling myself I had contracted paranoia from police work, until I entered the paved road that would carry me through dark, forest terrain to my own dirt road. There were no street lights here, and on a moonless night, it was pitch outside, occasional headlights the only illumination for miles. I glanced quickly and often in the rear view mirror. Every pair of lights behind me had turned off, except for the one far behind. It made no effort to pull close, and at times I lost it when

I went over a swell in the road. But I could see it again as soon as the road flattened.

Speeding up, I reached my turn off, then stopped a few yards under overhanging oak branches. Shutting off the lights, I gasped at the sudden darkness. I could see nothing, not even my hand in front of my face. I waited. I began to sweat and feel the closeness of the air. Reaching quietly under the passenger seat, I pulled out the holster with its black-handled pistol. Faint engine sounds approached on the paved road.

With one hand on the ignition, the other clutching the revolver in my lap, I stared in the mirror. A car slowed, then stopped at the entrance to the road. Without turning, it moved on. I breathed again, but waited. The engine noise faded into the distance.

Later that night, I lay awake in my swamp sanctuary, the heat pump putting out noiseless air conditioning. When I renovated the house, I had put in an alarm system and installed sensor lights. In a swamp, things moved outside all night long, triggering the lights. I knew this, and the clicking on of lights had become routine until tonight. Every time I sensed the disruption of darkness, I jumped. Once, I walked around the rooms, gazing out windows. The swamp, its thick vines and draping moss, stood guard, but I wasn't sure who it guarded—me or what? There were times I regretted the air conditioning that required me to close out the nightly chorus of frogs and occasional owl, the natural alarms of the forest.

At two, my body said to hell with it. I placed the pistol in the wooden box between my bed and the night stand, and pulled a sheet over me.

I thought about the past, the pleasant part, when Daddy had placed a scuba breathing device in my mouth and taken me, step by step, through the process of trusting it underwater. We had stood waist deep in the cold water near the landing. Minnows darted around our feet, but he said not to pay them attention. He demonstrated the mouth piece with his own equipment, and helped me with mine. I learned to make short dives at five.

By ten, I was way past the minnows. Three years later, Daddy took me with him to the big cave at Palmetto Springs. At first, the cold currents and dark space frightened me, but I soon marveled at the big catfish that sucked on silt at the bottom and the buried mastodon bones. When I flashed my light around the huge cavern, I felt like a princess mermaid in a white castle. I was hooked.

The following year, I went into a sinkhole. No longer afraid of the depths or the darkness, I still cringed at the slimy algae on top of the still water.

"It's not really still, Luanne," said Daddy, "you'll see when we get underneath."

And he was right. Dropping beneath the slime, I found myself in an underwater garden of green light. From the top, the algae roots draped and swayed like so many green ribbons. There was no slime here, only clear water and white limestone illuminated by spotty sunlight. Looking down, I saw darkness. Between that black hole and the surface slime lay a magical kingdom.

Suspended in this space, playing with brim that skipped across my fingers as they swam to the algae tips, I drifted into sleep at last. Somewhere, I heard lights click on, and a baby cry, maybe near the surface.

CHAPTER EIGHT

"You didn't sleep good last night, did you , ma'am?" Pasquin helped me into his boat at the bottom of my landing.

"How do you know that?"

"Too quiet, little bit of puffiness about the eyes. I know you, *belle dame*, too well."

"Yeah, well, I did have things on my mind." I lay back and let the sun hit my face. The river seemed sluggish, still, and a haze of mist floated on its surface in the early morning.

Tony had ordered both of us to meet him at the Wilburn house. We would do our search today.

"Think St. Claire will be there?" I let my voice drift into the gathering humidity. I felt anxious. I longed for a lazy day on the river, to lie with my face covered in a straw hat, to listen to the gurgling of turtles diving off logs and know it wasn't the sound of a drowning baby.

"Man like that has got to keep up his image," said Pasquin. "Bet he's done been there and cleaned up the house." He turned up the throttle, and we chugged over the main river, then down the deep water lane.

When we pulled into the cove, Pasquin tied the boat to a cypress knee. He held on tight as I moved to the shore. I pulled the boat toward me, so he wouldn't have to jump.

"This old river never changes, Luanne. Deep down there," he said as he pointed to the dark water. "Suck you up like catfish on bait."

We trudged through the foliage. Pasquin used his hat to bat at branches that grew in our path, holding them back for me. At the end of the path, I took him around the fenced garden and onto the lawn. Someone had recently mowed the high grass. We stopped in the grove of oaks when we spied St. Claire's camouflaged vehicle near the overgrown carport. He leaned against the rear, checking his watch, when another car emerged from the thicket of trees.

"Cut a new road through the forest, Mr. St. Claire?" said Tony as he handed the search warrant to the man.

"Had to. Just too hard on cars, even this thing, to run through all that mud and brush." He looked down at the warrant. "May I ask the specific reason for the search?"

"Suspicion of midwifing illegally, abandoning the mother, possibly dumping the baby, and as of seven-twenty this morning," Tony looked at his watch, "a dead mother."

I gasped. "Theresa died!"

"Bless her soul," said Pasquin and took me by the arm in the direction of the men.

"And you think the previous owners of this house had something to do with all that?" St. Claire shifted, his eyes opening wide.

"Yes, sir, I do. But until we search this place and do a few other things, I won't know for sure. Now, do you have a key?" Tony stretched out an open hand.

St. Claire said nothing, but deliberately pulled a key from his shirt pocket and turned it over to Amado. He turned to me, smiled gently and touched my arm. "Don't wreck the place, okay?"

"Mr. St. Claire, do I have your word you haven't disturbed

68

anything since I first told you I would search this place?" Tony frowned at the man's familiarity toward me.

"Haven't touched a thing," he said and climbed into his vehicle.

"Well, somebody mowed the lawn," I said as I watched St. Claire drive through the trees.

The warped door wouldn't budge until Loman pulled up on the knob and forced it with his shoulder. It opened into the hallway that stood barren of anything other than its worn boards. Tony began to open doors, then turned to Pasquin and me with latex gloves. "Here, put these on, but try not to touch anything without asking."

Pasquin donned his hat and pulled the gloves over aged, thorny hands. He smiled at them, holding up his palm spread-fingered as though purchasing a new pair of dress gloves.

Except for some fire irons and soot in one fireplace, the entire downstairs was clean. No furniture, belongings of any kind, and no dust. In the upstairs hall, a cheap 1950's chest of drawers leaned to one side, its broken leg lying in the corner. Inside the drawers, nothing.

The hardwood floors showed signs of recent scraping as though someone had run furniture across them. The closets stood bare, their doors ajar. Inside, unpainted for years, hanger scratches covered the rods, but no clothes hung there.

"We'll get the print boys up here, but I doubt they'll find much. Somebody left this place spic and span." Tony pulled out his cellular and called the crime scene unit. Frustrated, he stood quiet for a moment. "There's absolutely no sign of a baby or even of midwifing here."

"Yes, it's eerie," I said. "I'm going to look around outside." He tossed his head like he was glad to be rid of me. Pasquin tipped his hat and followed.

A breeze blew from the direction of the river. It cleared the humid haze and made the grass under the carport shimmy and relax in a series of movements.

"That's where I found the dog," I said, pointing to the area underneath one side of the house.

Pasquin stooped to look, then began sniffing. "Something dead around here."

"Probably a wild animal." I moved beside him, hoping it wouldn't be what was left of a newborn. The odor was more pronounced the farther I leaned under the house.

"Let's go around there," he said, pointing to the opposite side. He led the way, his nose slightly raised, resembling a trusty old blood hound.

"Man!" I said as I took a whiff of rotting flesh. "Something is under there."

The house on this side was raised enough for a human to walk underneath as long as he stooped over. The lattice work had been knocked out, something I hadn't noticed the first time I came here. I covered my nose and mouth with my gloved hand.

"It's here," I said, "looks like two dead and rotting dogs."

"I'll get the boss," said Pasquin. He slapped his hip as though whipping a horse.

While he returned inside, I pulled out my phone and called Kendall, the vet. I walked to the edge of the swamp where the scent was not so offensive, and stood beside tall flowering bushes.

"Pukey," said Kendall, "is doing fine. I call him that because puke is what he did the minute I placed him on the examining table. Coughed up chunks of cheese."

"I gave him that, all I had under the circumstances. What's the verdict?"

"He'll live. Getting better already."

"Could you come to the old Wilburn house? We've got a dead animal situation out here."

We agreed that Pasquin would pick him up at Fogarty Spring landing.

"There's some hardened food in a tin pan under there," said Tony as he emerged from under the house. He let out air and gulped in fresh oxygen. I walked with him to the edge of the property in back.

"Oleanders. At least six bushes, taller than six feet. These must have grown here for years." I looked up at the white and pink flower clusters among pointed green leaves. They waved gently in the breeze from off the river. "Beautiful, but deadly."

"You think the sisters used these on Theresa," said Tony.

"Possibly. Or she used them on herself. There's certainly enough material to work with."

A crime scene tech arrived on the new road at the same time Kendall trudged down the river lane. Pasquin followed, but I could tell he had tired. He sat in one of the plastic chairs and fanned himself with his hat.

"Yep, they're dead dogs, all right," said Kendall as he humped over the carcasses. "Here's the food they must have been eating. We'll need to take it back to see if it's poisoned. From the looks of these animals, I'd say that's how they died." He pulled out body bags and shoved the animals inside, then placed the food in another bag. "Better get Amado to take this pan to the fingerprint man." He shoved it from under the house, his latex gloves stained with dirt.

Loman helped Kendall pack up the remains while I gazed at the oleanders. "Can you tell if the dogs were poisoned with this stuff?"

"Well, somebody can. I don't have the lab equipment for it, but I know where to send it." He thumbed in the direction of the crime scene tech who would unload the food on Marshall's lab table.

"Pretty things, right?" I pulled a flower off one bush.

"Don't go putting that in a salad now," said Kendall as he loaded his findings in the trunk of a patrol car.

"Would Marshall also be able to tell if the poison came from one of these bushes?" I took one of Loman's empty bags and stuffed the flower inside.

"Don't know," said Kendall, "labs do lots these days."

"I think I read somewhere that DNA tests can be done on plants as well as humans." I wiped imaginary oleander sap off my jeans.

Pasquin chugged his engine to my landing, wholloping mosquitoes most of the way. As usual, I invited him inside.

"Lordy, this air conditioning do make a difference!" He fanned the cold air around his face with his hat.

"Then let's sit inside for lemonade, okay?"

We sat on either side of the empty fireplace, and listened to the quiet coolness of the house. Eventually, the lingering dead dog odor left us.

"Pasquin," I said, "do you know the Grassfield family?"

"Now, you know I've been trying to come up with that name, but I don't recall it. Except maybe on some gravestones over to the Baptist cemetery."

"You'll go with me, right?"

"Ma'am, you keep dragging this old man around, you'll have to leave him at the cemetery one day." He chuckled, but the thought sent a chill down my neck.

"Then get on the gossip line and find out something yourself," I said. He would do it, too. The river and the woods had their own primitive teleport, a sort of message system that could make its way across mud sinks from the cabin dweller on the north end to the converted trailer on the south. And if there was some lost baby out there, why hadn't the swamp people picked up on the rumor?

CHAPTER NINE

After a lunch of canned hash and fried eggs, Pasquin lay down on the sofa. He snored while I went to the kitchen to phone Marshall.

"Yeah," he said, "Tony already told me what to test for. I doubt I can tell if the poison came from those particular bushes, but I'll try. Could be some substance on them, not on other bushes. Of course, I have to test that food first. We'd have to get some DNA from a plant substance in the food in order to match it with the flower you sent. Besides, it could be some other kind of poison, if any. We got autopsies going on the dogs one door down from the humans."

People had been poisoning dogs for a long time, mostly because of their nuisance barking. I was thinking about the barking dog at St. Claire's place, when the phone rang.

"Luanne," said Tony, "we're going to ask you to go down with Harry again. The baby may have been in the cave and maybe the women, too. We need to be sure—cover our asses for the courts. Harry and one of his workers have dived a few more times and looked in some of the holes. One more afternoon should do it."

"Even if we find nothing doesn't mean they aren't there," I said. "They could have been washed down hole after hole until they're underneath St. Marks by now."

"Yeah, then you'd better check all the way to St. Marks. By four, okay?"

To get there by boat meant I would have to wake up Pasquin. I took the car instead. Tony promised to clear a car lane from the rutted road to the cabin. It wouldn't be much of a clearing, mostly chopped saplings and pushed-down brush. Since the graduate student had stored some tanks in the tent, I could walk through the swamp without the extra load of diving gear. I left a note for Pasquin and headed for the Honda.

Clear weather lives a tenuous life in this part of the state. A sudden cloud cluster can form and lightning flash without warning. The only indication is stepped-up breezes. They had begun, and a black cloud lurked far behind the tops of the cypress trees. I parked the car at the edge of the lane, pulled on swamp boots, and trudged through grass, mud, and nettles. In case I met up with a rattler along the way, I carried my pistol in one hand. In sight of the cabin, I remembered the screams and shuddered. Theresa Grassfield would never be able to speak for herself or her baby.

The cabin stood eerily quiet, yellow police tape across the doorless opening. I rounded the house, then tramped through more marsh grass and trees to come out at the tent. The graduate student worked at one of the tables. A familiar-looking young man sat on the ground and watched him.

"I guess the others will be along soon," he said. "I—we—just got here half an hour ago." He looked embarrassed and nodded to the young man.

"Don't I know you?" I said.

"Yeah," said the young man. He stood up and brushed dirt from the back of his shorts. "I'm Nick Summers. I audit your class."

I nodded. "Guess you feel better out here than in the class-room." I meant to be sarcastic, to refer to his lack of studious behavior, only it hit me that I'd rather be out here, too. I turned away from the shy smile and downcast eyes. He may have muscles like Mr. Universe, but he was still a kid.

At the edge of the lake, I looked down at the calm, deep water. On a shallow bank a few yards away, an alligator nearly six feet long basked in the afternoon sun. The clear weather had in-vited fishermen to sit in their boats, sip beer, and occasionally pull in a bass. Four boats sat in my line of vision, separated by half a mile of open lake.

The vibrating roar of a motor interrupted the silence and sent the reptile scurrying into the water. Harry, Tony, and Loman rode in a sheriff's department boat.

"Sorry we're late," said Harry. "I had to clear up some things with Tibby. She goofed on the mapping."

"Got other things on her mind," said the grad student un-der his breath.

We pulled on diving gear; Harry gave me details about some of the holes he had seen in another short dive.

"Loose silt on the walls. Be careful. Look first, then touch." He jerked up the full mask and tossed it to me. "You do the talk-ing this time, okay?"

I pulled the full mask over my face and tested it on the equip-ment that would listen and record what I said. We gave the signal to the student who would man the equipment, then Harry and I waded into the water, dropping suddenly into the depths. Nick leaned over the bank to watch us descend.

We headed for the cave opening under the marker flag and where the lifelines had remained firmly attached to the walls. Pretty soon we'd have to adjust depth gauges.

"We've passed the first inner opening," I said to the topside recorder, "and we're going to explore the second, smaller opening. Still have an outside light source." Something at the entrance caught my eye, but, concerned about catching up with Harry, I passed it.

Harry turned into the hole but swam too quickly and stirred up silt. He backed out and both of us suspended our bodies in the water, holding still to allow the silt to settle. When we could see the opening again, we noticed a section had fallen away. "That's the source of the silt, and it doesn't look safe."

I recorded this as Harry gave me a caution sign. When he tried again, another section came down, and, again, we waited. "We won't look here. It's too dangerous."

I backed away from the hole and moved closer to the first opening. Filtered sun rays lighted up the bottom just outside the cave mouth.

"I'm staying away from the walls. We don't want any more crumbling." I looked to my side and backward when the object caught my eye again. "On a solid-looking rock just at the opening there is something—dear God! Harry, Harry!"

I knew he couldn't hear me, that only those on the surface could. I dashed toward him and felt his arm before I could see him. "Pipe bomb! Pipe bomb!"

I screamed into the mask as I gave Harry the danger sign and pulled on him to follow me. I was ahead of him, swimming with all my strength toward the surface when I felt the wave effect, the tremendous force of water that pushed me into the shallows. The sound, a roar that could break eardrums, crushed at my chest. The mask left me, and I found myself lying belly down in muddy eel grass. I couldn't see very well, but I heard my own

77

screams.

"Harry! Where are you?"

"Luanne, listen to me!" It was Tony's voice, and it seemed far away. I blinked. Enough mud dropped away to see the lake again. I was nearly one hundred yards down shore in the shallows. When I could focus my eyes, I saw three boats on the lake. People in them were standing, looking toward us.

"Luanne, stay there. You're going to be okay, but don't move."

Half-submerged tree limbs blocked my view of the others. Fragments of motor boat floated around me.

Harry bobbed to the top, his face in the water, his tank missing. Throwing my tank aside, I pushed into the water and swam for him. Turning him over, I pulled on the collar of his wet suit until the student grabbed his weight belt and pulled him to shore. Tony and Loman lifted me up.

"Ambulance is on its way, Luanne, just hold on."

"It was a bomb, Tony. Somebody planted it down there."

Motor sounds from the fishing boats moved toward us.

"Check the boats, Tony. It had to be a remote from one of them out there." The student held a cola to my lips. "Harry?"

"He's breathing," said Tony.

I leaned back on the sand. My skin felt cold, and I could not stop shaking. "Thank God, Pasquin didn't come. He would have been sitting right there in his boat." A siren wailed from down river. Near the shore, swamp fishermen called out, "Is anyone hurt?" Then it felt as though my ears filled with rushing water. I closed my eyes when Loman placed a towel under Harry's head. The towel soaked up blood, reminding me of the one between Theresa's legs. I didn't think of much else until I sat up in a hospital bed.

CHAPTER TEN

"You can't stay out of trouble for a moment, can you?" A familiar voice sounded at the end of the bed. A friendly spanse of white teeth grinned like a Cheshire cat on its perch. Vernon Drake's bald pate lit up with the rest of his handsome face. He moved toward me and rested a gentle hand on my cheek. In spite of myself, I let a tear roll down and caress his knuckles.

"Harry is okay, Luanne. He's got some eardrum trouble, a couple of cracked ribs, but the head wound wasn't deep. And there's a broken leg. You're both pretty damn lucky you didn't end up in the chamber."

I pulled him close to me. The male scent of soap and sweat comforted me, and I thanked my stars my nose hadn't been broken. I clung to him, half crying, half laughing.

After rocking me in his arms, Vernon slipped his fingers into my hair and whispered, "Pasquin is outside. He says he has something to tell you."

"My God, Pasquin. He could have been sitting in his motor boat, sleeping with his hat over his face." I shivered again, but Vernon pulled me close.

"Do you want to see him?"

I nodded and let the tears flow when I saw the old man's skin folds spread into a grin as he removed his silly straw hat.

"Close call, ma'am," he said, "but you made it and pulled out Harry, too. You made your Daddy proud." He patted my shoulder, ignoring my sobs. Vernon handed me a tissue.

"There's something I got to tell you, about this case, but I'll wait if you want to sniffle some more." Pasquin's slow Cajun drawl was the familiar comfort I needed.

"No, tell me now. I need to take my mind off what could have happened."

"Well, I went to the Baptist this Sunday morning and took a look around the cemetery. Even talked to some ladies and a gent older than me." He grinned. I knew it took some doing for him to go to church. He would have had to take his boat to Fogarty Spring, then find somebody to drive him.

"And did you find anything?"

"Sure did. There's some old headstones with the name of Grassfield on them. I heard they did okay back years ago, but the modern lot ran into hard times and became a sorry bunch." He moved to a chair and fanned himself with his hat in spite of the cool room.

"You mean white trash?" said Vernon.

"That," nodded Pasquin. "Seems there's a man about seventy living on a farm near Havana. He's Theresa's uncle, but he didn't have anything to do with her. Surprised him when the law came asking. Said his brother—Theresa's father—moved away from these parts maybe fifteen, twenty years ago to a no-good farm near Mobile, Alabama. The brother and his wife only had one living child. That'd be Theresa. Her father died soon after they moved, then his wife a few years later. Far as he knows Theresa inherited what they owned, which couldn't have been much."

"You learned all this from church?" I had forgotten my tears.

"Yeah," he grinned, "better than the sermon any day. Congregations got a wife of a deputy who's gon' to put the department in jeopardy one day with her tongue."

"Does Tony know this?"

"Does," nodded Pasquin. "He's checking out Mobile right now."

"Theresa must have moved back here." I pushed myself up in bed, my sides and back sending sharp signals through all my nerves. "Damn! That hurts."

"Let us do the leg work, okay," said Vernon as he adjusted the pillows. "You fill up with pain killers until the soreness goes."

"Did anyone ask the doctor how long I have to stay here?"

Both men shook their heads. Vernon offered to find out and went in search of the man. Pasquin pulled out a piece of paper from his shirt pocket.

"A young woman by the name of Tibby—do you know her?" I nodded. "Said to tell you the archeology department has temporarily canceled the mapping project and all the stations are closed down. Said the stuff is still there, and she and two others have to check on it periodically." He looked up at me. "I suppose all that makes sense to you?"

"Yes. Did you tell Harry?"

"Gave the message to his nurse," he said as the doctor entered the room.

"Ms. Fogarty, you are lucky. Although I hear clever is a better word. If you and that other diver had been further inside those caves, we might be dredging the area for pieces of your body right now."

"Thanks. I love your bedside solace."

"Okay," he smiled, "stay out of water until I give you the go sign. That's going to be at least three weeks, maybe longer if the soreness doesn't clear up. You've got some nasty internal bruis-

81

ing, and I want to test your hearing. No eardrum bursts, but you must have got a heavy dose of noise. You'll stay here one more day, maybe go home Tuesday morning."

"What about the class I teach on Tuesday evenings?"

"If it's just stand there and lecture, okay. If it's swimming or diving, no way. And get someone to drive you. You'll be pretty sore in spots."

"I don't need you to tell me that." I leaned my head back on the pillows. "Vernon, want to go to a lecture in Old English roots on Tuesday?"

"You want us to bring you anything?" said Pasquin.

I thought for a moment. "Yeah. Could you go to the library and get some books on the history of the area, some with the names *St. Claire* and *Wilburn,* and possibly *Grassfield,* in the index?"

I lay on the pillows for an eternity, before Tony came in to tell me Harry would take at least six weeks to heal. The doctors couldn't tell him if he'd ever dive again. I knew better. Harry would go back in the water, bruises and all. I would, too. It was the only way to get over the fear. My daddy told me this, and I had once proved it to myself.

A teenager, I must have known everything there was to know about anything—especially diving. Cocky and headstrong, I did the one thing Daddy told me not to. I dived alone in the river off our landing. Near the dock, the eel grass and minnows in shallow water suddenly bottomed out to more than ten feet deep where the temperature dropped just as sudden. I had been there with Daddy, swimming deeper to the opening of an underwater cave and source of spring water gushing into the river. Past that, the river currents took hold. If you could make it across, you ran into an upward slope, then muddy water with nearly fifteen cypress trees, their roots like alien legs walking in the river.

The seasons had changed the currents, but I paid no attention. They hadn't been impossible the day I swam there with Daddy. I took off, swimming past the cave opening where I had to use all my strength to push against the current, into the open river.

The rushing water surprised me. It was nothing like before, and I could feel the downward pull. Panicked, I swam hard, but my tank and fins were hindrances. Several feet underwater, I knew I couldn't throw off the tank. Instead, I pushed on—right into a gush of current that tossed me head first into a multi-growth of cypress root.

I lost my mask somewhere in the river, and my mouthpiece came out. Retrieving it, I shoved it back into my mouth, tasting mud along with the air. Swimming upwards, I latched onto a cypress knee. The thought of water moccasins wiggled in my brain.

Providence must have been somewhere up that tree, because nearly an hour later, Pasquin and a fishing buddy came down the river. They had to slow down to avoid the trees and heard my yells for help. Bloody scrapes on my forehead and hands were all that later reminded me of the event—except my terror. I'd had enough of diving.

Daddy said no. I would go down again, this time the right way, and respect the rules of the sport from then on. He was right, of course. I've never made mistakes like that since, took chances when necessary, but no mistakes.

I'd just been stabbed with a pain-killing hypo when Tony called.

"We've called in the ATF men, Luanne," he said. "They'll want to question you."

"What's their interest?"

"We called them," he emphasized the *we*. "When somebody planted that bomb, we realized we've got a bigger problem than missing midwives and a baby."

My head buzzed, and my eyelids refused to stay raised. I wanted to give in to the drug, but someone entered the room with flowers.

"Harry?" I must have been dreaming to think he could be in the room.

"St. Claire, Miz Luanne. I brought you some roses. You're just too pretty to get messed up in something like this."

I shook my head, more in disbelief than is disagreement. "Like this?"

"Nobody wants to see scratches on that smooth skin."

I felt a male hand pass across my cheek and linger for a moment. A faded female voice spoke in the background. Something about putting those in water and sitting until I went to sleep.

CHAPTER ELEVEN

The nurse rolled the bed table across my knees and placed six books on top. "You'll have to make space for the meal tray later," she said as she watched me wince when I reached for a heavy volume.

"Could you find me a pencil and some paper?" I glanced at the phone table. A glass vase of red roses sat like a reminder of my evening haze. "Was there a card with these?"

"That man just brought them in himself. We had the vase behind the nurses' station." She left the room and came back with the paper.

Between shots of pain killer and catnaps, I managed to read about the St. Claire family. They had been farmers before the Civil War, the kind who rented both land and slaves from the big plantations. After the war, they moved in to claim not only their rented land but several hundred acres from the old owners. And their male members—down to the current St. Claire's great grand-father—were members of the Ku Klux Klan. Over the years, their land holdings had increased.

"And the current August is doing his best to make it twenty-fold," I wrote on the note pad. Most of the males turned into lawyers. Some cousins even spent time in the state legislature. August was the social animal, lawyering to senators, land holders, and bankers.

The few times I found *Wilburn* in the indexes, I discovered a similarity. They had been land renters, too, but after the war, they claimed only a few acres. In the middle of the swamps, it wouldn't produce much. No lawyers, not even a state congressman, came from that clan.

To my surprise, the Grassfield name cropped up in the same manner—land renters who had claimed a few acres. They had become dirt farmers, too. Among the three families, only the St. Claire's had profited.

I closed the final book, all six saying about the same thing, when I realized that all three families had rented from the same plantation owner before the war. I flipped back to the indexes, made notes, then lay back on the pillows.

"I bet St. Claire wished his ancestors had claimed some swamp land."

"Swamp land?" said the candy striper who wheeled in the food trays.

"Just thinking." I waited until she placed the tray on the bed table, then tried to sit up to eat.

"I hear you're a professor," she said. "I plan to go to college in September, but I'm not sure where yet. Probably I'll go two years to junior college first."

"Good idea. They'll help you find a suitable major." I stretched toward the phone. "Could you dial a number for me?"

After several rings, Pasquin picked up the phone.

"I need you to do something for me. Vernon will be diving now, and Tony doesn't have the staff." I could hear the old man panting.

"Ma'am," he whined, "I done run into this living room from tying up my boat. Ain't even had a chance to take off my hat."

"Then sit down with a pen and paper. I'll wait." I could hear noises in the background—drawers opening, creaking springs of his easy chair.

"Okay, what?"

"Go to the archives or wherever land sales are kept, and get information on the sale of the land around Palmetto Springs and River, but only the land owned by Grassfield and Wilburn. Got that?"

"I'm writing it down. Anything else?"

"Find out who bought it, and if you can, for how much."

"St. Claire bought it. You know that."

"I only know about the Wilburn house and the land around it. There's more, I'm sure. And, Pasquin?"

"Yeah."

"Find out all the land that St. Claire owns right now."

"I'll be in that city all day if I do this," he complained, but I knew he'd do it. "I'll have to catch a ride with somebody over in Fogarty Spring. Now, who's that going to be?"

Catching a ride into Tallahassee had never been a problem for Pasquin. I left him to his own resources, telling him to take the information to my house.

I dozed lightly until I felt the presence of someone near the bed and half-hoped it would be St. Claire. Opening my eyes, I saw a woman looking at the titles of the books.

"Excuse me, but those are mine."

"Oh, you are awake, good." She replaced the books, then turned to face me. "I see you're interested in local history."

"Why, Ms. Brennan, of real estate," I said as realization hit me.

"Yes," she smiled and stuck out her card.

"Just place it in one of those books," I said.

She adjusted her hair, and I could see where the narrow white streak of skin met the hairline. Glamorous now, she would be in the surgeon's office in a few years to rid herself of sun damage.

"I understand you were in an accident on Palmetto Lake." She looked away from me when she said that, her mascara weighting down extended lashes.

"Yes." I stared at her, but refused to offer any emotion.

"I," she hesitated and looked down at her T-strap heels. "I wanted to ask you if you think this will clear up soon. I mean I have clients, and I don't know what to tell them about the sale of the property."

"How should I know? Why not ask the sheriff?"

"He won't give me the opportunity." She hesitated again on that last word, which meant Tony wouldn't give her an answer at all.

"I thought Mr. St. Claire owned the property. Why would he want to sell it?"

She shuffled her T-straps, then moved to the end of the bed. "Well, he doesn't really. He's got partners, see, or potential partners."

"You mean he plans to go in with others to develop the land?"

She nodded. "Something like that." Her face changed suddenly, open-eyed. "Oh, I don't think they plan to clear out all the trees and build offices. Nothing like that. A club house, maybe."

"No vacation homes, restaurants, things tourists can move into for a weekend and feed leftover dinner rolls to the alligators?"

She paced to the window and back. Her expensive pancake began to run just above the lip.

"Nothing like that."

"Well, Ms. Brennan, you've come to the wrong place. I don't have the foggiest idea what's in store for the investigation. I'm pretty sore. If you don't mind, I'd like to sleep now." I relaxed on the pillows.

"Was there," she pulled her purse closer to her body, "really an underwater explosion out there?" Again she refused to look at me.

"Ask Amado." I closed my eyes.

"Please," I felt her looking at me now, "if you want to talk about it, call the number on the card."

I opened my eyes briefly and saw a frightened stare. I nodded, then pretended to drop off again.

Stretching for the phone meant a moment of agony, but I managed to dial Pasquin's number without help.

"Add something to that list. Find out what you can about Charlene Brennan, a local real estate agent."

"Ma'am, I'm over eighty years old!"

"And in damn good shape!" I replaced the phone and called for a pain shot.

Later that night, I asked the nurse to wheel me in to see Harry. He was a mess. Black threads stuck in rusty-colored iodine made a nasty gap in his thick salt and pepper hair. He wore a neck brace, and had some heavy wads of cotton over one ear. His heavily taped torso was partially draped in a sheet, but at its bottom, the lower leg cast protruded in a sling. His eyes were closed. I reached up and touched his wrist. He turned his head slightly, his eyes hazy. When he realized who I was, he smiled through the pain killer. "Luanne," he said, "I couldn't possibly make love to you right now." He made a half chuckle, then moaned.

"It's now or never, Harry. If you don't hop on right this minute, I'll not give you another chance."

"Just let me turn over, and you'll get the best lay of your life." He closed his eyes. "And end mine."

"You'll live, Harry. Just keep thinking sex and you'll repair in no time." I squeezed his wrist slightly, then nodded to the nurse to wheel me out.

The nurse, a rough woman who looked ready to retire from years of difficult patients, pushed me into the hallway. "That man's lucky he's still got a dick to dangle. Coulda blowed off in that water."

I laughed in spite of the pain, but in the back of my mind, I saw Harry's dick and a few other parts floating in cold water. Someone didn't want us down there and was willing to put a bomb together to make sure we didn't go down again.

The cave opening and possibly all its tributaries would be rubble by now, a pile of crumbled limestone. In time, the springs would force new openings and a new cave system would develop. In the meantime, divers would stay away until bomb detectors and probes could give the all clear. I shivered when I thought about Vernon. He would surely be one of the first divers down there with the ATF.

"I'll stay at your place for a while, okay?" Vernon grinned as he drove over my rutted road on Tuesday morning. Each bump jolted my ribs and shot bruising pains throughout my body.

"I'd like that. Actually, I'll like it better when I'm well."

"Too sore for romance. I see." He grinned again. In spite of the pain, I felt warm, comforted.

"And who is going to stay with me during the day?"

"Pasquin?"

"Vernon! He'll be half asleep most of the time, and he'll fill me full of hot peppers and strong coffee."

"Teasing, just teasing. Actually, Mama got somebody to drop in and help you a few hours. One of her waitresses, I think."

"Oh, great, some swamp woman who'll tell the world about the things I've got inside my new house." Secretly, I hoped she would bring meals from Mama's Table.

"You'll have to pay her, you know."

Vernon parked the car behind my Honda, which someone had driven back for me. I looked at my newly renovated family home that had recently been a tumble-down, termite-eaten swamp corpse. Its new boards, screened porch, and tiled roof spelled cocoon for me. The entire structure rested on new supports now, ones that would keep my living room above water level in the event of river flooding. The front porch steps, steep but nailed down firmly, sat between lattice work from the bottom of the porch to the ground. It would give during a flood, but it would keep out critters, or at least keep them away from human feet as they descended the steps. I once harbored a moccasin under my porch. He could still be there, but I was content to give him privacy.

Vernon carried the vase of roses with one hand and offered me his other for support. He made sure I could sit comfortably on the sofa in front of the television, the remote resting on the arm. He brought in iced tea and pain killers for me, a soda for him.

"I got you something," he said and reached behind the sofa. "It's real walnut." He handed over a dark walking stick, one with knots and curves and a carved gargoyle on the handle. "And I expect you to use it. If you fall, you'll bruise something else."

I looked at the thing. "Are you sure this isn't some kind of voodoo stick?" Its dark wood had varnish over some scratches.

"Could be. Ask Pasquin. It came from an antique shop out on the highway." He stood up, took it in one hand and walked across the floor, making thumping sounds on the hardwood. "Sturdy little bastard, too." He waved it about in the air. "Hell, you could kill snakes with this thing."

"Let me try," I said, and winced when I tried to get up alone.

"Here, use it to help you pull up." He handed me the stick so that with one hand on it and the other on the sofa arm, I pushed myself to a standing position without too much pain. I clacked across the floor like an aged hag.

"Okay, I've done it," I said as I moved back to the sofa. Sitting down seemed more painful than standing. "Oh, that hurts!" I grabbed myself around the waist.

"It's the internal bruising. Just lean back and let the pain go away." Vernon sat next to me, his warm breath near my cheek. I could feel tender kisses near my ear. "I don't know what I would have done had you been…" He couldn't finish the sentence.

"Killed?" I said. "Funny how that word hasn't registered in my head until now."

"Don't ever let it register anywhere, okay?" He began to nibble along with the kisses.

"If you keep that up, you're going to have to find a way to carry on," I said, stroking his muscled shoulder with the back of my hand.

"Anybody to home?" A voice shouted on the steps.

"Guess I won't keep it up, will I?" Vernon stood up to let in Pasquin.

"Mighty humid out there today. Bet it'll rain early." He pulled

92

off his hat and tossed it on a table near the window. "I done got some stuff for you, ma'am, but not from the library."

I wondered why he stirred early. Pasquin, notorious for puttering around late at night then sleeping until nine, scolded me every time I awakened him for a jaunt on the river. He plopped some brochures on the coffee table.

"Lady brought these over. Says she wants to buy my property and give me a whopping price for it, too."

I leaned over and took one of the pamphlets. "Real estate. The agent is Charlene Brennan. Did you invite her to your house?"

"Nope, but she showed up last night. Guess she saw the light on, so she pops in and tells me she's got a client who needs land in these parts and was I willing to sell."

"And?" said Vernon.

"Told her not to bother. I plan on living here long as the swamp god is willing to put up with me. And that's going to be a long time!" He chuckled, his entire face crinkling.

"Did she say anything about the dive, the underwater bomb?" My instincts told me the woman was fishing.

"Asked if I knew what they found out. Told her I only know that the ATF came in soon as something happened over there. Don't think that made her too happy."

"Yeah, I'll bet she worried about property values going down with criminal activity about," said Vernon who picked up a pamphlet.

"Vernon," I said, "could somebody develop these river lands into hotels, condos, and such?"

"Laws are clear on that. These are protected lands and nobody can build on them without permission, and permits aren't granted for hotels anymore."

"Then I built because I already owned this place, but I

couldn't put up a guest house?"

"Probably not, especially a large one. You renovated a structure already here."

"Pasquin, did you ask Ms. Brennan who her client was?"

"Well, I guess I told her who he was. When she said she had an interested client, I says 'and that would be Mr. St. Claire, right?' She just stopped talking a minute." He chuckled again, reminding me of a mischievous leprechaun.

"Is this man trying to buy up all the land on the river?" said Vernon, slapping the brochure back on the coffee table.

"Maybe," I said, "or she wants a sure-fire commission."

"You going into town today?" Pasquin turned to Vernon.

"Have to. You want a ride?"

"Got to get over to the archives for the lady." He nodded in my direction. "I'll need a ride home, too."

I tried to stretch my legs, but unbending them proved too painful. Near the window, the roses had opened their buds a little larger than last night. A dozen. Was that supposed to mean something? Vernon and Pasquin droned into the background, and I drifted into a nap.

At midmorning, a heavy-hipped woman climbed the steps and rapped on the screen. She carried a large paper sack in one hand, a small one in the other.

"I'm Tulia," she said, "not Petulia, Tulip, or Petunia, just Tulia, okay?" She moved toward the dining table without speaking to the men. "I got enough for your dinner and supper, but not for your guests. They'll have to make their own." She began unloading paper plates covered in foil. The odors of fried corn meal and peanut oil filled the room.

"That's Tulia, all right," said Pasquin. "I guess you'll see a lot of her these days." He leaned toward me, and lowered his voice.

"Ask her about Wilburns and Grassfields. She knows all the swamp gossip and can fill your hours with muddy dirt."

"We'll grab something on the way to town," said Vernon. He leaned over to kiss me softly. When he turned to my ear, I expected a playful nibble. Instead, he whispered, "I brought your backpack here yesterday. It's on that table. Your gun is inside. Keep it with you, okay?"

I nodded. "And the cellular?"

"There, too." He gave a gentle blow, and I blushed all over. "Be back late."

CHAPTER TWELVE

"You want more iced tea?" Tulia stood over me in the living room. She didn't wait for an answer. "I got to get you to the table. You ready?"

She offered both hands to lift me. I motioned to the walking stick and did it myself. Slowly. My muscles worked fine, but something inside was sore as hell.

"It's unsweet tea. Mama said that's what you drink." Tulia poured the dark liquid into a large glass full of ice.

"That's fine. Tulia, sit with me?"

"Of course. I got to eat, too." She pulled out a smaller bag from a fast food place. Displaying her burger and fries in front of her, she asked, "You got any soda?"

I nodded toward the refrigerator. "You're not going to eat that when you can have fried fish and hushpuppies, not to mention Mama's slaw."

"Yes, I am. I get full of that fish stuff when I work there. Now I got a reprieve to eat a burger. You don't know what a treat that is." She lifted the paper-covered burger and took a whiff, her eyes closed like a wine taster.

I motioned for her to sit down. She popped the drink can and poured cola into a tall glass.

"I appreciate this, Tulia," I said as I broke off a piece of fried flounder and popped it into my mouth.

"You'll appreciate it to the tune of thirty dollars a day." She bit into the thick, cheese-coated burger. "That's what Mr. Vernon promised."

I smiled at her use of the old Southern habit of adding the title to the first name. It was almost as quaint as Pasquin's *ma'am*.

"Of course, but you didn't have to do it, and I'm grateful."

She relaxed, jamming French fries into a glob of ketchup and wolfing them down. Her raw-red hands, signs of years in restaurant kitchens, set up a rhythm from table to mouth. She wore the double knit of the middle-aged swamp woman, blue pants, white top. Her hair, wispy and red, flared in disarray around the lined ruddy face. She wore no makeup, but her blue eyes sparkled with a life that refused burial in the hardships of poverty. Her sunburned nose and chapped lips formed perfectly under those eyes. She had been a beauty once upon a time in her life.

"You've lived in these parts a long time, right?"

"Since I was born right over there near Fogarty Spring. Born in the house I still live in. My kids were born there, too." She stopped and shook her head. "But their kids won't be. They all got trailers now, and plan to have their babies in a hospital. Got medical insurance and stuff." She shrugged and began working on the fries again.

"Did a doctor call when your kids were born?"

"Hell no. Couldn't afford none. That old man of mine didn't have a city job. Fished all his life. What did he know about insurance?" She leaned toward me. "I pulled them babies out of my belly in my own bed, same place as where I made them." She leaned back and laughed. "That's about all that man was good for—making babies."

"You had no help at all?"

97

"Just old Mrs. Wilburn. Knew just what to make me drink to ease the pain but not enough to hurt the baby. Didn't matter. I popped them kids so quick, the pain was gone before I could holler much."

"You don't mean Josie Wilburn?"

"No, she's my age. I mean her mama, the old lady. Died long time ago. I think she birthed most every baby in these swamps back in the fifties."

"I hear her daughters do the same thing."

"Yeah, but don't get much business these days. People go to clinics and hospitals now, use social welfare if they ain't got insurance. Women today don't want to face pain." She finished the fries, then picked up the last of her hamburger.

"There is ice cream in the freezer. Help yourself," I said.

"Yes sir, them ladies birth babies, but not like their mama did." She heaped three scoops of chocolate almond into a bowl, thought again, and added two more. "You got any bananas?" She spied some aging speckled fruit in a bowl by the sink. Before I could answer, she grabbed one, peeled it, and chopped it into her ice cream. "You want one of these?"

I shook my head. "Did you know Theresa Grassfield?" I pretended to be more interested in my hushpuppies.

"Oh, you bet I did! I heard about that stuff with her dying and all. Now those ladies done run off where nobody can find them."

"What do you mean, run off?"

"Just listen. Josie done been warned by the Midwifery Agency down in Tallahassee about birthing babies without a license. But, hell, she ain't gonna get a license. She just helps out women who ain't got insurance or maybe need a cheap abortion. Don't ask me what she was doing with Theresa Grassfield. I hear Theresa came back here about two years ago with money from her mama and daddy's farm. She didn't need no insurance to go to a hospital. But I figured she went to Josie 'cause that's who was renting her a room."

"Josie Wilburn rented to Theresa?"

"Sure. I think there's some kin there, second cousin or something. Anyhow, Theresa came back and moved in with the sisters." Tulia shoveled banana and chocolate ice cream into her mouth, savored it a while, then swallowed. Her blue eyes squinted in ecstasy.

"And her husband?" I knew Theresa had no husband. I also knew Tulia would want to tell me that.

"No husband. Poor kid. She comes here hoping for something good and gets herself in a fix." Tulia winked at me. "Know what I mean?" She stirred her ice cream into a smoothy, mashing the bananas to a pulp.

I laughed with her. "Then if she wasn't married, who was the father of the child?"

Tulia leaned over and in a loud whisper said, "People say it was some rich old coot from Tallahassee. I got my suspicions—about three or four of them." She smiled as again the smooth ice cream eased down her throat.

"Lawyers? Doctors? Governors?" I laughed with her.

"Maybe the first two. I don't think the governor does it anymore." She flung back her head and howled.

"Well, if she slept with a doctor, wouldn't he see to the birth?"

"Wasn't no doctor," she said. She grinned now, triumphant that she had the upper hand in the knowledge department. "Besides, wouldn't no married man want a swamp brat on his record."

"Married?"

"Yeah, kids, and grandkids."

I stared at her, smiling and lifting my eyebrows. "Couldn't tell me who you suspect, could you?"

"Won't say no names, but I'll bet you a hootie owl they came from that Hunter's Club."

"Palmetto Hunter's Club?" I knew about the cabin that bordered government land a few miles from the river. Some locals shared its upkeep and hunted deer during the season.

"No, that other one over by Calley's Slough."

Surprised, I wrinkled my brow. Tulia smiled and shoveled in more ice cream.

"Calley's Slough, the one near Hollowell Sink?"

"That's the place. Men go over there to play cowboys and Indians. Got them a tent and a few fancy campers. They're down there most weekends."

I knew Calley's Slough as a deep sloping tunnel under a natural bridge connecting two sinkholes. Formed by the force of flowing underground water, it was large enough for divers, one at a time. Dangerous, the water currents could flow either way, pounding the diver against dirt walls. It was a place for daredevils of the foolish kind. Three teens had drowned there over the years, each trying to prove he could make it from one sink to the other.

Hollowell Sink invited swimmers with its deep clear water. The state had made the area around it a wayside rest stop, setting up tables and trash cans. On any weekend, you could see young boys fly out on oak vines then drop into the bottomless waterhole. Parents guarded their children on these outings, but at night the drunks arrived. More than one had gulped down too much beer then stepped into the water, not realizing there was no bottom even at the edge. Unable to see in the darkness, they panicked, screaming to the fogged-up car windows of lovers in the dark lanes away from the picnic tables. If they heard, and if they pulled loose from each other to investigate, they found nothing in the dark water. The next day, sheriff's divers would pull a bloated body off a rotted tree limb deep below the surface.

Calley's Slough ran from Hollowell nearly two hundred yards to another sink, a small one with clear water that bubbled from a deep spring. Most people believed that eventually the sink connected to the Palmetto River, but no one could be sure. The opening leading from the second sink to the river was too small for a diver. But, the Slough wasn't the part that challenged pubescent boys into proving their manhood.

"They put up tents in the rest area?"

"No, ma'am. They cleared them out a space on past the trees. Can't nobody see them from the rest area. I know about it because my grandbaby tried to run off from me down there one day. Scared me to death! Thought he'd end up in that sinkhole."

"Did you know any of these men?"

She pulled back in a coy manner. "Seen some of them on the television news, but I don't *know* them."

I finished all I could eat and suddenly felt sleepy. The pain pill had kicked in. Tulia cleared the table, then helped me to a recliner near the stairs. I leaned back, my sore legs in the air, and felt the pain drift away.

"I'll just clean up a little around here, then I'll go. Mr. Vernon said he'd feed you dinner if he's not tied up. In which case I'll be back."

I must have mumbled an okay, because I heard nothing more from Tulia. Just before I drifted into oblivion, my head reminded me that grown men might play cowboys and Indians, but not at a hunt club.

When I heard the phone ring, my brain told me I needed to answer it, that I had to pull it from the backpack. When I heard my own voice telling whoever it was to leave a message, I realized it was the house phone, and the message sounded from the machine upstairs in my bedroom. The room had grown dark, and rain pelted the swamp floor.

"Ms. Fogarty, this is Charlene Brennan. I must speak with you about the Wilburn place. Could you get back to me? Use the cell phone number on the card I gave you. Hope you're feeling better."

I heard the voice differently this time, something, maybe arrogance, was missing. She sounded worried, and a little shaky.

Reaching for the lever, I tried to lower the recliner, but my aching muscles twinged each time I lifted my upper body. In desperation, I pushed hard. A sharp pain caused me to cry out, but it dissipated, and I thrust the lever downward.

My legs flopped to the floor and another sharp pain hit me in the back. With the stick, I pushed to a standing position. Just as I leaned over to turn on a light, lightning banged somewhere in the swamp. I jumped. The light wouldn't come on. "Damn power outage!"

I stooped slowly to the bottom drawer of the end table and pulled out a flashlight. Aiming it at my watch on the table, I found it was only three-thirty.

Outside, the rain grew fierce, and wind cracked in the oaks and pines. Thunder reminded me of the explosion in dark rushing water. The weather didn't add up to a bomb, but to a tornado. Somewhere, hot and cold air mixed and swirled in terrible force.

There was nothing I could do. We had no basements in the muddy soil of North Florida. Tornado warnings often came over the television, but rarely did one actually touch the ground. I moved to my backpack and pulled out the cellular. Sitting on the sofa, I waited. Within half an hour, the wind and pelting rain traveled on, leaving a soft drizzle. The sun peeked through lighter clouds, and frogs took up their victory chorus. Outside would be a muggy hell. If the power didn't come back on, inside would be just as bad.

Another half hour and thunder was only a distant rumble. I pulled Ms. Brennan's card from the bag and dialed her number on my cell phone. Nothing happened. After two more tries, I dialed the real estate office phone. While it rang, I heard the heat pump click on and realized the electricity had returned like a rebirth. Someone answered with the company name on the other end of the phone line.

"Luanne Fogarty. I need to speak to Charlene Brennan, please."

There was silence for a moment, then another voice, a familiar one, came on the line.

"Tony?"

"Luanne, what is it?"

"I was returning a call from Ms. Brennan."

I could hear him place his hand over the receiver and say something in the room. "Luanne, Ms. Brennan seems to have been in an accident. As soon as the storm clears, the divers will go after her. I'm on my way there now."

I was stunned. "Tony," I said, "she called here not much over an hour ago."

"Then she did it from her car phone. She and it are at the bottom of Hollowell Sink right now."

"Tony," I said, "there is no bottom to Hollowell Sink."

CHAPTER THIRTEEN

"Skid marks show she must have lost control out there on the road and didn't stop soon enough to avoid the sink. Flew right off the bank and into the water." The highway patrolman spoke to Tony as I sat in the car. "Family of tourists said they couldn't believe their eyes. The storm blew fast and crazy. They piled in the car to wait it out. Just as the lightning is flashing something fierce, this car comes racing through the trees like a bull elephant, tearing up dirt, and flying right off the edge."

"Did they hear another car, maybe on the road?" Tony asked.

"Couldn't. The storm made all the noise. Just zoom, through the bushes and, splat, into the sink." The trooper made a belly dive with his hand.

Tony moved into the car beside me. "Something's not right," he said.

"No," I agreed, "and you need to find that body." I shivered. Vernon and another diver were in the sink now, deep into darkness where they would find slopes and cave openings, old tree branches with years of debris wrapped around them. In the back of my mind, I saw a bomb in one of those branches. In front of me, I saw freshly broken tree limbs, their leaves still green. The sudden storm had ripped them from the mother oaks and strewed them across picnic tables and clear down the sloping banks.

Tony looked at me as I stretched one leg diagonally under the dash. "Doesn't that hurt?"

"Aches, but no sharp pains." I said as he stared at me. "Don't tell me to go home, Tony. I won't. What were you doing at her office anyway?"

"Checking out St. Claire's property buys. Just as we arrived, she called her office on her cellular. Said a motorcycle was tailing her, right on her bumper. Then the storm came. Knocked out the phone in the office. Little while later, I get this message from the dispatcher that her car had run into the sink."

"How did whoever reported this know it was her car?"

"License plate and rear bumper came off when she scraped a tree." He pointed to a series of three young pines, their bark skinned to raw innards. The trees wouldn't survive. Their dead trunks would come down in the next storm or the next wave of state cleanup. I saw crumpled wrap-around bumper on the ground. Ms. Brennan didn't drive anything cheap.

"My leg needs exercising," I said as I opened the door and pushed myself up with the cane. I hobbled toward the turn-off road that led directly into the rest area. A few yards away, it ran right into the paved road to Tallahassee.

"You can see where she skidded from the pavement then took off across the dirt," said the patrolman. He pointed to dark tire marks on the road, deep grooves in muddy ruts. "See how she tossed up dirt here? She really lay down on the gas to make these." He pulled out a tape and measured the height, the major part of the dirt formed the back of the rut. "Yep, blowed the octane right here, almost like she wanted to fly into that hole. Probably lost control when she went off the pavement."

The officer and his partner continued to snap pictures and take measurements. Tony went off to look into the sinkhole, hoping the divers would surface soon. Their converted Chevy Suburban with a small trailer behind took up most of the clear space near the tables. A young man with a badge stood guard over extra tanks and first aid kits. I stepped slowly through the grass next to the tire ruts, shoving the blades down with the tip of my cane. Still wet with rain, they emitted foggy puffs of humidity in the bright sunlight. A few yards away, sucker-footed frogs began their hop-and-hide dance on the forest floor. For them, the human drama wasn't much different from the natural one.

Keeping my eyes to the ground, I found myself at the edge of the pavement. Few cars traveled the road. The sun glared on the asphalt. Shading my eyes, I looked across the road. Something glared there, too. I looked both ways, then did a quick hobble to the other side where I found a piece of broken glass. And a few feet away, one narrow tire rut, not a full size car. Perhaps a motorcycle?

"Hey!" I shouted to the patrolman who seemed surprised I was over there. "Come look at this."

The crime scene techs took pictures, then bagged the glass.

"Could something have hit her?" I asked.

"That would explain the sudden surge of speed," Tony said. "Maybe we'll know if they ever get up here with her body."

I shivered. I hadn't thought of Charlene Brennan as a body, one that could no longer be coiffed and manicured.

From where we stood, it seemed as though a red mirage came ambling down the pavement, an alien on moon surface rollers.

"It's the crane," said Tony. "We'll need it to pull up the car if the divers find it."

They found it. Standing at the top of the steep bank, I thought it an eternity that Vernon had been below. Too many

106

things can happen down there, and I imagined all of them. I made a pact with myself to go down again as soon as possible, before I spooked myself into claustrophobia.

"It's caught on a slope with a bunch of roots and vines," said Vernon as he rested on the bank. "But if you don't pull it out soon, it'll sink clear to hell." He looked at the other diver. "You ready?"

The crane operator lowered the pulley, one strong enough to lift heavy safes, cement blocks, and drowned autos. Vernon and the other diver went below. They would carry the hook to the car, latching its pulley on the axle or something intact. Finally, both divers emerged and Vernon gave the pull ahead sign.

At first the crane's heavy cable moved almost silently, then the entire machine began to moan and jerk, then roll backward. A great slush sound came from the hole, and the back end of an expensive white car rose out of the depths. From where I stood, I saw a human female slumped over the wheel, her hair limp as swamp algae.

"It's Brennan, all right," said Tony as he pushed the head back to look at her face. "And it's no accident."

Forgetting my sore leg, I moved forward. Charlene's tanned skin was darker now, caked with mud. Her eyes, wide open, saw nothing. Her red lipstick smeared down one side of her face. Red appeared on the other side, too, near the neck. "There," I said and pushed my finger close to her skin without touching it. "A bullet hole, I'll bet."

Tony frowned then walked toward the highway patrolman standing near the pavement. After a short conversation, he nodded to another patrolman. They both moved with him toward the road beyond the blocked-off entrance to the rest area. One law enforcement agency had just turned over command to another, not something often done around here without a lot of male posturing.

"Get Marshall Long out here," Tony shouted above the noise of the crane that was pulling the car to a more secure position on the bank.

"Tony," I said, "Hollowell Sink is state-owned. No way would Charlene Brennan's firm be handling a sale. What was she doing here?"

"The paved road goes on around to Palmetto Springs. Maybe she wanted to see the lake land again." Tony tugged at his stiff shirt collar. Under the circumstances, he should have been covered in mud. Not a speck showed on the shirt or the creased pants.

"Not in that car, unless she had her off-terrain parked somewhere down there." I remembered the four large tires on the open vehicle. Something like that would require a flatbed truck or a large pick-up to take it to the edge of the forest. Charlene must have had a stash place. "I'm going to walk a while, Tony. Don't leave me behind."

Leaning on the cane, I followed the dirt road a few yards until it met with the paved one. Turning right, I walked on a high grassy bank that dropped off to a deep drainage ditch, then rose again to meet the pavement. The storm had left the ditch nearly full, its muddy waters rushing to the culvert, carrying broken tree limbs and a couple of dead armadillos.

Tall pines grew near the ditch. I had maybe three feet of grass on which to walk clear of them. One slight curve, and I was out of eye range of the goings on at the sink. Two more steps and I entered the silent world of no cops or cranes, and, because the paved road was now blocked, no traffic. The forest of tall pines and spreading oaks thickened and I thought of turning back, when

I spied a clearing. The trees skipped a few feet then started up again, thicker than before. I pushed forward, turning my ankle once in the heavy grass.

"A road to where?" I said as I stood looking down at two muddy ruts, recently used. The tire tracks appeared to be those of swamp riders, large tires that raised a truck high in the air to avoid scrub brush.

I turned down the road, walking on the edge where the mud mixed with grass. There wasn't much room here as the road backed right up to heavy tree trunks. I was in snake territory. Glancing often at the ground, I kept the cane ready. Not far away, the sound of a heavy vehicle engine approached. I ducked into the underbrush, scratching my arms and stepping in mud.

A camouflaged converted Hummer passed in front of me, its tires riding high. Military green and white also decorated the clothes of the two men inside. The vehicle traveled slowly after the rains, sloshing through deep puddles. I couldn't clearly see the men's faces, but one seemed middle aged. The other one was young, with a shaved head and bulging muscles. When I heard the Hummer reach the pavement, I stepped toward the road again.

A green lizard darted from a tree and landed on my pants leg. Startled, I stepped backwards and felt the sharp twinge in my calf. I went down, cane, hands, and butt into mushy vegetation.

"What the hell?" said Vernon as I hobbled back to Hollowell Sink. I had wrenched something that ought not to have been wrenched, and mud caked my pants.

"Don't ask," I said. "Just help me sit somewhere."

Leaning on the Suburban, I bent over while Vernon poured sinkhole water over my muddy hands.

"You run off like that again, we may not find you for a week," he said.

"Stop patronizing, Vernon. I always take the cellular with me. You know that." I looked into his face, his grin the best peace offering I know. My insides warmed for a moment, and I forgot the ache in my leg. Vernon had never let me down. Always the up-beat smile, the handsome strong body that caressed me as a lover as well as a reassuring friend. I knew how lucky I was.

"You planning on telling me anything about this?" he asked.

"Have you ever swum through the slough?" I used a towel to rub off smeared mud from my pants.

"Once, and was it spooky," said Vernon. "Some stupid kid got himself caught in it, stuck sideways while his buddies got through ahead of him. We pulled him out, but he had swallowed half the water and all the critters in it by then."

"Did you go all the way through to the small sink?"

"Never did that. Don't want to, okay?" He started toward me when I winced at a pain in my leg, then stopped and looked around him. "You better stay off that for a while."

I smiled at him. "Embarrassed to massage it in front of your buddies, aren't you?"

"I'm on duty, Luanne. Don't go rubbing a sick leg against my thigh." He moved a step away, out of my reach.

"Have you ever been in the small sinkhole?" I leaned over and rubbed the leg myself.

"Not in it, but I saw it a few years back. It's hidden in a lot of trees. I wouldn't go walking back there if I were you."

"Why not?"

"Luanne, don't scare me anymore, okay?" Vernon bent over me, his voice lowered to a whisper. "I nearly died when they called me in Jacksonville and told me about the explosion. Don't go anywhere without me or Tony, not while you're healing." He leaned near me, almost close enough to kiss. "Promise me."

110

"Promise the man anything, but let him get back to work," said Marshall as he approached me. His unbuttoned white lab coat blew outward, away from his sides. Sweat poured off his layers of face flesh. He held up a briefcase with one gloved finger. "Woman's case was waterproof. Ain't that grand?"

"She lives in North Florida where it rains. Why would that be unusual?" I said.

"Isn't. It's just that inside, the papers didn't spoil in all that sinkhole water. And look at this, a list of phone numbers and names."

Marshall balanced the case on the trailer edge and laid open two sheets of handwritten numbers. The writer had used a thin black felt marker.

"My phone is here. So is Pasquin's. Why would she keep a record of all these numbers and times?"

"Ask the man," said Marshall and thrust the papers back into the case. "Just thought you'd like to know."

"Oh, hell, let me glance through the whole thing, Marshall. For heaven's sake! You're just like Tony, tease me, then drop the whole issue like you don't know why I'm curious." I reached for the case with an ungloved hand. Marshall pushed me away and reopened it.

"These names," I said as I let my eyes run down the columns, "Look!" I locked on to Wilburn, Alberta, a date, time, and number with a Georgia area code neatly printed next to it.

"Why would Ms. Brennan be making calls to any of the Wilburn's, and only yesterday?" said Marshall as he pretended not to see me scribble the number on a scrap of paper. When he poked the papers back in the case, a stack of business cards slipped loose. "Damn! Lots of Miami clients." He picked up one that had turned over and read, "place for children," scribbled in pencil.

"Great! Turn the swamp into an amusement park. Make the gators mechanical robots" He nudged the cards into the opening and closed the flap.

I waited nearly an hour before one of the officers drove me home. As we left Hollowell Sink, I turned toward the woods, back where the slough ran underground and wondered if any more camouflaged men lingered there, wondered if they watched the white coats take great care of the items pulled from a dead woman. And, I wondered if Alberta Wilburn, whoever she was, would hang up when I called her.

CHAPTER FOURTEEN

Somewhere in the bowels of Georgia, the phone rang twenty times before I gave up and took a bath. My leg ached; I popped some pain killers and dozed in the recliner. When I awoke, I felt dizzy, like the swamp dirt still crept through my pores. Two more futile tries, and I decided to call the next morning. Pouring a giant glass of cold tea, I moved to the front porch, hoping Pasquin would come by and tell me if he knew Alberta.

The sun moved behind the river. Its setting fireball gave off a boiling red light. The rest of the swamp darkened with shadows, and insects began to sing, their hairy legs sawing together like out-of-tune fiddles. I dozed, but my skin prickled with heat. In the distance I heard a boat motor. Thinking it might be Pasquin, I left the porch and walked to the landing.

With my cane in front of me, I felt like a blind woman, one who by instinct knew the exact path to a familiar place. I stood on the wooden slats and listened to river water lap gently against the sandy shore. When the sun made its final bow, I could barely see the tree tops. Turning back, I saw the lamp light in the living room.

Had I left the light on? Something wasn't right. Swamp creatures had ceased their noises. I froze on the landing, my cane raised slightly, ready to jab or pound into an unseen threat. I heard movement in the thick foliage to the right of the lane that led back to the house. I stared at the spot, swearing I could see a pair of legs, bare and muscled. When another sound came from the road, the legs moved away.

"Hey!" I cried and tried to run after the legs. Instead, I tripped over my own cane and fell into the water.

"Luanne?" Pasquin's voice whispered in the dark. He clicked on a flashlight and shined it around the landing.

"Down here," I said and pulled myself onto the stairs. "Get me inside."

"Who the hell was that?" he said as I fell into a rocking chair on the porch.

"Did you see him?"

"I heard this movement on the landing just as I walked up to the porch."

"What you got here?" Pasquin put his hand toward my arm, then pulled away.

I looked at my wrist. A redness began at the bottom of my palm and ran up my arm. "Oh, damn!" I said and slumped back in the chair. "Poison ivy. Can anything else go wrong?"

"Sure is," Pasquin drawled as he stared at the rash. He began to nod. "Glad I wear long sleeves. Do more than just keep out the sunburn," Pasquin said. "Don't like the poison ivy. You're going to itch child, hoowhee!" He watched as I tread upstairs for calamine lotion and dry clothes.

"I got this when I fell in the swamp near the slough," I yelled from the upstairs bath, my skin feeling as though it would raise off my arm. I pulled a denim shirt from the closet. Doing my best to keep it from touching my arm, I put it on. So far, the rash hadn't spread above my elbow.

Vernon and a deputy came when I called about the intruder

in the woods. I knew they wouldn't find him. The swamp has a way with people like that, hiding them along with venom and powerful teeth, then spitting them out when they make a wrong move. If this man didn't know the swamp, he could be knee deep in mud by now.

I secretly hoped he'd fall into a muddy section of a stagnant pond where mudpuppies slithered just below the surface. They weren't poisonous but they could bite and hurt. More satisfying was the fear they instilled in even seasoned swamp people. He'd think he was in a snake pit.

"Nothing, Luanne," said Vernon as he joined me on the porch.

"Probably had a boat waiting somewhere," said Pasquin.

"Might have been some tourist walking around the swamp. Stupid as that is, they've been known to go out looking for gators on their own." Vernon moved near me, putting his arm up to surround me.

"Sorry, but this stuff is going to prove to be a big problem around here," I said as I leaned away and revealed my arm. I stared at him and he stared back. We gave each other weary, helpless looks.

All four of us jumped when a voice came from the front steps. "Miss Fogarty! It's me, Tulia. You want to come open this door?"

Standing on the bottom step, under the porch light, Tulia's red hair looked as though the afternoon lightning had shot it through with electricity. She still wore her white uniform from Mama's Table. Two large bags sat on the ground behind her.

"I got some food and some sleeping stuff for me. Folks over to the restaurant said you're going to need help tonight. I'm here to stay." She pulled up the two bags and squeezed past me.

Disregarding the men, she talked straight to the kitchen. "Don't expect me to stay past six a.m., though. I got waitress duty all day tomorrow. Promised Mama I'd be there to help with seven o'clock breakfast."

"Tulia, Vernon is here, so I…"

"Might get called out during the night. You need somebody with you. And I got this." She opened the top of the bag and pushed aside a cotton nightgown. A large caliber pistol lay at the bottom. "Don't you worry none. I killed many a rabbit with this thing."

"I don't eat rabbit…"

"Didn't say you did. It's for them two-legged rabbits, if you get my meaning." She began storing food inside the refrigerator.

"I got your meaning. What I'm trying to say is, I think I'll be fine by myself." Actually, the thought of Tulia sleeping over seemed intrusive. I wanted to be with Vernon, poison ivy and all, not with Swamp Lady.

"Show me where you want me to sleep."

There was no driving her away. I pointed upstairs. "Turn left at the top, then left again. The guest room is there. Sheets are in the closet."

I sat in the recliner. All three men, dumbfounded by matronly assertion, grinned at me.

"What can I do?" I shrugged.

Vernon turned to Pasquin, "You need a ride home?"

"Plan on walking. Thanks just the same. Just brought over some nice tomatoes from the garden, Luanne." His eyes looked startled for a moment. "Damn! I left them on the path when I heard the splash." He darted out the door, faster than any other octogenarian ever could. In the silence, we could hear him mumble.

"Look at this!" He held up a paper sack, full of squashed

tomatoes, red mixed with bag brown. "Some fool done stepped on it."

"Let me see," said Vernon. He grabbed a magazine and held it under the bag. Turning it at a slant beneath a table lamp, he said, "Wasn't one of us. We all have on shoes. See this." He pointed to muddy indentations where the tomatoes had been completely smashed. "Toe prints."

Vernon kept the bag. Said he'd get it to Marshall and see if anything could be done. We all guessed it would sit in the evidence refrigerator for months.

Tulia, who had watched the whole bag incident from the kitchen door, mumbled, "Damn! If I ain't seen it all."

That was the signal for the men to head outdoors. Vernon squeezed my hand and said, "Later."

I watched the patrol car back down the road, then turn around in a clearing. Soon, even the tail lights disappeared in the bends of trees. Pasquin saluted with his hat and placed it on his white hair. I walked him to the porch.

"Pasquin," I said as I latched the screen door behind the men, "who is Alberta Wilburn?"

He turned, then shook his head. "Nobody I know. Must be related to the sisters if she's from around here."

I watched him walk a few steps away from the house. Pasquin disappeared into the forest. Within seconds, heavy darkness covered all trails. Only the sound of a fading motor signaled human presence in the woods.

"Well, I guess I know who Miss Alberta Wilburn is," Tulia's voice, strong and determined, startled me from behind.

"Don't do that, Tulia. That's enough to make someone shoot at you."

"You're not toting a gun, are you?" Her blue eyes widened,

spreading the ruddy crows feet like sections of a fan.

"Well, not right now, but I have been known to."

I moved into the house, suddenly weary. My leg ached and my arm itched. It would be a long night.

"Now, you just sit there," Tulia said. "I'll get you some warm milk and tell you all about Miz Alberta."

"Cold milk, and bring me a pain pill while you're at it, okay?"

Tulia made a "poor folk's milk shake" by adding some sugar and a drop of vanilla to the tall glass of cold milk. I sipped it slowly after popping the pill, feeling like a child again. My mother had died when I was young, and Tulia was nothing like her, but both women made the milk shakes and catered to me. It felt nice, for a while.

"Now, to Alberta Wilburn," I said.

Tulia pulled up a chair to face me. She held a glass of tea encased in a dish towel. "Well, she ain't living no more, I can tell you that."

"What?" I rubbed my poisoned arm gently on the recliner upholstery.

"She died a long time ago. She was old Mrs. Wilburn's sister-in-law. Lived up in Valdosta. Never married, but I hear tell of a kid, maybe adopted. He don't look nothing like the sisters. He's dark, kind of gypsy-like. Well, he stayed in the old homestead up there. Fact is, most of the Wilburns are buried up there—I hear tell."

She leaned back and took a long swig from the tea glass, then swiped at the condensation with the towel. "Now, I don't think Josie and Sadie liked that adopted kid much, but maybe they made up in time. We all kind of lose our prejudices when we get older, kind of mellow out. And he was a cousin of sorts."

"Would they have run to him after this problem with

Theresa?"

"Can't say. Haven't heard about that side of the family for years. To be frank, I ain't heard much about Josie and Sadie much either, until this latest stuff happened. Some say they're at the bottom of the river."

"Valdosta," I could feel my eyes getting heavy. "Guess I'll have to make a trip up there."

"Now don't you go running off by yourself. Come on. I'm going to get you into bed." She stood up.

"No, I'll wait here for Vernon. You go on up."

She stood over me, her hands on her wide hips, the red hair like a fresh bonfire around her head. She began to blur.

"Well, all right, but you call out if anything happens."

The pill knocked me out. Somewhere I thought I heard a phone ring and Tulia's voice, but I couldn't pull out of the stupor. *These pills are dangerous,* I remember thinking as I drifted off again.

"Better get up, Miss Luanne," Tulia's voice backed itself up with rhythmic stomping across the floor from kitchen to living room. "I guess Mr. Vernon had to work all night. You were so sound asleep, I left you alone. You stiff from that recliner?"

"Haven't tried to move yet," I said, then pushed against the arm. My neck wouldn't cooperate and my leg was numb. "Damn! Can you give me a shove?"

"Told you being alone is dangerous," she said as she slipped one hand behind my neck and gripped my shoulder with the other. Cartilage cracked and snapped. Together, we got me sitting straight up. My legs, down now, tingled as they filled with blood.

"I'll get your breakfast, then I got to go." She handed me the cane and headed for the kitchen, already dressed in her waitress

119

uniform.

I staggered to the downstairs shower where I stood under hot, steaming water until my neck and legs moved without sound effects. In the kitchen, Tulia greeted me with warmed over fried fish and hushpuppies, and strong black coffee.

"Enough grits on these fish to make your breakfast," she said. "I got to high-tail it out of here, but listen. Mr. Vernon called last night. Said to tell you a woman from the Department of Midwifery would come by this morning. You're to tell her all you know."

The Department of Midwifery had quarters in an old shopping mall that had long since converted to a state office building. I knew little about it, except it licensed trained midwives all over the state. My image of a midwife was the Wilburn sisters.

I made it to the top of the stairs with my cane. My arm, red blisters running into each other, itched beyond belief. Sitting on the bed, I managed to draw on a pair of elastic waist pants. The shirt wasn't so easy. It had to be long sleeve or I would repulse half the people I met, not to mention rupture and infect the blisters. I found a white cotton thing and eased it over the rash. I was buttoning the front, when someone knocked on the door.

It took me just as long to go back down the stairs. A few jarring twinges as I bumped the sore leg against the wall stirred up a curse or two. The caller pounded on the door just as I jerked it open.

"I heard you had another accident. You are having a time of it, aren't you?" August St. Claire and his suit and hair stood on my screen porch. He smelled of after shave that cost money, and he held yellow mums in one hand. "Thought you needed some cheering up."

I froze. His blue eyes pierced through me and shook my

nerve. "Would you like to come in?" I felt silly, like the kid who didn't know what to say when the football hero asked her to dance.

St. Claire nodded and held the door for me as I slowly moved out of his way. He placed the flowers on the fire mantel, then with the straight posture of a dancer, took hold of my hand—the undiseased one.

"I was afraid you had been disfigured with a rash." He coddled my hand in both of his, staring at my covered arms. He smiled and said, "Please, sit down."

"I'm sorry I can't fix you some tea or something. You're welcome to get your own." My breath came in wisps. *Why did this man make me nervous?*

"Why, of course." He patted my hand and rose to go into the kitchen.

"How did you know I got poison ivy?"

"Lawyers hear things." He looked out a window. "You know, you really need a guard out here. I can arrange for one, you know." He brought iced tea glasses and sat them on coasters.

"Why would you do that?"

"I believe in protecting lovely ladies." He pulled a flask from his suit. "This is as good a pain killer as there is." He held it towards me.

"No, thanks. I'm taking pills."

"Then I won't either." He closed the flask and replaced it in his pocket.

"You heard about Charlene Brennan?"

"Oh, dear, yes. Best real estate woman in town. Drowning like that, such a freak accident."

I kept quiet. There had been no news media at the scene, probably because of the storm. St. Claire didn't seem to know about the shooting.

In the distance, we both heard a car approaching. St. Claire placed the tea glass on the table and stood. "Well, I can't stay long. My wife and grandbaby are waiting for a boat ride. Just thought I'd see if I could do anything for one of my prettier swamp neighbors." He took my hand in both his again and squeezed it. He cocked his ear slightly, then hurried to the door.

I stood on the porch and watched him get into his car, thinking about him leaving me flowers then running off to his wife. He saluted my next visitor as he pulled into the rutted drive.

"Nothing like a kiss and run," I said. "I'll have a house full of flowers if he keeps this up."

"Miss Fogarty?" A classy version of Tulia stood on the steps. Slim, she wore an expensive green polka dot dress pulled in at the waist with a black patent leather belt. High heeled shoes matched the belt. The ruddiness in her face evened out with pancake makeup, and the blue eyes sported eyeliner and subtle shadowing. The red hair, tame and sprayed, had been piled softly on top of her head, fastened by some invisible pin. The whole Southern fashion plate threatened to melt in swamp humidity.

"I'm Luanne Fogarty." I leaned on the cane.

"I'm Patricia Echols, investigator with the Department of Midwifery. I believe you were informed I would be here today?" She over-pronounced the drawl. I cringed.

I held the screen door for her. She didn't bother to help. The cane meant nothing to her, and a mad moment tempted me to goose her with it, but I held back.

"I'd offer you tea or something, but I'm not in the best of health right now." I motioned for her to sit on the sofa. She took a chair instead.

"Just some cold water would do," she said as she opened a small, leather notebook. Without looking up and in the same tone, she asked, "Was that August St. Claire who just left here?"

"The same."

"Oh, I don't mind getting the water myself," she said.

I stared at her for a minute, wondering how much different it was to pour water than tea, then told her to sit still and limped to the kitchen. As I filled a plastic glass from a fast food take-out, I looked back at Ms. Echols. She wrote in the notebook, her nails manicured and polished in a peachy color that matched the dominant tone in her skin. I wondered if she had visions of being discovered by some passing Hollywood producer who would cast her in a Southern soap opera. Balancing the water in one hand, using the cane with the other, I hobbled into the living room. She frowned at the plastic glass, but took the water. *This is not going to be easy,* I told myself.

Ms. Echols made a dot with her pen and caressed the notebook page with her manicured nail. "Is he a friend of yours?"

"Just an acquaintance. And you?" I envisioned her at a debutante ball for aging belles.

"Always thought he was a self-serving lech who couldn't keep his hands off young lady's butts." Ms. Echols redeemed herself. I guessed I wasn't the only victim of his aristocratic charm.

When she began to talk about her job, she wasted no Southern charm on preserving dignity. If I could get past the facade, I would be fine with Miss Patricia.

CHAPTER FIFTEEN

"There are many illegal, and downright dangerous, so-called midwives out there," she said, her brow wrinkling. "They take advantage of anyone who thinks she doesn't have enough money for a doctor. Then there are the ones who advertise themselves as midwives to sucker the 'naturalists' into contacting them."

"These sisters seem to have performed a needed service to lots of poor women."

"Those services are, and have always, been right there in Tallahassee."

"I take it, then," I said, "that you wouldn't go the midwife way in having your own baby."

"Hospital all the way for me, you bet your life." Her makeup turned pinkish, hiding the hot anger that would have stood to attention on Tulia's face.

"Well, I don't think the Wilburn sisters did any advertising. Not in the commercial sense, anyway."

"We've dealt with them before, you know." Patricia leaned over and touched the table. Her perfect nails clicked on the wood. "Neither of them is properly trained or licenced. Josie is the real one on this. Sadie comes along to help out. Would you believe Josie actually uses the term 'nurse' with her?"

I shrugged. What else would you call someone who aided a

midwife? "Why would they abandon a mother who had just given birth?"

"I understand you interrupted them."

"I did."

"That's why. They knew they were in deep horse hockey when you came in. They hightailed it out of there."

I nearly laughed out loud. This picture of doll-baby perfection used "horse hockey" in her description. I began to like the woman in spite of her pancaked skin. "What's the next step?"

"Well, let me ask you some questions about that day. Tell me all you know, then we'll go from there." She flipped to another page in her notebook.

Patricia Echols spent the next thirty minutes taking detailed notes of my encounter in the swamp cabin, the baby, the underwater bomb, and the search of the Wilburn homestead. When she finished, she hadn't moved—her legs, crossed at the ankles, her back straight as a ballerina's, and her red hair still in its neatly pulled-up bun. The humidity that had formed on the makeup at the front door had long disappeared. I wondered if she ever gave some guy the roll and tumble, then came up in pristine shape. A quick glance at her ring finger showed a dainty, expensive blue stone, nothing that looked like a wedding ring.

"If you were right and Josie did run away with a bundle that was a live baby, then we have to ask what she wanted with it, and where did she take it."

"To the bottom of the river, along with her sister and herself, maybe," I said.

"Until we know that for sure, we have to believe they took the baby somewhere—maybe even kidnapped it."

"Why? They are two old ladies."

"Lots of younger ladies want babies, Ms. Fogarty. You might

125

know that yourself."

I shook my head. My own biological clock ticked loudly sometimes, mostly when Pasquin nagged me to get married and produce. I couldn't believe I'd ever want a child bad enough to steal one.

Ms. Echols continued, "Now, I have to find out where they went. I'll run a state search and go after them with local law enforcement." She closed the notebook as though she were dressing a painful wound.

"What if you find they went to another state?"

"I'd have to work with people there, if they have a midwifery department, and local law, of course."

"They may have gone to Georgia, possibly to Valdosta."

She looked up, surprised. "You didn't tell me this."

"I'm telling you now." She retrieved the notebook and opened it up again.

"Okay, where, and how do you know this?"

I began with Charlene Brennan's murder and the phone numbers in her briefcase. "I called the number several times, but no one answered." I didn't tell her Tulia's gossip about Alberta Wilburn dying years ago.

"Well," she closed the notebook again, "I'm going to have to notify Georgia, then make a trip up there."

"I want to go with you."

"You?" She opened her blue eyes wide. From the way the light shone on them, I could tell she wore blue-tinted contacts.

"And so would, I imagine, Tony Amado from the sheriff's department. If they aren't dead, these women are criminal suspects. I don't think it's a good idea for you to go alone." I watched her wide eyes narrow to a squint.

"I'll do my preliminaries, then call you. Could you meet me

at my office, with your detective?"

I stood on the front porch and watched Patricia Echols drive her air-conditioned Buick onto the swamp road, then move around the bend, out of sight. She was a Columbo, disguised as a bubble-headed Southern belle. She could size up the situation and draw a gun on you in a second, both without your realizing she was willing to break a nail in the process. "*My detective,*" I chuckled. "Tony would love that one."

"You want to travel to Valdosta with that leg and your itchy arm?" Tony stood behind his cluttered desk. His eyes darted from one stack of files to the other, but never looked at me. The mess he made of his office was the antithesis of his clothes, and he seemed bewildered about how to resolve it.

"That's what I said, Tony." His habit of questioning every decision I made infuriated me. He never did it to the males around him, simply accepted their word as fact.

"You know, some of the deputies around here are getting a little out of joint about you hanging around all the time."

"They are? Or is it you? Look! I found these women with Theresa Grassfield, and I nearly got killed on this case. If you don't take me to Valdosta, I'll drive my own car." My ears burned with anger. "Besides, you always tell me that when I do anything for your office, I'm an agent of the law!"

"All right!" he leaned forward, his eyes meeting mine for the first time. "When Miss Echols calls you, let me know. If she has something to investigate, I'll travel to Valdosta with you."

"What about local law?"

"I got a buddy on the sheriff's department there. Don't worry about it." He pulled out a file and spoke to it. "Thank God! I thought I'd lost this sucker."

I eased back into my Honda station wagon. My sore leg didn't like it, but at least there was less aching. Placing the cellular on the seat beside me, I headed home. When I came to the fork, each road heading in a different direction around Palmetto River, I took the one away from my house. Traveling south, I slowed as I approached the entrance to Hollowell Sink. The crime scene tapes were down now, the road no longer blocked to traffic.

I turned left. No one lunched at the picnic tables. Only scraped tree trunks, lush vegetation, and the big water hole sat in front of me. Even the ruts from the police vehicles were nothing but mud puddles now. Southern earth covered up its sins in a hurry.

Stepping from the car, I stood at the edge of the steep bank. In the oak limbs, a gentle breeze stirred the moss. Occasionally, a bird sounded a snake warning. Staring into the dark water, I imagined Charlene down there, her tanned face covered in swamp mud that mixed with the blood flowing out of her neck.

If she had died suddenly, it wouldn't matter. But if she were unconscious, then revived by the cool water just in time to die far below the earth… Like a child, I built horrific scenarios, but this was a scenario I knew well. A diver, trapped alive in a cave, disoriented, panicky. Death was always the way out, the answer to a foolish turn. "And what foolish turn did you make, Ms. Brennan?" I asked aloud.

My gaze drifted above the sink and onto the opposite shore. I stared into green and brown shades of oak, pine, palmetto, all still and unrevealing of their secrets. The silence surrounded me like a vacuum until a loud pop broke in the distance. Frightened birds scattered into the sky. Men shouted. It came from the deep wooded area to my right, the section near Calley's Slough.

At first, the voices sounded threatening. Moving to the other side of the sink, I stood between the steep bank and the woods. The voices took on a gleeful quality, like playground noise. I couldn't make out the words, but I could hear more pops and shouts, sometimes a crushing of undergrowth. I reminded myself of Tulia's words. Somewhere in the distance, grown men were playing cowboys and Indians.

The distance between me and the men grew narrower as I heard someone tramping through the bushes. With my cane, I pushed aside some brush and hid behind a clump of trees just in time to see a hefty middle-aged man in camouflage come bouncing over a log. He slipped to the ground, his shirt riding upward to expose lots of hairy belly. With a quick jerk he rolled over and propped his upper body on the log. With a gun in one hand, he searched the forest with his eyes. With my eyes, I saw pants that didn't quite cover a tail crack.

"Gotcha, sucker!" I lowered my voice and poked the end of the cane just above the crack.

The man froze, then made a quick turn over to expose his belly once more.

"What the hell!" His eyes widened when he saw a female.

I used the cane to knock the gun from his hand and toss it into the woods. Placing the tip on his stomach, I could feel the flesh quiver.

"Playing games, are we?"

"So what?" He said and grabbed at the cane.

I moved it downward, pressing into the flesh just above the groin. "Do that again and I'll shove the family jewels back into pre-puberty."

The man stretched his arms outward in surrender. "What do you want, lady?"

"Who's out there?" I nodded toward the sounds coming from the slough.

"Just a bunch of men. We play war games. That's all. What's your problem?" He squirmed but didn't fight each time I pressed on his bladder.

"Give me some names, and I'll let you go."

"Uh-huh," he shook his head, rolling it back and forth across the log that was now his pillow. "I can't do that."

The men's voices came closer. I raised the cane and pretended I was going to slam it into his genitals. He cried out and grabbed himself. I took the opportunity to slip back into the tree coverage.

"What's going on here?" said a voice. Several men in camouflage and caps surrounded the man on the ground.

"Just slipped. Help me up." The man raised a chubby hand, and two others about the same girth as he, pulled him up. "Get my gun over there." He pointed to a tree where I had tossed it.

The group strolled back toward the slough, their game burned out for the day. As they went, the man turned back and looked in the forest. I knew he wouldn't relate the incident. No macho warrior would admit to being held down by a woman with a cane.

"Arnie Newsome's got the next game set up. Let's go," said one of his fellow warriors.

Before they left my sight, a pager beeped in someone's pocket. When the man moved into the light to see the display, he jerked off his hat. I almost shouted out loud when I recognized him—Robert Boseman, the dean of my college.

Tulia returned for the dinner part of the evening then took off for a church meeting. "I'm leading prayer meeting tonight," she said. "We're between preachers." The mental picture of Tulia shouting prayers in Holy Roller style, her red hair shooting off in all directions around her face, gave me pause to smile. "We'll say a prayer for the Wilburn sisters and for that poor little baby."

I relished the solitude. My arm still itched, but its crustiness indicated healing. Pulling on a long-sleeved flannel gown, I watched myself in the mirror. Once totally brunette, my head was now streaked with ribbons of gray, hairs that seemed courser than their dark neighbors. I tugged on the elasticized wristband and moved the sleeve carefully up my arm. The red nastiness of the poison ivy had begun to fade to a raw pink, and dead skin peeled at the edges. Highly allergic to poisonous plants, I had lived with the burn-like scales twice before in my young life. Once, while romping through the woods with a friend to find the perfect Christmas tree in an especially warm December, I brushed against some poison oak. My right arm endured the itchy mess, and I ran a fever for two days.

Later, in my teens, I forgot myself in the throes of a hormone attack. I flirted with a classmate by taking off through the same terrain, ignoring my previous bout. He caught me, as planned, and we landed on the ground in a thick brush. Snakes and palmetto bugs be damned, we wanted each other. Well into groping, we heard voices. Jumping to a stand and reattaching clothing, we presented ourselves to Pasquin and his fishing buddy who were taking a short cut through the swamp. Pasquin tipped his hat and smiled.

The next day, my guilt stood out for the world to know. I had bright red itching death clear down one side of my body, arm pit to buttock. My friend in hormonal jeopardy had the same, only his ran from under one male teat to a hip bone. My father said nothing, but took me to a doctor where I suffered the embarrassment of a lifetime. He had just treated my boyfriend. His parting comment was, "This stuff has prevented more pregnancies than you'll ever know."

I reached down and pulled up the gown to look at the side where I suffered my teenage romp. The skin, white and smooth, surprised me. I had found tiny varicose veins on the backs of my knees, but none sprouted here, and no scarring. I laughed and wondered whatever happened to that guy who almost deflowered me in a swamp bed.

A knock at the door jarred me into the present. On the way downstairs, I heard a key, then saw the door open.

"Sorry," said Vernon, "I thought you might be in the shower."

I had given Vernon a key a year ago, a gesture that sealed our familiarity. Neither of us had made a verbal commitment to anything, but we drifted in that direction.

"You're just in time," I said. "I've bathed and covered up the plague."

"Good! Give me ten minutes."

He darted upstairs and into the shower. I waited for him in my room, my sanctuary from swampy turmoil. The air conditioning unit pumped cool, noiseless air onto yellow curtains. The king-size bed sat squarely in the center of two windows, its quilted coverlet matching the soft ivory in the two chairs. I had painted the old wood slat walls a faint peach, and lined them with pine furniture. A soft room, it leant itself to love-making, a far cry from poisonous forest growth.

"Why are you smiling?" Vernon asked as he swiped at his scant hair with my brush.

"Just thinking how nice this is," I said, preferring to let my memories stay mine.

"And not enough of it," he said. He winked at me as he removed the towel and slid onto the cool sheets beside me. I kept the diseased arm in the nightgown sleeve but the rest of me belonged to Vernon. We shared bodies, swimmers' bodies, the way we dived together. Teamwork, watching where the other person went, caring for the other's well being. This was no practice dive. We touched the right muscles, breathed the right rhythm, and paced the right strokes. In the end, we had swum as though our lives depended on every move.

I lay awake, still in a golden stupor, and listened to Vernon's contented breathing. Outside, the katydids chirped loudly, and I pictured them making love to other katydids. Squirming, I pulled on the nightgown again and settled against Vernon's bare back. His solid muscles pressed against me, and for a moment, I lost myself in his protective maleness.

The phone rang.

"Tony here, Luanne. Are you awake?"

"No, but talk to me anyway," I said, my hand reaching to caress Vernon's stirring arm.

"It's Harry. Somebody paid him a visit in the hospital, and tried to knife him."

I sat up straight, shocking Vernon into the same position.

"He's bruised a little more, but okay," continued Tony. "He wants to see you, and he's damned mad about this. Refuses to take a pain killer until he talks to you. Haul yourself out and get down here."

I shrugged as I replaced the receiver. Vernon read my expression. "Get dressed," he said. "I'll drive."

At the hospital, Harry sat up in bed, his face full of scratches and some additional bandages on one arm. I recognized the anger in his wide-open eyes. He winced when he moved one side, but he moved it anyway.

"Damn about time!" he said when we entered. Tony nodded at us from his chair at the foot of the bed. Vernon leaned against the wall near the door.

"I live in the far side of the jungle, Harry; what can I say?" I moved to the side of his bed. Leaning over, I saw blood ooze through a heavy gauze bandage. "Shouldn't the nurse take care of that?"

"Needs stitches," said Tony. "He doesn't want any needles right now; he made them hold off."

"Damn woman!" said Harry.

"Now wait a minute," I said.

"Not you! Tibby. She brought a friend of hers with her, some guy she dates. Said he was interested in diving. Muscular fellow. They left, but he came back later. Said he had a message from her, then came up next to me. He pulled a knife. Thank God I was awake. I smashed him with the T.V. remote control."

"He managed to dodge the knife except for that slash on his arm. Nurse heard the shouts, and the guy ran. We've got a description," said Tony from his chair.

"Maybe this wouldn't have happened if you hero cops had been on duty." Harry leaned back and grimaced.

"Have you questioned Tibby?" I said.

"We will as soon as we find her," said Tony. "She's not at home."

"I can't believe she'd be a party to violence," I said.

"I doubt she knew what she was doing," said Harry. "She's been an airbrain from the start. Never trusted her diving, now

134

this. Fell for a set of muscles. Dinghead!" He tossed back the sheet, revealing tanned thighs in between bandages from the blast. The short hospital gown barely covered his groin. He placed his bruised hand in a strategic location.

"What did this guy look like?" I asked, focusing my eyes on his face.

"Typical jock. Wore a tee shirt that stretched on his biceps. He works out somewhere. Short hair, nearly shaved off. Tall as I am, about thirty."

"Any other description—other than jock, that is?"

"Didn't notice any scars if that's what you mean."

CHAPTER SIXTEEN

"You want me to sit in on your class?" Tony looked up.

"If he did it, what are the chances he'll really show?"

I had told them Harry's description of his visitors sounded a lot like Nick Summers.

"I'd sure as hell like to be there. Any way you can arrange it?" Harry waved away the nurse who approached his bedside with a filled hypodermic.

"Not hardly," said Tony. "Let's talk, Luanne." He stood and crooked his finger toward the door. With his other hand, he motioned for Vernon to follow. "Nurse, get those stitches in this man, now." The woman, without hesitating, began rubbing Harry's shoulder with alcohol.

"The dean said he'd meet me in his office." Tony spoke inside my car. The three of us decided not to attract attention by showing up in police cars. If a student knew my Honda, then that's what he would see tonight. "You two go on to class, but Vernon, you wait for me in the hallway, preferably looking like you attend one of the other classes." Tony stumbled from the back seat and entered the Gothic-style brick building. I drove slowly into the parking lot.

"I don't see him around anywhere," I said as I twisted in the driver's seat to stare at students and faculty members hurrying toward buildings.

"Okay," said Vernon, "you walk toward the building. I'll watch, then follow you."

I slipped out after I made sure the inside light wouldn't come on. It still wasn't dark, and wouldn't be for nearly two more hours, but when I returned after class, it would be pitch black. I wanted no vulnerability, and the inside car light prevented me from seeing what immediately surrounded the area. I carried a partially unzipped briefcase in my left hand, empty except for the automatic that I could easily grab with my right hand. My job would likely be in a stew if university officials knew I had it. The cane stayed home tonight.

On the walk to the classroom, I chatted with some students. Sure that Vernon kept watch somewhere behind me, I placed the briefcase on the desk, the opening facing me. A student pulled the lectern next to the desk. I stared at the expectant faces. Students had their pens poised, their blank sheets of paper ready to fill with facts about the Viking influence on early English. No one sat in the back seats.

Until the break, Vernon wandered the hall, passing the open door twice to nod the all clear to me. By break time, Tony had joined him.

"I got the dean on the phone and told him to get down here." Tony's jaw moved when he wasn't talking, grinding teeth, a sure sign he was pissed. "We're going to meet him in half an hour."

"Muscle man didn't show, either," I said.

"I know. Vernon's already told me."

"And how am I going to finish this class and meet the dean

at the same time?"

"You're not. Cancel the thing." Tony paced the hall. His quick glances at me brought on the usual female guilt. Had I put him up to doing something completely worthless?

"Nobody outside fits the description. Of course, it's pretty dark out there," Vernon said.

I met the class and gave them a reading assignment. Begging off and pulling up my sleeve part way, I pleaded pain from an injury. Two girls in the front row gasped as they stared at the crusty red streak. Either they thought it was a burn or they had suffered the same stuff on their butts. The class filed out, some offering me condolences and wishes to get better. One even suggested he walk me to my car. If he had only known that an automatic lay less than two feet from his nose.

We sat in the car again, in front of the same Gothic brick building. Tony, angry and insulted, wanted to surprise the dean when he pulled into the driveway.

"That's him," I said as a new black Mercedes parked in a lined spot with the dean's name printed in white letters on the curb. The three of us met the man on the steps.

"Sheriff's department, sir," said Tony as he made a show of his badge directly in the bright foyer light. Vernon held his up, too. "Just lead us to your office."

Dean Boseman, gray tufts of hair poking from his sideburns, and dark strands carefully combed on top of his head, breathed heavily, and said, "Yes, this way." His shoulders stooped as he walked ahead of us, like one marked for doom.

"I'm not allowed to give out information regarding students." Sitting at his desk, he rubbed his hands together and refused to look at us.

The dean looked nervous, tired and vulnerable, unlike the

confident man I'd glimpsed in the woods.

"Sir," I said, "Someone could be involved in a capital crime—about as capital as you can get. You'll have to speak to the police sooner or later."

Boseman's head shook a couple of times, his eyes watered. "Murder?"

"Possibly." All three of us stared at him.

He swiveled his chair, touching a Christmas cactus plant he had placed on top of a cluttered table. Vernon's hand went immediately to his waist, and I placed mine on top of the briefcase.

"Some men around the county. We play games at a camp." He jerked around to face us again. "You know, put on camouflage and chase each other around the swamp with paint guns. Afterwards, we drink beer and cook venison over a campfire. It's just weekend fun."

"Weekends?" I asked.

"Yes."

"Only weekends? At Calley's Slough?"

He sat up straight. "You know about us?"

I leaned forward. "I know it's not only on weekends that you play games out there, and I know it's not paint guns you use. I also know you have at least one Hummer vehicle. I even know a fat guy who stumbled over a log and one muscle-bound shaved-head type. I saw you with them."

His hands fidgeted with a pencil. He didn't wait for an answer. "Yes, well, we do go out there other times, but most of us can't get away until the weekends."

"Your wives go with you?" said Vernon, his towering stance forcing the dean to look upward.

"It's not their thing."

"Who are these men, sir?" Tony's face was pure stone.

139

"Look, unless they have committed a crime, I can't give their names. We made a pact not to."

I leaned forward. "Does August St. Claire play these games in the woods?"

The man's face paled and he stared back at me in silence. When no one else spoke, he closed his eyes and nodded. "And he brought in the fellow from Montana."

"Montana?" said Vernon. "Are you sure theses games aren't real militia—supremacist stuff?" He turned back to looking out the blinds, a movement that seemed to terrify the dean.

"It's not! I assure you." He stood up halfway and looked toward Vernon. "Is there something out there?"

"Is something supposed to be out there?" Vernon kept looking, moving his head as though searching for a better view.

The dean sat down and sighed. "We play games out there. That's all."

Tony stood up. "Yeah, well sometimes little boy games get out of hand." He placed his palms on the desk next to the dean's, then leaned close to his face. "Tell me, what's the man from Montana's name?"

The dean shook his head. "I don't know."

I asked, "Is it the man in my class?"

"Arnie Newsome is taking your class?" the dean said in surprise.

Tony and Vernon looked at each other.

I stood as though ready to leave, then turned to the dean. "You wouldn't happen to know where the man from Montana is tonight, would you?"

"I think he got into a little accident—twisted his ankle he said."

I drove back to the sheriff's office where the three of us sat

140

in the parking lot for nearly half an hour.

"He's going to run back and tell his buddies," Tony said. "That's good. Get them scared. We'll have to watch their movements. All I need is some crazy militia blowing up state buildings."

"I know what you're thinking," said Vernon. "That blast at the cave had the markings of a white-boy nut case."

The next morning I planned to ease myself back into the water. Vernon would meet me at the Sheriff's Department computer room later in the day.

To cover the streak of poison ivy, I pulled on a long-sleeved tee over my bathing suit. I trudged to the landing, the cane and my face mask in one hand, tank and fins in the other. I sat the equipment on the boards and brushed the water with the tips of my fingers. The iciness moved up my arm and somewhere in the pit of my stomach, I felt the old ache to swim, to be a part of the river again. I rolled into the water and let the cold envelop me until it felt natural. Floating and splashing like this for half an hour brought back the confidence. Soon I was gazing into dark water where I'd use the tank.

I couldn't go into the cave not far from the landing. I needed a buddy for that. But I would use the tank and go to the entrance, check out an area that had once been used to hide drugs.

Back on the landing, I took my time pulling on the fins, strapping myself in the tank and practicing breathing in the mouthpiece. I had the mask raised when I noticed bubbles from the middle of the river. For a moment, I trembled. "Stop it, Luanne," I said. "It's a turtle." I shoved on the mask and eased into the water.

The warmer shore water gave way to dark cold depths. I pushed slowly downwards until I needed the headlight. The currents gripped me, and I struggled to keep them from curling round me and bundling me off to some cypress root cluster. When I reached the narrow entrance to the cave in mid river, I stared into an area that resembled a gargoyle smile. Shining the light around the edges, I looked for bombs. Finding none, I moved my head inside the hole. Darkness prevailed except for the narrow beam of light. I knew the cave tapered into a tiny spring outlet, one that no human could ever fit through. For a brief moment, I felt a pang of sadness when I imagined a tiny newborn trapped in this darkness. I had to shake it or I'd be back where I started. I stayed in the spot until I felt at ease with the watery cocoon.

Topside, I stripped off the equipment and lay back on the dock. The hot Florida sun felt good after the cold water swim.

"Miz Fogarty," a voice sounded from one end of the landing.

I raised myself and in the glare of sunlight, saw muscles and a bald head. "What?" I sat up quickly, preparing to defend myself.

"I just came by to let you know I decided not to take the class after all."

"Nick Summers?"

"Yeah. You remembered my name." He grinned. "I got a part-time job at Palmetto Park, cleaning out grass from the springs. That's why I gave up the class." He grinned and lowered his head. "Besides, I'm not much of a student."

"So you dive?" I touched my tank, ready to hurl it at him if I had to.

"Yeah, but not on this job."

I fidgeted, not knowing whether to keep a protective stance or relax on the landing. "How did you find me?"

"I get around the swamp." He grinned. "Saw you swimming here once before."

"Do you ever play war games in the woods?"

"Me? Played with paint guns once. Why?" He sauntered toward me a few steps, grinning like a pleased child.

"But no militia games?"

"Never." He looked puzzled.

"Nick, how did you get here?" I waved my hands around me. "I'm not too far from the springs, but…"

"We're working a grass puller up that way." He pointed down the river. "They don't need me right now. Felt it was a good opportunity to let you know about the class."

I nodded, and Nick walked into the forest.

"Arnold Newsome," said Vernon as he read the glaring print from the computer screen, "football star in high school, spent two years in the army—hey! a sharpshooter—son of a Montana rancher. Okay, here is the good stuff." He sat up straight and I leaned over his back. "Drunk and disorderly, three arrests, one conviction. Sentenced to six months for battery on a woman— suspended sentence. Moved around the country selling exercise equipment wholesale."

"There's got to be more," I said when the computer refused to scroll further.

"Nope. Not on this file." Vernon hit *print* and waited for the laser copier to spit out its data. "It's getting late."

Tony nodded when he skimmed the printed sheet. "Meet me here at eight tomorrow morning. We'll need you to ID the women if we find them. We're going by to pick up a Miss Echols and see what we can find in Valdosta."

CHAPTER SEVENTEEN

The road from Tallahassee to Valdosta, in spots, smacks of Kentucky bluegrass country. Vast fields of grass blanket rolling hills, fenced off with sturdy oak posts. Inside the fields, sleek stallions graze on the blue-green foliage. Besides the large oaks, weeping willows touch the grass in spots by running creek beds. A white farmhouse, or maybe a newer brick one, sits in a grove of trees on the edges of the fields. Vernon squeezed my hand just as we passed a chestnut mare with a colt.

Tony drove, and Patricia Echols sat in front with him. She had been waiting for us in the Sheriff's Department lobby when we arrived at eight. Dressed in a baby-blue cotton dress and those damned high heels, she was perfectly coiffured again. Her little blue stone ring still graced her finger, but her nails had changed to colorless polish. When I wasn't taking in the lovely countryside, I stared at the way she had tucked in the red hair at the back. It wasn't quite a French roll, but it folded in like one. I saw no evidence of pins, but they must have been there. The translucent skin on her neck accented the blue collar of the dress. My eyes wandered to the back of Tony's neck. His dark olive contrasted with the stiff white collar of his dress shirt.

Something was happening here. I had felt it when we waited for Tony to join us in the lobby. He nodded to Vernon and me, but actually smiled at Patricia Echols. She had held out her hand and said, "Good morning, Tony." Tony? Why not Mr. Amado, or even Detective Amado? In the car, she had insisted on reading the data she had on the Wilburns, though all of us knew it already. Without his usual squirming impatience, Tony often nodded in her direction. I eyed Vernon once. He winked.

When we pulled up in front of the sheriff's office in Valdosta, Patricia made some comment about hurrying up because she was just going to be a puddle on the car floor in all this humidity. "Then you'd better come inside," Tony said and nodded for all of us to follow him.

"Good thing she's along," I whispered to Vernon. "We could go into shock from sunstroke for all he cares."

"Civilizing hormones," he grinned.

Tony appeared relaxed when we were all inside. He exchanged shoulder slaps with a uniformed man.

"This is my buddy, Lieutenant Palmer," he said. "He'll be the official at the Wilburn estate." Palmer shook hands all around then introduced us to the two uniform deputies who would accompany us. The three men of the same height, weight, balding pate, and fuzzy sideburns, stood like triplets, unsmiling and ready. Palmer placed a wide sheriff's hat on his head, and his men mimicked the gesture with theirs.

"Follow these guys," said Palmer in a deep Southern drawl. "I'll ride with them. Now if anyone is there, and they agree to talk to us, we'll let you do the questioning. My guess is, however, they're going to hightail it off somewhere, or refuse to say a word. Then we got to look at a warrant, and I don't know if I can get one too quick, based on what I know so far." He looked at each of us like students in a classroom.

The patrol car pulled in front of Tony's unmarked car. Palmer sat in the back and waved for us to follow. We eventually ended up on a road that took us by the university, a group of brick buildings in an open field off a tree-lined street. Nearby, large, aging, white wood-frame houses stood as reminders of the sixties when whole groups of students would commune in one house. No one locked the doors back then, and residents constantly dragged in strangers to stay over. *Peace, love, happiness—where did it go?*

We were in true country in a short ten minutes. Only an occasional vehicle, usually a logging truck carrying heavy pines, passed us in the opposite direction. Finally, the left signal on the patrol car began to flash. We tailed it onto a dirt lane. The high grass between the two tire ruts indicated little car travel.

"Get ready," said Tony. Vernon's hand went automatically to his gun. He touched it as though to make sure it was really at his waist. I had chosen to wear linen slacks and a short sleeve cotton blouse. Reluctantly, I pulled on a matching jacket. Patting the pocket, I felt the metal bulge. In the other pocket rested the small cellular phone. Patricia picked up her notes and tucked her purse under the front seat.

The deputy driver motioned for Tony to pull to the end of the drive and stop. He backed his car up so that the two cars together formed a vee. On each side, deep culverts filled with recent heavy rain completed the barrier. Anyone trying to escape by car would have to crash through the vee or risk drowning.

We stood before an ancient house, a gray-board mansion that had lost its glamor in years of neglect. Nearly covered in trees and kudzu vines, only the windows on each end were visible. From the rear, it looked as though the heavy forest foliage would eat it alive. It was Old South, long dead.

"Straight out of Faulkner," I said.

146

"Well, I wonder if they have an idiot to tell a tale inside there," said Patricia as she dabbed at her upper lip with a lace handkerchief. It startled me a little to realize the woman actually read anything outside romance and midwifery reports.

"We'll see to the front door," said Palmer and motioned for Tony to go with him. "You two take the rear if you can get through all that brush." He pointed for the two deputies to walk around one side. "Maybe you should watch the other side, although I don't see how anyone could get through that stuff." He spoke to Vernon as he nodded toward the under and overgrowth that clung tightly to the side of the house. "And you two ladies stay near the cars."

"At least he didn't say 'little ladies,'" I said.

We watched them walk to their stations. "I don't suppose you have a gun on you?" said Patricia.

"I do, why? Will we need it?"

"Don't know, but it's always nice to come prepared."

"And how did you prepare?" I expected her to whip out a notebook with a dainty zipper.

"Right here, and if I don't get into some air conditioning soon, I'm going to shoot somebody for sure." She pulled up the flap on one large cotton pocket of her dress. I saw the handle of small caliber gun resting inside a white half holster. "It's concealed, isn't it? I wonder what Georgia law says about that?"

I didn't answer her, silently betting she could hit somebody between matching earrings at fifty feet without shedding one female tear.

A scraggly-haired girl in dirty shorts appeared at the door. Her eyes widened when badges flashed before her. I could see her turn and say something to someone inside. There was a wait, then suddenly the girl slammed shut the door, and Palmer yelled, "Hey!"

Vernon jerked his head around as the kudzu vine shook behind him. He drew his gun and yelled for the others. The two men on the porch leaped off the end, and the three of them disappeared into the foliage.

"Nobody is going to run through vines like that," said Patricia. She dropped her notebook on the hood of the car and started around the other side of the house. I had just caught up to her when two familiar women headed straight toward us.

"Watch the well!" yelled Josie to her sister, and Sadie parted from her, trotting off at an angle.

"Just hold it right there," I said as I caught up to the terrified woman less than ten yards into the swamp. She threw her hands into the air even though I never pulled the gun. "Back up against that tree and don't move." She did as I said, her chest heaving from the short run.

I could hear underbrush crushing as Josie thrashed into the woods. The two deputies, hearing the commotion, drew their guns and came running from the back of the house. Patricia's two high heels lay on the unmowed grass; she had leapt into the brush after Josie. I could hear her screaming.

"Stop! You goddamn, friggin' bitch! You got some answering to do. Now, stop!"

The older woman couldn't move as fast, but she knew the forest better. Making a meandering pattern, she came into my line of sight several times, Patricia closing in behind. Suddenly, Josie halted behind a tree on an embankment. A sinkhole, nearly six feet in diameter was at the bottom of the bank.

"Patricia!" I yelled. "She's at a sinkhole. Watch the tree."

The next time I saw Patricia, she was coming up behind Josie from the other side. When the older woman saw her, she made a move to run. Patricia flew through the air, and made a

148

tackle that only a Florida State Seminole football player could analyze. The two of them fell, and I heard both scream as they slid down the embankment and hit sinkhole water.

I yanked off my jacket and tossed it to one deputy. "Keep an eye on her," I said, pointing to Sadie who still had her hands raised in front of the tree. Briars tore at my pants legs, and I wondered how much more poison ivy I touched as I thrashed toward the sink. At the embankment, I leaned back and slid down the muddy side into a blanket of algae. Both women were holding onto tufts of grass that grew from the nearly vertical embankment, their faces and hair covered with green strips of slime. I swam to them. Josie's frightened face begged for rescue. Her grip on the grass slipped and she went under a couple of times. In her panic, she dug into the dirt on the bank, trying to grasp something that was not there.

"I'll take her first," I said to Patricia. "Are you okay?"

"Damn okay. Just get that cow out of here." Her words dared the sink to drown her.

"Lean back and let me float you to the other side," I said to Josie. She tried but wouldn't stop trying to grab at the bank. "You'll have to let go and let me take you." She let go once, her head slipping under as far as her mouth. She spat out green algae and clung to the side again.

"Just lean back, bitch, or we'll let you sink in this bottomless pit!" Patricia yelled like a shrew.

It worked. Josie's body relaxed a little, and I slipped my arm under her chin.

In seconds, we were on the less steep side where Vernon and the deputy pulled her up. I treaded water until she was able to rest on the bank, then turned back to Patricia. But the midwifery agent had already appeared at my back. When Tony and Palmer finally reached the action, we were standing on the bank, resembling two rare swamp creatures.

"We don't have a bathroom here," said Sadie as she stared at her sister and two other women pulling off strings of algae from head and shoulders. "There's an outhouse."

"Running water," I said. "Do you have that?"

"Well, yes, we have it in the kitchen, and there's a hose." She pointed to a green coil near the front steps.

I pulled on the hose that was attached to a make-shift pipe under the house, and turned it on over my head. I could feel my clothes stick but I could also see clumps of algae drop to the ground. Patricia joined me, and we giggled in the spray until we realized five men were having a free show.

"Take your sister inside, and clean her off," I said to Sadie. "And Palmer, get on your radio and get us some dry clothes."

The two deputies escorted the sisters to the kitchen sink. Tony pressed his lips together and tried not to smile. Vernon, on the other hand, grinned from ear to ear. "Never had so much fun in my life," he said. "Just sit right here on the porch and let the sun dry you off." He brushed next to me and casually mopped a few drops with his hand. "You getting cold?"

I sent out a dirty stare, then burst into laughter with him. We sat on that porch for thirty minutes before a marked patrol car turned onto the lane. By that time Josie, in a dry dress, and Sadie had been seated in dining chairs brought from inside.

"Damn! What have you men been doing to these ladies?" said the female deputy, her dry, crisp uniform looking comfortable even in the heat. She held a large paper bag in one hand. "This is all I could find. I hope they fit." She handed over two pairs of jeans and two tee shirts with *Lowndes County Jamboree* printed across the front. "No underwear, I'm sorry."

Thanks to elasticized waists, the jeans stayed put. I put on my jacket to cover my braless-ness. Patricia had no jacket, but she did have firm breasts that stood at attention in spite of no support. I had visions of new implants every time she visited the manicurist. When she came out in her shirt, Vernon poked me in the ribs. Tony tried not to look, or at least limit himself to furtive peeks.

The Wilburn sisters wouldn't talk about the midwifing incident. Josie threatened a couple of times to sue if she caught some disease in the sinkhole, but she clammed up, turning her eyes away, when asked about birthing babies.

"Miz Wilburn," said Palmer, "you do realize that I'll get a search warrant for this place, and you'll probably be sent back to Tallahassee to answer for this incident?"

"I don't realize nothing, sheriff. You got a cause to arrest me, then do it. I'll get me a lawyer, and be back here in no time." Her sharp nose reddened, the only color in a gray face.

"Miss Wilburn," I said, "aren't you worried about leaving your Florida house unattended?"

"What house? I sold…," she stopped, her eyes startled at her own words.

"To who?" asked Palmer.

"Don't know his name. Some fellow with money down there." She turned her head and glared at her sister who paled.

"Just tell us what you did with the baby," said Tony.

"Don't know nothing about no baby."

"Miss Fogarty walked in on the whole thing. We have a witness."

"Her word against ours. Two against one." The woman spoke in staccato and refused to look at us.

Sadie blinked tears from her eyes as she looked from us to

151

her sister and back again.

Vernon stood up and moved to the bottom of the steps. He propped up one leg, leaning toward one knee. Looking up at Josie, he said, "Actually, Miss Wilburn, somebody tossed it into a water cave. Did you do that?"

A gasp rose from Sadie who stared at her sister.

"He's lying," Josie said and stared back.

"But, how does he—?" Sadie stopped as Josie shot her a wide-eyed nasty look.

"How do I what, Miss Sadie?" Vernon's position allowed them to look down at him, but it was like looking down at a rattler.

The woman shuddered and shook her head. Her sister continued to stare at her.

"Well, looks like we got cause to take you in, at least," Palmer stood and took hold of Josie's arm. She jerked away and rose by herself. He held out a hand to the other sister, "Miss Sadie." She wasn't so feisty. Allowing him to help her, she stood while he read them their rights. It would be the last time for a while that they were together. Palmer made sure one rode in front, the other in back. At the sheriff's office, they occupied separate interview rooms.

"Ms. Fogarty," said Palmer, drawling it out longer than normal, "is this one of the ladies you saw in the cabin, delivering a child?" He spoke to me but faced Sadie who sat at a metal table and shook like a bad student in the principal's office.

"She was there. They said they had delivered a child, and the woman on the bed had obviously given birth." I tried to stare at the woman as I spoke, but she shifted her eyes to her rough hands.

"You got anything to say about that, Miss Sadie?"

Sadie shook her head, then suddenly looked up at me, her eyes pleading. "I never said there was a baby!"

"Then you were in the cabin?" asked Palmer.

Sadie looked from him to me, her ruddy complexion even redder. She trembled like a cornered rabbit. "But I never said there was a baby." Tears dropped across her cheeks.

Palmer nodded and motioned for me to follow him outside. "Talk to me, Luanne."

"Josie said Theresa Grassfield had called her in as midwife. And she carried a bundle like it was a child. I could swear it whimpered, but I never actually saw it. But Sadie's statement, as you so cleverly pointed out, puts her in that cabin, right?"

"Probably," he said, pulling the word out into its three syllables. "I got to find a cause to hand them over to Amado, though. You see the legality, don't you?"

"Oh, come on, Palmer, you've got plenty of cause. Hell! We have a dead woman in Tallahassee and, at least, evidence of a baby's body. Get on with the extradition!"

Palmer stared at me, then broke into a grin, revealing a shiny gold tooth. He began nodding his head, then said, "Amado said you was scrappy!"

It would be at least forty-eight hours before the judge would sign the paperwork turning the two sisters over to Amado for transport back to Tallahassee. So far, the sisters refused a public defender. Josie said they would take their chances on someone in Tallahassee if they had to return there.

"Whether the judge makes up his mind by tomorrow or not, we're coming back to Valdosta to watch Palmer and his men search that old house," said Amado. "And that little girl who ran for the woods, we need to find out what she knows. You'd better come too, Luanne, in case we need to see what's in that sinkhole."

"Well, I just hope you're going to charge those women with double murder!" said Patricia, her face furious.

Tony looked at her and smiled. A gentleness I had never seen in him spread over his face. "Will try to oblige you, Miss Echols." Then, he blushed! Actually blushed, his olive skin taking on a sunburned hue.

On the way to the car, I leaned against Vernon's arm and whispered, "Something's happening."

Vernon didn't comment, only grinned and stared straight ahead.

CHAPTER EIGHTEEN

Patricia Echols wasn't about to ruin another pair of panty hose. She dressed safari style for our return to the wilds of southern Georgia. Everything matched in ecru—cap, shirt, pants, shoes, and canvas bag. "I've got some things in here, just in case I have to dive into that filthy sinkhole again." She waved the bag around, then tossed it on the floorboard before climbing in beside Tony.

"Guess we get the back seat again—on this double date," said Vernon as he held the door. "You brought your suit?"

"Yeah. It's all there." I pointed to a square bag that carried my diving equipment—wet suit, bathing suit, fins, mask, weights, lights. Tanks were being loaded in a small trailer behind a patrol truck. "But I'd like not to dive in that hole."

"If anybody does, it'll be us," he said. "Tony has loaned us to Palmer."

Patricia talked incessantly at Tony about how the Wilburn sisters had violated the midwife regulations. Anyone else would have gotten the tightened jaw, pitch-black stare, and a clenched teeth, "cut the gab." Patricia got smiles, nods, even a one-syllable comment once in a while. Beguiled by this well-dressed vixen, he sighed almost audibly when he got out of the car in front of Palmer's office.

"You love it, don't you?" I whispered as I exited from the

seat behind him. He shot me an unsmiling glance, then turned away and walked inside the building.

Patricia sat still inside the car, her temple beginning to drip a little tear of sweat, which she dabbed with a tissue from a cellophane wrapped package. Vernon and I leaned against the car, our only relief from the heat the sweeping branches of an ancient oak.

"Warrant was easy," said Palmer as he and Amado joined us in the parking lot. "I got a feeling extradition will be the same. Seems these ladies don't want a lawyer from here. Keep saying they can get a good one in Tallahassee."

"Did they," I asked following a hunch, "say anything about a Mr. St. Claire?"

"Didn't mention anybody's name." Palmer turned toward me. "Who's St. Claire?"

"Just someone of the more patrician gentry whose name sort of pops up every time we run into these two sisters. Says he bought their property."

Tony eyed me suspiciously. I knew my questions often agitated him, but I also knew he would be curious enough to follow my lead. Vernon stared, then nudged my side.

"Let's get going," said Tony. He sat in the driver's seat and waited for Palmer to pull his car in front of us. Two deputies who doubled as crime scene techs rode with him.

The old Wilburn house may have been a hundred years old— or a neglected thirty. It was hard to tell under the kudzu growth. If anyone lived in the Wilburn house in recent years, he had done it in absolute solitude, with a few reptile visitors for excitement. My own renovated swamp home could have looked like this, only worse, with a few more years of neglect.

"If the sisters sold their own property, why would they live in something like this?" No one answered me.

Palmer walked to the front porch and knocked. The door stood slightly ajar. When no one answered, he pushed on wood that had warped and wouldn't budge. Pulling up on the rusted knob, he nearly fell inside the house when the boards gave up their grip.

Inside, the darkness engulfed us even though the sun shined brightly in the front yard. Through dirty window panes, we saw entwined leaves thickly meshed; they appeared as an intricate print on drapery material. A green lizard darted across one vine and briefly attached itself to the window glass.

"Nothing here," said Tony. "Nothing but kudzu and mold."

The deputies and Palmer headed back inside to explore the upstairs rooms. I wandered around the outside, my mind alternating between childhood fears of what could be under all that kudzu and the possibility of a path a child might take through the forest. From the attached outhouse, I followed the kudzu vines until they joined the heavy oaks. The stuff could snuff the life out of the trees, but these oaks, and a few pines, grew strong and green. On closer inspection, I could see why. The edges of the vines had been sliced off clean. When I moved them with my arm, they opened like a vegetable door. Inside the darkness, I saw the path.

"This is how that girl got away," I said as I aimed Tony's flashlight at the path. "Shouldn't we follow it?"

"We'll do that, ma'am," said Palmer. "Let's finish up in the house first."

In a large pantry off the kitchen, the deputies found the sisters' clothes and toiletries. In a crib meant for firewood, they found a supply of canned goods. Empty cans ended up in a cardboard box a few yards away.

"Looks like they opened the cans, warmed them on the grill,

then ate right out of the tin—like Army rations," said Palmer.

"And upstairs?" I asked.

"Can't get up there. The steps are falling apart and two of them are missing altogether. We'll get a ladder and search, but I'm betting they never got up there."

"Palmer," I said as I pulled out a slip of paper from my purse, "I called this phone number and it rang. There are no phone wires here; where do you think this might be located?"

Palmer looked at the number, then nodded and moved away from us. He sat in his car nearly twenty minutes. "Under the name of Alberta Wilburn all right, but the billing address is a trailer park not far from here."

"Maybe at the end of that forest trail?" I asked.

We squeezed through the kudzu gate and, single file, pushed into the heavy growth of a South Georgia forest. Palmer and his deputies led the way. Patricia followed Tony who would occasionally turn around and hold a briar vine for her to pass underneath.

Suddenly the path widened, and then abruptly halted at the cement stoop of a rusty trailer. There were two small plastic windows on the back side of the single wide vehicle, which had obviously not been towed in years. The lower part of the siding showed the brown jagged edges brought about by alternate extreme muggy heat and cold. The whole thing rested on algae-covered cement blocks.

The deputies moved to opposite ends, not an easy task as they had to push between undergrowth and around heavy tree trunks.

One deputy whispered back to Palmer. "Must be four, five old things like this one. Some kids playing in the sand in the middle. Wash hanging on a line in front."

"Dial the number," I said.

Palmer jerked his cellular phone from his pocket and punched out the number I had given him. Holding it up to his ear, he said, "It's ringing."

I leaned my ear against the trailer, and from somewhere within its tinny bowels, I heard a phone ring. No one was picking up.

"No answer," Palmer said and let Tony hold the instrument to his ear.

"None inside, either. This is the place." I stepped back and waited for the Georgia cops to do their thing.

Palmer rested one foot on the narrow steps at the front door and rapped on the torn screen. When he got no answer, he moved to a side window and attempted to look in by cupping his palms around his eyes. He rapped again, on a window this time, but still no one came. From my side, I heard a rustle. She couldn't see me, but I was staring at the profile of a skinny girl, no more than thirteen. Dressed in dirty shorts and a tee shirt, she carried a plastic bag containing a large bottle of soda. When she saw Palmer, she dropped the bag and turned to run into the trees. Instead, she ran into me.

"She's here!" I cried as I held the squirming girl around her slight waist. She fought at me, making low guttural sounds of "no, no."

"Okay, sister, hold still," said Vernon as he caught her upper arms and pulled her back. She started to fight again, but the deputies grabbed hold until she calmed down.

"What's your name, girl?" said Palmer, his badge and uniform towering above her.

"Don't have to tell you nothing." She turned abruptly toward the toddlers as both began to cry. "I got to tend to them." She tried to jerk away but found herself in a hard grip.

159

"Sooner you give us answers, sooner you can see to them. Otherwise, we call Children's Services and let real adults take them away." Palmer said this calmly, then took a step toward the sandy area.

"MaryBeth!" the little girl yelled, her eyes terrified.

"MaryBeth what?"

She breathed deeply. "Russell."

"You got a momma or a poppa?"

"Momma's working. No poppa."

"These kids your brother and sister?"

"No. I take care of them for those two trailers." She pointed toward the rusted twins of her own abode.

"Their parents are at work, then?" Palmer walked to both trailers and knocked. No one came to the door.

"Everybody's at work. Including me." MaryBeth twisted both shoulders in an attempt to shove off the deputies' grip.

"How old are you?" Palmer stood over her again.

"Twelve and a half." She shoved her bare foot into the dirty sand, spraying grains onto Patricia's ankle.

Patricia shot her a glance that hid curse words.

"Does Georgia allow this kind of thing?" she said, leaning over to dust the unsoiled cuff.

I wanted to ask if she meant kicking sand on her slacks or leaving babies in the care of a minor, but I resisted.

"No, ma'am, Georgia doesn't, and I'm getting somebody out here right now."

He turned to MaryBeth. "You any kin to the Wilburns, child?"

MaryBeth's eyes widened, then scowled. She shook her head.

"You do know them, right?"

She refused to look at him, forcing her gaze on her bare toes.

When he called his office to order Children's Services to the trailer park, Palmer got the news that extradition was in order for the Wilburn sisters. Tony called Tallahassee deputies to meet him at the state line. Palmer had agreed to take them that far.

"And the kid?" I asked.

"We're going to stick around and see what her momma has to say."

MaryBeth's momma had lots to say about pulling her off her job at the motel. She hadn't finished cleaning her rooms and would be docked for it. Her wailing didn't stop there. She wanted all this to be over by six so she could report to her night job, bar waitressing at a joint near the state line.

"What's your relation to the Wilburns?" asked Palmer.

"They're my great-aunts, why?"

"Your daughter ever visit them?"

"She had a little job helping them out in the house. They gave her pocket change. Anything wrong with that?" Mrs. Russell glared at her child as though she had deliberately brought these lawmen to her house.

Palmer leaned close to the woman's sweaty face. She stopped fanning and stared back at him. "Now, Mrs. Russell, you got a charge of child neglect on your hands, not to mention those other two mothers who left their kids in the hands of your kid."

"We'd like to question your daughter, maybe even have her give us a tour around the Wilburn place. We need you along to do that." Palmer stood tall, his thumbs in his belt, and waited. It wasn't a long wait. Mrs. Russell nodded twice.

"We'll have to come back tomorrow," said Tony. "Can you arrange things by then?"

We headed back to Tallahassee, traveling behind a patrol car that carried the Wilburn sisters to the state line where Loman met us and took custody.

Josie Wilburn would say nothing at the Sheriff's Department except to insist on her phone call. A deputy stood beside her while she dialed a number. I leaned against the wall around the corner from the phone where I could hear the woman's nervous breathing.

"Tell Mr. St. Claire," she had cuffed her hand over the speaker. "that this is Josie Wilburn, and I need that lawyer he spoke about."

CHAPTER NINETEEN

"Where the hell is that lawyer?" Tony's agitation infected all of us as we sat in his cluttered office. Josie and Sadie had refused to speak. Josie had been clever enough to let us know she and her sister would be represented by the same man and no way were they going to be hauled off to separate questioning rooms.

"Sadie would talk if her sister weren't around," I said.

"Yeah, but find a way to pull her away from Demon Midwife." He held up a hand as if expecting me to scold him. "Patricia's title, not mine." He sat down hard in his swivel chair, his taut jaw moving back and forth with gritting teeth. His usually cluttered desk seemed mysteriously uniform today. All the file tabs turned the same way.

The Wilburns' lawyer, Gerald Hawkins, didn't appear until seven o'clock.

Vernon sat with Loman and Tony in the conference room, but I had to wait behind the two-way mirror. Hawkins eyed the three law men as he leaned over to speak to Josie who sat between him and her sister. Sadie's eyes widened, almost unblinking. I could see a slight trembling when she placed her hands on the table, then jerked them back again to her lap. Hawkins pulled out a yellow legal pad from a shiny, tan leather satchel. After he ran a finger under the tight neck of his shirt, he nodded toward Tony.

"We're ready, sir."

"I'm recording this," said Tony as he punched the machine in front of him. Giving the time, date, and those present, he looked up at the two sisters. "Do you want to make a statement regarding Theresa Grassfield and her baby?"

Sadie jerked and put one hand toward her throat, then thought better of it and pretended to scratch her chin. Josie's eyes stared fierce hatred at Tony, even while Hawkins leaned over to whisper in her ear.

"I've advised my clients to say nothing," said Hawkins, his pencil working in broad strokes over the legal pad.

"I saw no one speak to Miss Sadie Wilburn." He stared at the man, an even, unbreakable stare.

"Her sister speaks for her," said Hawkins, his pencil suddenly halting on the paper.

"Miss Sadie," said Vernon, "are you comfortable with this?"

Sadie hesitated, then nodded.

"This is being recorded, ma'am. Please say something out loud." Vernon looked toward the recorder.

"Yes," said Sadie, the hoarseness belying her confidence.

"And, as I said before all this began, my clients are saying nothing." Hawkins placed his pencil on the yellow pad.

"We've got a witness and prints, plus some other evidence we're running tests on right now," said Tony. "Your clients won't be free to go. I'll have to arrest them. Given the late hour you probably won't be able to bail them out until morning."

"We'll see about that," said Hawkins, smiling as though he knew a secret.

"Well, there is another matter," said Tony. He turned to

Loman. "Ask Miss Echols to come in here."

Hawkins sat up straight, his boyish face frowning but looking more like a pout.

"This is Patricia Echols, investigator for the state midwifery department. She has dealt with the Wilburn sisters in the past, and is most concerned with the death of Miss Grassfield, and her baby." Tony motioned for Patricia to take the vacant seat.

"She has no jurisdiction here," said Hawkins as he tried to scratch information on the yellow sheet.

"No, but she's got a reason to be here. Like I said, we have a reliable witness who can identify these two who were practicing midwifery—without license—on Miss Grassfield."

"And the mother died as a result of such midwifery," said Patricia. She assumed her most officious air after she laid open her folder on the table.

"Mr. Hawkins, the baby was never found, but we've got evidence it may have been dumped in the river. If your clients are found guilty, you know where they could end up."

"This could be first degree murder. Are you prepared to defend your clients for that?" Tony looked directly at the young lawyer who half-nodded. "Then, Loman, read them their rights again, and take them to their cells."

"Oh, no!" cried Sadie as Loman stood up and faced the women.

"You have the right to remain silent, to…" Loman read from a printed card.

"No! Wait!" said Sadie, both her hands gripping the table.

"Shut up!" said Josie. She clamped her hand on Sadie's arm.

"Let go!" Sadie snatched her arm away; the older woman's nails scratched across the skin. "I want another lawyer! I didn't agree to this one!" Sadie nearly fell as she moved sideways out of her chair. Josie, in hot pursuit, grabbed at her with both hands.

"You do as I say, Sadie! This lawyer is paid for. Who do you think is going to pay for another one?" Josie tried to stand, but Hawkins, by now on his feet, placed both hands on her shoulders.

"Calm down!" he yelled, his own face dripping with sweat.

Loman stood motionless; Vernon and Tony stayed seated.

"Miss Sadie," said Vernon, "as the Miranda rights say, you have the right to an attorney even if you can't afford one. Do you want your own lawyer?"

"Now wait," said Hawkins.

"Do you, Miss Sadie?" Vernon held her eyes.

"Yes!" she screamed. "I want to be away from her!" She pointed at her older sister in a act of defiance that overturned years of elder sibling dominance.

Josie leaped toward her sister, upsetting her chair and banging her shins. "Sadie, you can't!"

Hawkins leaped after her and tried to pull her back, but a uniformed deputy appeared at the door and stood between the women.

When silence again overtook the room, Tony spoke. "Detective Drake will escort you to another room and arrange for the lawyer. As soon as they are out of the room, Sergeant Loman will continue reading the rights to Miss Josie Wilburn. If they and their attorneys agree, Miss Patricia Echols will be present at all questioning sessions."

That seemed to end it. Vernon and Sadie left the room. Loman read the rights. Hawkins nodded a disgusted approval, and Tony ended the tape.

I breathed rapidly as though I had been part of the ordeal. I was the witness Tony mentioned, and would have to make good on testimony. As for Vernon, I had a new-found respect for the way he had gently, for the second time, exercised cobra-like charm over Sadie Wilburn.

"At least we've got them in separate cells, and we'll have them in separate conference rooms from here on out," said Tony as I joined him in his office. He presented a clean chair for Patricia who wrote down notes in one of her leather books.

"I'm going to check with my superior to see where we go from here," she said, gently closing her notebook and looking up at Tony. Generations of Southern charm training began to click into motion, and Tony ate it up. He met her eyes, and turned to mush, unable to speak for a moment. The good fairy who had straightened his desk clutter must have been Patricia.

"Uh, I don't think we'll get anymore out of these women right now. Plus, Sadie's lawyer won't be here until morning. Maybe we should call it a night." He looked directly at me. I nodded and smiled, then stood up to leave.

"Sleep well," I said to both as I went out the door.

I found Vernon typing a report. "Let's split," he said.

I waited in the car while he spoke to a colleague. That's when I spied Tony exiting the front door with Patricia. He actually touched her back as he guided her to his car.

"The man is falling hard, I tell you," I said as Vernon slipped into the driver's seat. He bent over to watch them drive away together.

"Yeah," he smiled, "and he'd die if he knew we knew."

"Wonder what he sees in her?"

"Maybe they admire each other's creases." Vernon's grin vanished. "It won't last, you know."

"Why not?"

"Tony's marriage is this job. He was engaged a few years ago, but she bowed out when he broke one date too many. Ms. Echols doesn't look like the type to be stood up more than once."

"Yeah," I said as I leaned my head on the back of the seat, "it's not much of a world out there for marriage—for anyone, really. Life just gets in the way."

Vernon leaned over and squeezed my hand. His silence agreed with me, and I relished the lack of commitment, the relationship without the pressure to produce a wedding ring.

We passed few cars this time of night as we headed for my swamp house. When Vernon slowed for the fork that lead to Hollowell Sink, I sat up.

"Stop! Let's turn off and head for Calley's Slough. I want to see if any of the swamp warriors are there. Please?"

He gave me a wary look.

We turned onto a narrow dirt lane flanked by tall pines, a few spreading oaks and thick underbrush. I tried to spot the area where I fell into the poison ivy, but even with my flashlight, the opening had refilled itself with heavy brush.

"Don't see any lights up there," said Vernon as he let the car headlights guide him through the pitch darkness.

"Keep going," I said and shined my light on both sides of the car.

When we finally reached an opening large enough to stand in without touching trees, I opened the door.

"Get back in here!" Vernon's hand grabbed at my waist.

"Just keep an eye on me," I said. "I want to check out the slough." I refused to let him pull me back.

Instead, I slid off the seat and moved to the side of the headlights. I could see better there, and after moving between two trees, I spied the water-filled hole where the slough came to the surface. No one outside the area would ever believe that an underground water tunnel led directly back to Hollowell. I saw it, however, because only small shrubs grew over the slough. The dirt wasn't deep enough in places to hold the roots of larger oaks. I wanted to walk it in daylight, to see exactly what one could tell from topside.

"There's a camper over there," Vernon whispered at my side. He took my flashlight and shined it through an opening in the trees. I saw the camouflage, the dark green vehicle, and a line strung from one tree to another.

"What's that for?"

"Could be anything from a clothesline to a place to hang small game."

"Come on," I whispered, "it looks like no one is here."

We moved to the camper where I shined my light in the cab windows. The camper was Army-style, camouflage canvas draped over metal beams. The back flap wasn't fastened. I shoved one edge aside with my flashlight and peered in to see a shamble of clothes and bedding. At the top end, I spied a white box that must have been a first aid kit, and a familiar bottle.

"Calamine lotion! Maybe one of these oversized toddlers fell in the poison ivy, too."

Vernon took down the license plate number. He tried to focus the light on the registration through the windshield, but he could see nothing. "I'm calling Tony," he said. "If this belongs to Newsome, we should stake out the woods."

I moved around the camper as Vernon spoke to Tony. Another muddy opening, created by a smaller vehicle, showed up near the front fender. "Vernon! Doesn't this look like tire tracks?"

"Yeah," he said, "motorcycle, most likely."

CHAPTER TWENTY

"They're relatives, all right," said Palmer as once more Vernon and I stood in the front yard of the Valdosta Wilburn estate. "Old Alberta lived in this house until she couldn't take care of herself anymore. Her adopted son bought that trailer and moved her in there until she died. He, shall we say, *co-habitated* with the Russell woman, and little MaryBeth is the outcome. Then he took off somewhere west, and MaryBeth and her mother just took over the trailer. Even kept the phone in Alberta's name." He stopped and scratched his chin. "Come to think of it, they're not really kin at all. If Alberta's son was adopted, then any kid of his wouldn't be no blood kin of the Wilburn's."

"Can MaryBeth's mother tell you where he is?" I checked the gauges on my diving tank.

"Nope. She don't want to know, neither. The trailer is hers as far as she is concerned. He grabbed all his clothes and took off when the kid was a baby. Legally, she don't own the place, but she'd have a case in court if she went after it."

MaryBeth and her mother sat on the worn steps of the ragged board house; both stared at Vernon as he unloaded diving equipment.

He turned to MaryBeth. "Now, MaryBeth, tell these two swimmers everything you told me."

"Well," she breathed deeply and took on an adult attitude, "the old ladies paid me to run over to the mini-mart and buy food."

"Did you ever see the ladies with a baby?"

MaryBeth looked puzzled. "A baby? No sir, I never saw no baby. They said part of my pay included a little cleaning out, so they gave me some things to get rid of. Only, they said they didn't have any car to take the stuff to a dump, and for sure there ain't no garbage trucks coming by here. I could help them put it in the sinkhole."

"What did you put in there?" Vernon asked.

"They just gave me a full-up plastic bag, you know, one of those big things you use for garbage cans, and told me to drag it to the sink—only they called it the well—then wait for them."

"Wait? Why?" Vernon knelt, pretending to work on his equipment but placing himself in that tricky position again, just like he did with Sadie. He looked up at MaryBeth.

"They was bringing something else, some kind of wire. They pushed the wire over the side then told me to ease the bag down the bank. Oh, yeah, I had to tie a brick to the closing, first."

I nodded to Vernon and slipped away as MaryBeth continued her garbage bag story. Retracing my steps from our nasty rescue, I stood at the edge. The holes we had made in the algae-slime had disappeared, and a green film covered the water again. The grassy edges were like little cliffs that dropped off without warning. In the dark, someone could tumble right in, and if he didn't keep his wits about him, he'd never get out, drinking in a mass of surface slime then sinking into bottomless dark water.

I squatted and leaned toward the surface which was at least four feet from my face. Searching the banks, I waddled around the circle like a duck. Near the tree side where the bank was steepest, my fingers touched something besides grass and dirt, something metal.

"Over here!" I cried. Vernon and Palmer joined me. "There's a wire curved into the bank like a hook. It goes into the water." I pointed to the faint dirty silver line that pressed down through blades of grass. "It's holding onto something at the other end."

Vernon knelt and grabbed hold of the wire with both hands, his knuckles digging into the dark, damp earth of the bank. "Maybe we won't have to dive after all," he said and yelled for Palmer to join him.

The two men, on their knees, grasped the wire and tugged its hooked end from the earth, then pulled gently. Like an emerging demon, a large plastic bag surfaced, the brick dangling from the tied end where another, larger, wire hook had caught hold and kept it from sinking into oblivion. Green algae clung to the black plastic as Vernon reached over and gripped the bricked opening. He pulled hard, and soon he and Palmer were struggling with the fat end on the bank. I pulled it away from the edge. When I dropped it to the ground, water trickled out the torn opening where the hook had latched onto the brick, then caught on the plastic. I had visions of finding a newborn inside the bag.

"MaryBeth!" Palmer yelled at the girl who had resumed her seat on the steps. He stood and dusted wet grass from his pants. "Is this the bag you dumped?"

The girl, her eyes wide with wonder at retrieving something from a bottomless pit, nodded silently.

"Wait," said Palmer. "I'm getting gloves for all of us."

Latex gloved, we took hold of the bag. Vernon pulled up the bottom and tilted it towards Palmer and me.

"Rattles like pots and pans," he said, as heavy clear plastic came tumbling out.

"Something wrapped inside this stuff," Palmer said as he knelt and began unfolding the clear covering.

"It's the birthing pans!" I said, recognizing the old galvanized bowl-like pans the sisters had used to gather water from the lake. "I'll bet it's the same ones."

"What's this?" Palmer retrieved a pair of metal tongs.

"Forceps?" I had never seen the real thing, but the nearly two-foot scissor configuration with circles at one end and curved metal pieces just beyond the joint couldn't be anything else. I shuddered thinking of Josie ramming them into an unsedated Theresa, then yanking the baby away.

Vernon closed the clear plastic over the pans and forceps, then shook the water from the black bag. Folding it over, he placed both bundles in the back of the car. "Let's get some scene tape around the sink, and an official statement from the kid."

By the time we secured the sinkhole, returned to the sheriff's office and took MaryBeth's words down on tape, it was mid afternoon. When Palmer was satisfied with the rudimentary paperwork of a small town sheriff's bureaucracy, we headed for Tallahassee—birthing pans and forceps in the trunk, a small trailer loaded with full diving tanks attached to the rear.

"I'm starving," said Vernon. "We haven't eaten since breakfast."

"Nothing but country joints on the way home. You want to stop at Tom's?" I referred to a tiny, wooden store that sold homemade sausage, fresh ham, and cold sodas according to the ancient sign tacked to the front wall.

"Why not?" He pulled into a dirt drive just across the Florida border and parked in a grove of oaks, their moss dragging across the car. "You watch the car. I'll grab some grub."

Grub consisted of pure cholesterol—long, hot sausage links,

fresh-baked corn bread, two six-inch pecan pies, and orange sodas.

"This'll stick your ribs together, not to mention your blood platelets," he said as he sat the box lid of Southern cuisine between us on the front seat. He drove; we ate.

"We'll have to do three days' dive to work this off," I said as I bit into the iron skillet-baked bread, its crusty side revealing the pork grease that had been used as shortening. The sausage, a pure meat concoction, had been warmed in a microwave. I ate it like a banana, biting off a bit at a time.

"This is pure heaven," said Vernon. He finished his sausage, then slid the pecan pie from its tiny pan. He drove with his left hand, shoved in the food with his right. I stayed with him, holding his soda while he brushed his hand on a napkin. "Like it?"

Yes, I liked it, the whole thing—eating fatty Southern food, watching him stuff his mouth, sitting beside someone who made me comfortable but in a flash could excite me to frenzy. For a few contented moments I forgot the battering of an underwater explosion, and the feel of slime on my face.

"Love it."

We drove through the blue grass, then across hills covered with spreading oaks heading for the sheriff's office.

I asked Vernon, "Has anyone called Tibby?"

"They've tried to reach her but she isn't in her apartment."

"It's likely the stuff they used to deliver Theresa Grassfield of her kid," said Vernon as he handed over the evidence to Loman. "Get Marshall Long on it right away."

Vernon plopped in his office chair to write a report of our morning in Valdosta. Tony was in the field. I stepped into the basement to see what the computer operator had found on Arnold Newsome.

"He's not a Southern boy," she said as she pulled up the stored data. "Although he was born in Alabama, he moved with his parents to Montana when he was only seven. He's got a record—you know that—it's minor. But," she dragged the word out, "he's got this pappy who belongs to the North Mountain Militia, and I'll bet you know what that is."

"A white supremacists' group?" I suddenly felt a chill.

"You got it! They meet up there and talk about how superior they are to people like me." The operator waved a dark-skinned arm toward me.

"They tend to convince themselves of it, too," I said. "And Arnold—was he part of this?"

"Data doesn't say so, but I'd guess he was. Like father, like son, most of the time. I'd keep an eye open for it, anyway."

I sat down hard in a swivel chair and let the operator go back to her regular work. The Hummer, the military games in the woods, the white supremist background—Arnold was sounding more and more like the homegrown terrorist.

A local newspaper lay on a table between terminals. Someone had opened it to the community section where pictures of local VIPs wearing suits and low-cut dresses grinned. In one, the governor stood between the first lady and Mrs. August St. Claire. Her curled gray-blond hair surrounded a wide smiling face. Diamonds circled her neck. The caption described an event to raise money for the nature museum.

"Yeah. Put them in museums so you can build stuff on their natural homes," I said. I tossed the paper aside and closed my eyes.

In the quiet of the room, I tried to put my thoughts in order.

175

Harry and I dove into a planted explosion. Someone fitting a body builder's description attacked Harry in the hospital. And Tibby—no one's seen her since then. Arnold is the son of a white supremacist. Arnold plays military games in the woods, we think, with St. Claire and the dean. But then Nick knows the river and the woods.

"Good, you're already here." Tony removed a file from under his arm, rifled through it, then said, "That camper you and Vernon ran into at Hollowell Sink—it's registered to our lawyer buddy, August St. Claire."

He closed the file, then looked me in the eye. "Look, Luanne, we've got some problems here. St. Claire is paying for Josie Wilburn's lawyer. He's not going to want to talk to us about Newsome or any other toad from the jungle."

"This is swamp talk, isn't it, Tony?" I referred to the people who live deep in the swamps, like Tulia, like Pasquin, and like me. And like the Wilburn sisters. Messages travel through those snake-filled vines like any small village. If you knew how to listen, you'd find out what you wanted to know.

"Could be," said Tony. "If I knew those people, I'd treat them with great respect right now."

He might as well have said, "See Pasquin, and go from there."

I nodded, then stood to head for my swamp. With a missing baby, an underwater bombing, and a murdered real estate agent, St. Claire—if he was connected—was worried about more than a little development project.

"I didn't send you, Luanne," Tony said, almost as an afterthought.

When Pasquin didn't answer his call, I headed for the place where he could usually be found—and where Tulia would most

176

certainly be working—Mama's Table. When I turned off the two-lane paved road onto the scraped dirt lane that lead to the dock, I watched a blue egret take off, his stick legs like twigs floating above the reeds. After nearly a mile, I pulled under a thick grove of mossy oaks and parked alongside cars and trucks—some towing boats—and walked a few yards to the dock. Atop wooden stairs, a battered screen door led to the best-smelling place on Palmetto River. The aroma of fried mullet hit me in my appetite center.

"Well, glory be! It's Miz Luanne," said Tulia as she placed bowls of cheese grits and cole slaw in front of two men in fishermen's caps. "If you can't catch 'em, you sure can eat 'em," she said to the men, whose red faces were either sunburned or bloated with afternoon beer.

"Over here, child," came the familiar Cajun drawl from a back window. Pasquin sat in a booth overlooking one edge of the dock. "I got Mama to try cooking real New Orleans-style shrimp." He forked the white flesh covered in tomatoes and peppers and slipped it into his mouth. "She's out of practice, though. Not as good as her fried stuff." He pulled out a clean paper napkin and dropped another shrimp on it, then pushed it in my direction.

"Too hot," I gasped as I sat in the booth and rolled the shrimp in my mouth. "She put nearly a ton of Tabasco on it." I swallowed, my eyes watering from the spice.

"You gonna need this," said Tulia as she plunked a glass of cold tea in front of me, then waited until I had swallowed some. "You want to eat?"

"Maybe some fried grouper fingers and grits, if they're any left," I said.

"And some key lime pie later, I'll bet," said Tulia. She shuffled off to the kitchen, her broad hips making rhythmic ups-and-downs that stretched her white skirt to its limits.

"Pasquin," I said as I placed my fingers lightly on the back of his hand, "can you stop contemplating hot food long enough to listen?"

"I can eat and listen at the same time." He started to deposit another hot shrimp onto my napkin, but I shook my head. "Guess I got to eat it all myself."

"Well, you asked her for it."

"Didn't ask her to bring up the fires of Hell, did I?"

Tulia returned with my grouper fingers and a bowl of cheese grits. Mama followed right behind her, fanning her round, clear face with her apron.

"What's this, old man? Too hot for you?"

"Like sand fleas on a sunburn," Pasquin said. "You try this before you brought it out?"

"Just cooked it like you said." She reached over and fished out a shrimp with her fingers, then popped it in her mouth. Tilting her head slightly, she said, "Right, too hot. You want me to try the recipe my way?"

"Just stick with what you do best—the more Protestant fried stuff."

"Fine." Mama acted disgusted, but the corners of her mouth twitched, indicating perhaps a deliberate sabotage of anyone attempting to fiddle with her menu. "Anyone for key lime pie? It's fresh-made today."

"Good idea," said Pasquin. He nodded, and pushed the hot shrimp dish toward her. Tulia reached around Mama and plopped it onto her tray.

"More ice tea, Luanne?" Mama said, and when I nodded, she turned her body toward the kitchen.

"Okay, shoot," said Pasquin in a voice so slow and matter-of-fact that anyone else would wonder if he cared at all. I knew

178

better, of course.

"Can you get the swamp vine going?"

"Could, if I knew why and what I was supposed to find out."

"As much as possible about the connection between Theresa Grassfield, the Wilburn sisters—and Mr. August St. Claire."

"Better add that Miz Brennan in there. And—" he leaned toward me, "a little something about your co-worker down at the Springs."

"Harry?"

"The lady."

"Tibby?"

"She's the one." Pasquin smiled without looking at me. His pie arrived and he played with the meringue.

"Stop teasing, old man. What about her?"

"Got herself beat up around the face a little last night—so I hear."

"Who?" I felt a silent alarm.

"She wouldn't say. Came running up to one of the tour boat guides while he was swabbing the glass bottom. Said she just wanted to be safe. Guide didn't want no involvement with the law; told her to sit in the boat. Said some fellow jumped on a motorcycle parked up near ya'll's camp and took off."

"Did he see the guy?"

"Nope, but when they heard the cycle leave, Tibby said that was him, and she'd be okay now."

"I guess I'd better find her," I said and kicked myself for not looking for her sooner.

"Said she wasn't going to stay around. Had somebody down state and planned to go there."

"And, of course, the guide just let her go."

179

"Did," Pasquin nodded.

I knew the older swamp people. Many of them took wife—and girlfriend—beating as part of the domestic scene.

I pulled out my cellular phone and dialed Harry's room at the hospital.

"Haven't checked my machine since I've been in here," he said. "Guess I'll do that now. Stay put, and I'll call you back if there's anything on it."

I ate the rest of my grouper and scooped up the last of the grits with a spoon. Tulia had just brought my key lime pie when the phone rang.

"Oh!" said Tulia, startled. "Them things scare the girl out of me. Can't get used to telephones on the table with the food."

"Tibby said she wouldn't come in for at least a week. Said she was headed for Lake City to see her mama. I think most of her folks are from there. Can you check it out?"

"I intend to do just that."

I invited Tulia to sit next to Pasquin for a moment, then motioned for Mama to join us. She stood at the end of the table and pushed back her bottle yellow hair with her wrist.

"I need help—swamp people help."

CHAPTER TWENTY-ONE

I stood in front of a screened porch that fronted a newly painted white board house. The carved molding and green window trim had seen generations of care. Flat-top hedges and quail rows of pansies welcomed anyone who came around the bend in the sidewalk. Everyone in town would know this family.

"Could I speak to Tibby?" I said to the blue-haired woman who came to the screen. "I'm Luanne, her co-worker."

"Well," the woman hesitated slightly, then true to her nature of trusting people, she opened the screen door and let me walk onto the porch. "I'll tell her you're here." She hesitated again before she went inside. "Would you like some lemonade out here on the porch?"

I gushed, "That would be nice," in my finest Southern drawl. The woman nearly bowed as she moved through the door. She must have spoken in low tones because I heard none of Tibby's whine from my position. A bruised face poked around the corner of the door and looked up and down the porch before joining me.

"Sorry," she said. "I was checking to make sure you were alone." She sat in a rocker next to mine, both padded with cushions carefully fashioned from blue gingham.

"You really got it, didn't you?" I couldn't take my eyes off the green-brown skin around both her eyes and the nasty dark red gash near the right corner of her mouth. Her lips were swollen to a permanent pout.

"Bastard!" she said quietly, as this was not a word a sheltered lady used in a proper Southern home, even if she were speaking of the real thing.

"Tibby," I began and had to stop while her mother entered the porch with a wide tray loaded with lemonade glasses, the pitcher, and some square pecan coffee cakes. I smiled politely as she sat them on a matching round table in front of us.

"I'll just let you girls gab, if that's all right," she said and headed for the living room. I knew the type. Seemingly ignoring her daughter's scarred face, she gracefully made her exit just as she would with any group of gentlemen who wanted to talk business. But, she wouldn't be ignorant. A choice spot near the front door would give our voices enough amplification to hear it all. Later in the evening, she would sit down and discuss everything with her daughter.

"Did your boyfriend do this?" I nodded toward her face.

"Arnie, yes." She bowed her head and waited for more questions.

"Could you describe him?"

She began with the body-builder biceps and flat stomach. "Not like most of these beer guzzlers who ask me out," she added. I thought for a moment about how much they looked alike, all these young men with carefully trained bodies and shaved heads.

"You know, Tibby, he could be the one who planted the bomb and nearly killed Harry and me."

A tear rolled from one black eye. When she reached up to brush it away, she winced in pain. "What can I do?"

"File a complaint so the sheriff has a legitimate charge against him. When he's arrested, he can be questioned."

"That means facing him in court. Oh, God!" She bent over in pure fear. "He nearly killed me this time, Luanne."

"This time? He's done this before?"

"Twice, but he socked me other places—the stomach, my back—where you couldn't see." She pushed up a tee shirt sleeve to show me a faint green spot near the shoulder. It could easily be a diving bruise.

"What sets him off?"

She shrugged. "I started talking about that woman who died giving birth and wondering what happened to the baby."

I nodded. "And he didn't like that?"

"Said I better mind my own business, said I got too whiny and just had to shut up about it." She lowered her eyes.

"Were there any witnesses to this beating?"

"The first time, some man who dropped by the site—I think he's important or rich or something—stopped him after he hit me once. After that, Arnie made sure no one was around, until I ran to the tour boat guide."

"He'll testify if called, but what about you? Do you have the guts to carry through with this?"

"Will you and Harry be around? I mean, will I have to do this alone?"

"We'll be around and so will several sheriff's deputies." I waited until she nodded assent, then added. "Get a pair of sunglasses, some clothes, and come back to Tallahassee with me. I'll bring you back here if you feel it's unsafe to stay in your apartment."

I ended up helping two women pack: Tibby and her mother. They would stay in her apartment, but her mother would be there as comfort and someone who could wield a pistol in case of another threat made on her daughter. Gentle Southern motherhood had the strength of front line warlords.

Later, Tibby sat in front of Tony and dictated answers to a deputy who had been called in to take the complaint. When the man left to issue an APB for Newsome's arrest, Tony shoved a photograph across the desk and asked, "Now, the 'important' man, do you see him here?"

"There," she said, placing a finger on a smiling August St. Claire who stood behind his wife as she held a plaque for environmental concern and shook the governor's hand. "He is important then?"

"You might say that," said Tony and pushed the photograph into a manila folder. "And he's going to be pulled in as a witness—which I know he's going to love."

The house had come far since we last visited Mr. St. Claire. Mrs. St. Claire stood with a woman inside the foyer. They had fabric samples spread across the backs of dining chairs.

"My husband is inside with someone right now, but do go on in," she said. "My grandbaby is in there, too. Probably driving the men just crazy." She laughed.

We moved inside where workmen busied themselves with sanding floor molding. St. Claire stood in the doorway of his office. He held the toddler in his arms.

"Mr. St. Claire?" Tony said. "We need to speak to you about an incident you witnessed a few weeks ago. Is there somewhere we can talk?" said Tony.

"Why, Ms. Fogarty, how nice to see you. Did you enjoy the flowers?" St. Claire moved around the men and took my hand.

Tony glared at me.

"Sir," he said to Tony, "I'm just a bit busy right now." He bounced the child in his other arm.

"You'll either talk to us now or you'll talk in *my* office." Tony's irritation, either with me or with St. Claire, showed in his voice.

The fabric lady stopped talking when St. Claire handed over the child to his wife.

"Out here, gentlemen." He ushered us to the giant oak that graced the front lawn. Not being one of his *gentlemen*, I followed anyway.

We stood near thick, heavy roots that protruded from the rich, dark soil. Lengthy strands of gray moss graced our shoulders when the wind blew gently through the forest. St. Claire, annoyed, grabbed hold of one clump and jerked it from the tree, ripping the moss apart like pulling hair.

"Okay, what can I do for you?" he asked.

"Arnold Newsome," said Tony and waited for a response.

St. Claire's eyes widened slightly

"Who?"

"Ever hear the name before?" Tony stood in front of him, Loman and Vernon to the rear and each side of Tony. I had placed myself to one side and closer to St. Claire. It was all calculated to make him feel caged.

He shrugged. "I might have heard a similar name somewhere. There are lots of Newsomes around the county."

"Arnold Newsome—muscular, probably late twenties, close cropped hair. Rides a motorcycle." Loman clicked off the data without lifting his eyelids.

"Could be, but if I know him, it's not well." St. Claire frowned, fidgeted, yanked on more moss.

"You ever let him use your camper?" Vernon spoke from behind.

"No—well, I often leave my camper at Calley's Slough. Friends there are welcome to use it when I'm not with them."

"He's your friend?" I said from the side. St. Claire jerked his head toward me; spasms twitched at the edge of his eyes.

St. Claire looked down at his feet, then shifted his stance, resting both feet on the root growth. He teetered back and forth, occasionally placing his hand on the tree trunk for balance. "I know the guy, okay? He's a newer member of our hunt group."

"Hunt group?" asked Tony.

"Well, we hunt—or pretend to—enemies." He blushed, stared at the ground again, and hesitated before admitting what they really did at the Slough. "We play games, military games. But!" he looked at us directly, "it's only games. We don't shoot real ammo."

"Just a bunch of old guys playing sergeants and generals, right?" Loman asked.

"I guess you could say that," St. Claire nodded. "We don't harm anyone, I assure you."

"Did we say you did?" Tony never removed his eyes from the man's face.

"Well, no, but—look, you asked about Newsome. I know him from that group but not much more. He's younger than most of us out there."

"Ever see him slug a woman's face?"

St. Claire stiffened, then shook his head.

"Mr. St. Claire," said Tony, "this talking under an oak tree is not going to be enough. Can I count on you to come in voluntarily?"

"I don't see what more I could tell you, but if you insist…"

"I insist. Tomorrow afternoon, my office?" Tony handed him a card. "Don't let me down, sir."

We moved away in a group, solidarity on our side. I said to Tony when we were out of earshot, "He'll bring a lawyer if he comes at all."

"I know. He'll come, but with the lawyer he'll have to talk or refuse to say anything. If he refuses, he'll reveal he knows something. If he talks, we might get stuff we can use."

When we reached the car, Loman leaned over to open the door for me and dropped his notebook in the process. I picked it up.

"There's nothing here!" I said as I flipped through blank white papers.

"Never has been. I just like intimidating people with the thing. It's like those old mystery shows. People really believe them." His eyes twinkled under the heavy lids.

We bumped and ground across the rough forest terrain again before reaching the dirt road. When we hit pavement it was like the tempest had suddenly stopped blowing hard winds—smooth sailing back to Tallahassee.

I wanted to rest, to stop thinking about dead babies, crazy old men in army fatigues, and midwives. My arm was nearly well, but had left a peeling, crusty mess of skin under my long sleeves. Vernon, still on duty, promised to come over and stay the night. We had been near each other every day, but the nights had been a void and both of us needed the closeness. Right now, my swamp house with its newly painted walls, refinished floors, and silent air conditioning in the middle of a natural greenhouse, beckoned to me.

I drove the two paved roads, then turned onto dirt ruts. Rounding the bend of heavy oaks, pines, and some cypress, I spied a man and a dog on my front porch. A small, paneled pickup truck with *Veterinarian* printed on one side, sat in my yard.

"Kendall, what the hell?"

"He's well," he said and pointed to the sickly mutt I had rescued from the Wilburn house. He had filled out some, and his coat looked sleek and shiny. But, the best parts were the alert eyes and wagging tail. He came toward me, his head down then bobbing up to grin and hassle at me. Instead of jumping up and landing dirty paws on my legs, he touched my foot with one of his. I couldn't resist. Bending over, I scratched his ears while his entire body quaked with tail wagging. "He's well and needs a home, Luanne. You've got all kinds of space here." Kendall waved his arm to indicate the entire swamp.

"I don't own it all," I said and watched the dog shake itself in ecstasy.

"You want me to take him to the pound?"

"Kendall, you bastard. I don't need a dog. I'm away from the house a lot."

"You need a protector. He's smart. A real learner, and I'm estimating he's around two. He's got lots of years ahead of him." Kendall leaned over and petted the dog on the back. "Give him a good name, a good home—you've got one hell of a great companion."

"Not now, Kendall, maybe when this mess is cleared up. Can't you keep him for a few more weeks?"

I stood on the bottom step, my faithful dog at my feet on the ground. He looked up at me instinctively when I looked down at him. The tail swayed slowly in response to my eyes. "Will you protect me?" The tail wagged harder.

Kendall waved out the car window as he drove off with the healthy mutt in the back seat. The dog watched me through the window, his tongue hassling. I felt a pang of guilt knock me in the chest.

From the upstairs window, I gazed toward the dirt road. The only evidence of Kendall's truck was dust rising between the trees. I turned toward the river where I could see the water side of the landing. A grass puller floated by, its dual paddle wheels doing their best to yank up the alien growth that had nearly taken over when some fool dumped Brazilian aquarium grass into the area. The grass had nearly ruined the habitat for the local birds, choking out the snail habitats, thus removing part of the food chain.

Two men sat on the puller, one driving, the other tending to the conveyor belt that pulled the grass to a storage area. He faced me and waved toward the house. Could Nick Summers actually see me standing in the window?

CHAPTER TWENTY-TWO

According to Vernon, if Southern gentry ever popped its bottled-up secrets, it would look just like August St. Claire in a sheriff's questioning room. At best, he squirmed; at worst, he threw up his shaking hands and massaged a sweaty face. His carefully, and recently, groomed hair took on a nervousness of its own and disheveled itself. His expensive gray summer suit hiked up, wrinkled around the middle, the sleeves refusing to stay down even though he tugged at the cuffs. It would have been better had he worn the overalls of a dirt farmer.

Vernon would sleep at my place for the next few days; He had brought over his gear from his lakeside house. But, he had not appeared last night as planned—worked too late, he said.

"I almost got a guard dog," I said as I handed him an iced tea. "May still get him one day soon. He's the one who was near death at the Wilburn place. Kendall wanted to dump him back on me. And he does grow on you."

"Just so he doesn't grow on you more than I do." Vernon smiled and leaned his head back on the rocker. He looked content, like he was meant to sit on my front porch.

"Tell me about St. Claire," I said.

"He and his lawyer looked like twins, like they buy those expensive suits for uniforms in his firm." His laugh sounded like a sneer. Years of dealing with defense lawyers who earned big money and got criminals off had hardened him against the whole breed. "That suit crumpled right along with him for a while. Said Newsome had joined the hunt club about nine months ago. Tried to tell us he was some kid who sold motorcycles over near Quincy. They let him in because he knew how to arrange war games. Did it somewhere out west, he said. And Theresa Grassfield. Said he didn't think he knew such a person. If the man took a polygraph, he'd be in hot water so deep he'd be a pink lobster."

"The dogs?"

"Said he didn't know about dead dogs, but was glad they weren't around anymore. They barked at his workers and scared his grandbaby. He's scared shitless," he said. "Tony wants us to swamp ride."

That meant find out what the swamp people were saying about the city people. We'd spend hours, maybe days, on motor boats, swimming in springs, and listening to dock talk. It would all be hearsay, but it would be a starting point for detectives.

"Let's invite Tulia over here tonight, and Pasquin," I said.

"Just make sure they go home to sleep in their own beds."

Vernon sighed relief inside the cool house. I leaned over him from the rear of the sofa, and placed a gentle kiss on his tanned bald spot. "No way is anyone going to share our sleeping time tonight." He pretended to shudder. I headed for the phone.

Pasquin arrived with Tulia in his boat. Her fuzzy red hair stood like so many warning flags in open boat racing. She had packed a cooler full of fried shrimp, grits, biscuits, and slaw from Mama's Table.

"Damn old fool nearly dumped the whole business in the

river," she said as she stumbled up the stairs. "Don't know how to slow down."

"Needed to get it all here 'fore it got cold," Pasquin drawled, then shook Vernon's hand.

"It'd be cold all right, wet and cold at the bottom of a river cave." Tulia refused anyone's help with the cooler as though it was her cross to bear, and lugged it to the kitchen. "I ain't staying the night!" she yelled back at us.

"I know you're not," I said softly. Vernon winked.

"Guess you'll have to ride back with me," Pasquin didn't raise his voice, but the sound carried to the kitchen.

"I'll take over the motor this time," she said.

"Oh, no," he said, shaking his head, "nobody takes that motor but me." He fanned himself a few times with his straw hat, then hooked it on the back of a straight chair. Taking a seat in the recliner, he leaned his head back. "Got lots to talk about, Miss Luanne. That woman in there got lots to say, too. Better get some peach iced tea if you want to hear it all."

I smiled at Pasquin's preparation, his Cajun attitude of take it all in, but don't let it grind on your guts. During his eighty-plus years, he had seen more bodies in the springs and snake bite victims than I would ever read about; yet it never made its mark on his psyche. From what I could gather, he had nurtured his laid-back demeanor since he rode the river in his teens.

Before I could find a comfortable position on the floor among a pile of throw pillows, Tulia entered with a tray full of glasses, peach tea in a jug, and some miniature homemade biscuits. "Mama down to the restaurant has been experimenting again. She sent along these for your taste test." She found a spot on the sofa and poured the tea in the glasses. "You ready to talk, old man?"

192

"Done been," said Pasquin, and he slurped out loud on the tea. "Give me one of them biscuits first." He sat on the edge of the recliner seat and popped a biscuit in his mouth. "Damn, good, yeah," he said quietly.

"Without Tabasco, I hope," I said and wolfed down one myself. Heavy on butter, it melted away before it could be chewed. "Heaven," I added.

Vernon propped himself up on the floor pillows with me, his tea and biscuit still untasted. "What's been happening around the cypress circuit?" he asked.

Pasquin nodded to Tulia who placed her glass on a coaster. With a frown on her brow, she began. "Well, I needed some home-grown tomatoes the other day. I headed over to the stand on the paved road. Old man over there sees everybody go by, strikes up conversations all the time. And," she emphasized the *and,* "he's some distant kin to the Grassfields—so I hear. Anyhow, it gave me a way to ask, so I says, 'You any kin to that Grassfield girl who died a few weeks back?' He just looks at me, then says, 'Think I could be. She's in an album I got at home. May be my third or fourth cousin. Didn't know her though. Did see her once along the road. She's kind of pretty, but not so pretty as to hunker up to the man she was hunkering up to in that expensive car.'"

"Did he tell you who that was?"

"He said that Lincoln Towne Car belongs to the man who done up and bought all this property around here."

"August St. Claire?" I said, not ever remembering a car like that at the house restoration.

"Just the one." Pasquin chuckled lightly, then took over. "He got this lad, you see, who delivers some old lumber from another site to the restoration. Does it by boat because the old lumber came from a river house torn down a while back. Lumber is good still, thick, carved stuff that's hard to buy these days. Old boy said St. Claire wanted it to fix up something in the den of the house he's working on." He gazed at the floor, lost in thought.

"Lumber, Pasquin," I said to bring him back in focus.

"Old boy got this boat, see, and he passes me on the river ever now and then. We stop for a little river talk, if you know what I mean. He tells me about the secret nookie old St. Claire is getting from the Grassfield girl. Said the Wilburn sisters let them use the house for a few hours at a time." He chuckled quietly again. "Old boy says he was supposed to deliver some of the lumber to the Wilburn place. He couldn't get it ashore by himself. He hikes from the landing to find a helper. Instead, he walks in on the two doing their *for—noo—ca—see—on.*" He slapped himself on his knee and let out a whoop.

"Did St. Claire see him?" laughed Vernon.

"Did he? Jumped up bare-assed and projectile-like." Pasquin laughed out loud.

"Old man, you just making that up," said Tulia, forcing herself not to laugh.

"No ma'am, it's the truth, according to my friend. Said the man tried to hide his family jewel with his hand but the treasure chest was just too full!" He began to cough along with the laugh.

"What did St. Claire finally do?" I asked.

"Yelled at him to get the hell out of there. Didn't have to, though. My friend done run halfway back to the boat about that time." He dried the corners of his eyes with an index finger. "It was later St. Claire told him to keep mum about the whole deal. Gave him something extra when he paid him that day."

"But he told you anyway," said Vernon.

"That was after St. Claire told him he wouldn't need him anymore and hired two young kids to haul the rest of the lumber.

Made him mad; he figured all deals were off."

"Are you sure it was Theresa Grassfield?" I asked.

"Sure was," said Pasquin. "My friend recognized her right away—even if he saw more than her face."

"Now this story don't end here," said Tulia, sitting rigidly in preparation for her chapter of the tale.

"There's more?" Vernon finally bit into his biscuit, found he liked it, and popped the whole thing into his mouth.

"More and more," she said. "Theresa finally had her a fancy man, one who'd bring her play-pretties in exchange for being one herself. Poor girl. Didn't have nothing all her life and now she's hit a gold mine." She shifted to the edge of the chair, the excitement showing in her body movements.

"Now, I hear tell the Wilburn sisters, who had rented her a room, took most of any money the fellow poked down her bazooms. Then Theresa kind of disappeared, or stayed out of sight. St. Claire stopped going to the Wilburn house. I got this acquaintance, see, who don't want to be named, I'm sure. She walks through that area sometimes when she hitches a boat ride. Said one day, she came by and saw Theresa in the back, hanging out some clothes. Pregnant out to here!" Tulia made a gesture with both hands. "Theresa didn't see her on account of my acquaintance stayed behind the bushes. One of the sisters might have seen her, though, because somebody yelled from an upstairs window for her to get back inside. Called her by the name, Theresa. That's how we know it was the same person."

"Your acquaintance is reliable, I assume," said Vernon.

"Oh, yeah. She tells me a lie, and I'll bust her lip." Tulia raised a fist in the air. Her red hair stood on end, almost in unison.

We listened to a little more gossip about how St. Claire offered to buy the Wilburn place and let the sisters continue living

195

there. No one, it seemed, had any idea why they quit the place so suddenly.

"Better ask the next time you see her," said Pasquin.

For now, we wouldn't take the names of these informants. Instead, we settled for names like *Pasquin's Friend* and *Tulia's Acquaintance*. If we needed them for court, we could ask. Until then, it was information gathered the old-fashioned way.

After Tulia and Pasquin left, both fussing about who would drive the boat, Vernon and I eased back on the cushions. I had hooked the porch screen door, but left the main door open. Night time and humidity began to fill the room along with swamp sounds—owls, an occasional baby gator calling for its mama, katydids keeping up a monotonous rhythm, and intermittent toads croaking out their beats near the front steps.

"You know," I said. "I miss the days when I had no air conditioning, when I could listen to the songs of the swamp."

"When you could sweat gallons all over the sheets and have to change them daily or sleep in mildew." Vernon pulled me onto his chest, a solid one, full of swimmer's muscles. "Not to mention the moisture two passionate bodies could manufacture in less than ten minutes."

I fell into his caresses. The hard floor felt fine as long as we bolstered it with the pillows, and soon we manufactured the sweat—*sweet sweat* Vernon had whispered in a particularly passionate moment. The katydids sang louder as we encircled each other in a rhythm as old as the river current itself. We became one another, bursting into a chorus of our own.

We lay for a countless time on the soft pillows. I stroked Vernon's baldness, his few strands of hair wet now from body heat. The room had become dark when the sun set behind the river, and neither of us wanted to rise to turn on a lamp. When Vernon shifted to a cooler position, I looked toward the screen door across the porch. In the back of my mind, I wondered why the air conditioner hadn't switched on. Pitch blackness lay beyond the living room door—and the katydids were silent.

"Listen," I said.

"I don't hear anything," Vernon said as he raised on one elbow.

"That's just it. The noises have quit." That meant an intruder. Maybe a wildcat, a buck deer, even a Florida black bear.

"Careful," Vernon said as he quietly untwined himself from me and silently pulled his gun from the holster he had placed under a rocking chair.

I turned over and, without a sound, raised to my hands and knees. Vernon had already reached the open front door and was peering around it onto the porch. "I thought you had sensor lights," he said.

"I do." They weren't on. Almost anything moving within ten feet would set them off. I looked to my right at the television set with its videocassette recorder on top. "Damn! The electricity is off."

Vernon flipped the wall switch. Nothing happened. "Could be a power outage, but there's not a drop of rain out there."

We both knew what it could be—a human storm that knew how to cut wires. I reached inside an end table and pulled out a flashlight. Crawling around the pillows, I pulled my nude body to a standing position behind Vernon. He took the light, then moved to the front porch and switched it on. Holding it away from his body, he flashed around the porch steps, then both sides of the house. Nothing. He turned it off, and we listened. The katydids did not resume their song.

I moved next to Vernon and whispered, "I know someone is out there. I feel it." He nodded, holding the pistol in a ready position.

"What the hell!" he cried out as a light flashed from a clump of bushes near the porch.

"Back inside!" I yelled. Two more flashes broke the darkness. We slammed the door. "Somebody just took pictures of us in the nude!"

Vernon and I stood in the darkened room. We couldn't see each other.

"Someone is out there, Vernon. He may have come in a boat. I'm going to rouse Pasquin's river brigade."

CHAPTER TWENTY-THREE

"Couldn't see a thing," said Vernon when he returned from a quick search of the outside. He had grabbed his pants, and with the gun and flashlight, headed outdoors while I called Tony. "We need better lights, and I don't want to tramp over footprints." He tossed the flashlight onto the sofa in disgust. "You look just fine for catching a peeping Tom," he said, smiling at my nudity.

"Depends on who's doing the peeping, Mr. Lech," I said as I jerked up my clothes from the floor and began dressing.

"Why would someone want our nude pictures?" I said, knowing full well St. Claire could embarrass the department with the things.

"I just hope we see them before they appear in a local paper—or before a court. St. Claire's friend, Newsome, sounds about right for this kind of thing." Vernon pulled on his shirt and tucked it into his pants just in time for the electricity to come on again.

The lamp that was always on a timer clicked on, and we could hear the kitchen microwave beep. The VCR began to flash 12:00 a.m. Relieved, we knew the outage wasn't due to cut wires.

"Let's get those porch lights on," I said and headed outside to make the sensor lights come to life. They would allow us to see any prints in the muddy dirt near the house.

A moonless night in the swamp is like a dungeon with moving walls. Noises, some indistinguishable, sounded warnings all around, and the mugginess closes in, pushing the poisonous factions ever closer. It's not a place to step frivolously. The sensor light flashed on and cast an eerie blue glow over the black mud, dark green river grass, and palmettos that grew in thick bundles. I leaned over and moved slowly, hoping to catch the muddy indentation of a footprint. Instead, I encountered the frog choir gathered for practice. At each of my movements, two or three jumped in unpredictable directions, one nearly squashed as I struggled to balance myself without stamping him.

"Try over there," said Vernon. "I think that's where the flashes came from." We moved across the beaten lane where Pasquin often walked when he came to visit. "Here." Vernon shined the light on one deep print in the mud. "Looks like running shoes to me."

"The militia men usually wear boots." I said.

"We need to secure this," Vernon said as he picked up some sticks and laid them end to end around the print.

"There don't seem to be any others," I added, "but the grass is pressed down a little here. I'm betting he high-tailed it to the landing and onto a boat."

"We didn't hear a motor."

"If he was smart, he wouldn't use one until he got further down the river. I'll bet he had oars." I took the flashlight and moved toward the landing that had belonged to my family since before my father was born. Shining it back and forth, I looked for prints, but the grassy path and patched boards revealed nothing in this light. Standing on the landing, I saw no sign of a boat tie, no evidence of anyone ever having been there.

"We're going to have to wait for daylight," I screamed back to Vernon. "Let's hope it doesn't rain before dawn," I added silently.

I joined Vernon back on the front steps where we waited for a patrol car to make its way down the rutted lane. Its row of blue and red lights blinked in the darkness like a silent alien ship descending on the most primeval of earthscape.

Tony arrived alone just as Vernon asked him to over the phone. The veins on his olive neck seemed locked in place as he grit his teeth.

"This is just about stupid, Drake. You're a deputy; she's an adjunct. The two of you screwing for photos. How dumb can you get?"

Vernon's mouth turned up at the edges. He knew Tony well and would get a laugh out of this reaming. I burned just as hot as Tony did.

"It's not as if we were posing!"

"You might as well have. Why the hell didn't you close the door?"

"This is my private home, Tony Amado. I'll open the doors whenever I feel like it." I seethed, not only at his anger but knowing too many people would see too much. My female ire rose from a pit in my stomach as I imagined the good old boys in uniform gawking at my pubic hair.

"Private or not, you've got me and a lot of others in deep shit! If the department gets hold of those things, I won't be able to mention your name without a joke. You're a valuable diver, Luanne, but just how valuable?"

I started to protest, to take on this battle, but Vernon placed his hand on my good arm.

"And," continued Tony, "what if this is St. Claire's work? What if his lawyer gets this stuff in the papers?" He slammed his fist on the table and paced the floor. "You're going to have to stay away from the office for a while, Luanne. Just don't come around. Some of the guys are already bitching about your influence."

Vernon sighed and walked to a window. I moved to the kitchen and made coffee.

We sat at my kitchen table, waiting for the air conditioning to cool down a house that had been hot for too long. Drenched in sweat, I removed some ice from the refrigerator, dumped it in a glass, then poured coffee over it. An unsteady silence had entered the room.

"The brigade is out," I said to Tony.

"I don't want to know," he answered, holding up one palm.

The brigade was not a body of legals who could act as agents of the law. They were regarded as a vigilante group, although it was doubtful any of them would actually take on a criminal. No one knew swampy hiding places like they did.

"Are the Wilburn sisters still at the jail?" asked Vernon.

"Nope. Couldn't hold them. Sadie's lawyer is working on a plea bargain. If she tells what she knows about the midwifery, she'll get off."

"Even if she's involved in murder?" I asked.

"Probably. We believe Josie was the instigator."

I closed my eyes, suddenly sleepy as we waited for the morning sun. Vernon's voice trailed off, then Tony's took over, along with a sweet whiff of—what? I opened my eyes.

"Do I smell perfume on you, Tony?"

He blushed, or what he passed off as a blush, a sort of puffiness of olive skin. He avoided my eyes.

"And why are you dressed in a suit?" I noticed for the first time that he wore a tie with a dress shirt and suit pants.

"I wasn't too far from here when you paged me," he said,

staring at his cup. He wouldn't look at Vernon.

"Where did you leave Miss Echols?" asked Vernon, forcing himself not to smile.

Tony looked up at him briefly, then sipped from his cup. "Dropped her by her house. She lives between here and the coast."

"You've been dancing by the Ocholockonee, haven't you?" I said. "Took her to the look-out over the bay. And used a patrol car!"

"At least we wore clothes," he said.

"For how long?" said Vernon.

"We saved her from a fate worse than death, I'd say." I stood up and poured more coffee over ice, then filled the glass to the brim with milk.

Tony glared at me, but refused to say anything else about Patricia Echols. Their fastidiousness of dress, the ever well-pressed look, would click. I wasn't sure about the rest of their lives. His office had shown signs of female nesting. Maybe he was fair game after all. I'd give anything to see photos of their love making. Would the sheets be neatly turned back and scented, she in a pushed-up silk gown, while his freshly washed pajama bottom lay atop the dresser like a tossed file?

The ringing phone jarred us into seriousness again. The voice on the other end first informed me that the electric company verified there had been an outage in the area. We could rule out vandalism. The rest of the message played better.

"It's Loman," I said. "They've arrested Newsome."

When Tony finished speaking to his assistant, he told us he would travel to Lake City, seventy miles east of Tallahassee and bring back the man who had socked Tibby.

"In the meantime, you two can call in the other divers and search the cave area where the bomb went off," he said, his veins popping up again. "Under no circumstances are just the two of you to dive together. Get somebody else, and see if the explosion threw up anything."

"It'd be in minute fragments," said Vernon.

"Just do it!" Tony slammed the screen door as he stomped down the steps.

"Get your gear ready for tomorrow. I'll call in the diving unit." Vernon turned serious. "He'll confiscate those pictures if he can."

I took the lead into the murky water near the shack. Debris had blown into the grass near the shallows, but you couldn't see it now. The river has a way with disguising its pain, and the constant currents from the aquifers deep below the surface cleaned the scene of any visible crime.

The ATF had come and gone. Only muddy, crushed-down grass near the shoreline gave any sign they were ever there. We had checked the river, anyway, to make sure no fishing boats sat in view. We couldn't be so sure that someone wasn't in the woods, waiting with a remote to blow us all to fish bait.

The slope to the cave area was longer now, shallower from the chunks of limestone thrown up behind as Harry and I had been tossed to the surface. When I reached the old opening, sand and rocks formed a long curving barrier, like a smiling monster who had swallowed something precious. We used our lights, even though the sunlight still shined dimly in the water. I nodded to Vernon and the other diver to search each end of the pile while I searched the center. The third diver wore the full mask and spoke into a microphone for the deputy on shore.

We sifted, then rested to let the silt clear from the water.

Our mesh evidence bags floated from our waists like fresh water jellyfish. There was nothing left of anything that had been tossed into this cave—not even pieces of pipe that held the bomb. It was either buried deep in the debris or on its way to the Gulf.

Vernon gave the upward sign. I held my hand over a few spots that bubbled, places where the spring source still pushed its way to the river. In time it would force another opening, maybe not wide enough for a diver, but certainly big enough for a newborn.

CHAPTER TWENTY-FOUR

I lay on the bed, the gentle air conditioning forcing cool air without a breeze. In my drowsy head, I remembered my father reading to me shortly after my mother died. The fact that my mother was gone forever didn't make an impression on me then. Forever never existed, really. She had left for somewhere nice, and the family had given her a great going-away ceremony. I could see the abundance of flowers surrounding her casket. They were mostly yellow, her favorite color. My father had rarely read to me before then, but afterwards, he came to send me off to dreamland. Stories of princesses in danger, saved to live in a glorious castle— he made them all sound like he was talking about me.

A year later, I realized my mother wasn't coming back to sit in the rocker by my bed.

In my fuzzy brain, a tear dropped onto my cheek. *I need to wake up,* I thought.

I pressed the remote and brought the morning news to life on the little television in my bedroom.

The viciousness of a newly caged bobcat couldn't match Arnold Newsome's rage as he pulled himself, cuffed, out of Tony's car. He jerked his arms away from the uniforms who guided him into the station, causing one to yell, "hey! hey!" and grip him by the back of the neck. Newsome kept up a verbal barrage of "government harassment! Your guts will fly for this!"

A local reporter stuck his microphone between the deputies who finally brushed him aside. Newsome took advantage and jerked himself into the camera range just as a uniformed foursome bodily moved their prisoner into the back door of the sheriff's department.

Newsome, who like Nick shaved his head, wore a tight fitting, short-sleeved tee shirt. His muscles bulged with defiance, and a bright red rash stood out on one arm. "Poison ivy!" I whispered to myself.

The two young men looked alike but I could finally see for myself the difference between them. Newsome wore his anger in the lines of his forehead, while Nick's was as blank as a baby's.

Loman looked around when the reporter shouted at Newsome, "You have anything to do with the cave bombing?" Loman's eyes lit upon a car that had pulled up behind them.

Harry—I hadn't thought about him in a few days. The usual pang of—what was it?—guilt, embarrassment, still-burning flame, whatever, it flared up when I saw two uniformed deputies offer to help their passenger pull himself out. Loman waited with a metal walking stick. His leg was in a cast, but he had managed to pull on a pair of jeans by slitting the leg up one side.

Tony's call came about an hour after the broadcast.

"I thought I was supposed to stay away from the office for a while."

"Tibby wants you here, says you promised her." His voice strained against his own orders. "Just don't say anything to anyone about nude photos."

"Any evidence that they've turned up?" I visions of St. Claire's lawyer slamming them down on a conference table.

"Nobody's mentioned the track of your poison ivy yet."

I ran into Harry the minute I reached the inner offices. He sat in the hallway, his leg stuck out in front. He motioned for me to take a seat beside him.

"Tibby's going to identify him, right?" He asked.

"And carry through with the complaint, I hope." I turned to him. "The real grabber is if you can identify him."

Harry nodded. His face looked strained and he closed his eyes for a moment. When the deputy came, he stood as though waiting for the pain to rush down his leg, then pushed through the door. I followed him and the deputies to a room where we would await the visage of Mr. Newsome, where Harry could name his attacker and Tibby could accuse her beater.

The deputies left us alone in the room. An uneasy silence prevailed until Harry broke it with a question.

"Is any mapping getting done?" He winced in pain.

"I don't think so. The students are keeping an eye on the camp and catching up on paperwork. One of us needs to get back to them, but Harry…"

"I know, I know," He looked weary and fished a prescription bottle from his shirt pocket. "I wanted to get along without these, but macho hurts." He dumped two capsules into the palm of his hand and threw them into his mouth.

"Just a minute," I said and went in search of liquid. I found it in the soda machine near the parking lot door. Retrieving the aluminum can from the slot, I popped it open just as a frightened Tibby entered with a deputy. Her mother followed, holding a sweater over one arm. It must have been for a too-cold air conditioner, because the outside air hung like a wet cloth on a giant line from Hell.

"Luanne, you're here." Tibby took hold of my arm, then removed the sunglasses to reveal nasty green-black eyes. Her face swelling had reduced but it still had a moon quality to it.

"Harry is here, too. Both of you can identify the man." I let the deputy lead us back to the room where Harry sat on a chair and leaned his head back on the wall, his eyes shut.

"It won't be long," said another deputy who had been sent to instruct us. "You're both going to a room with a mirror. You can point out the man if you see him, and don't worry, he can't hear you. I'll take you in one at a time." He turned to me. "Miss Fogarty, they want you right now." I watched him closely. Was there a gleam in his eye like he had seen a photograph of middle-aged boobs on a darkened porch?

I followed him down a long hall, then into a room that blackened as soon as the door closed. I heard voices. Through the mirror, I could see a long table where Newsome sat with Tony, Loman, and a uniformed deputy. A recorder rested in the center of the table.

"Were you looking for your girlfriend in Lake City?" I heard Tony ask, knowing he was referring to Tibby.

"He has waived his right to an attorney," said the deputy who stood next to me, "says he wants to represent himself."

"Did he make any phone calls?" I asked.

"None yet. Said he may want to do that later."

"Try to find out who he calls," I said, wondering if August St. Claire would provide services again.

"I am supposed to ask you for an I.D. on him," said the deputy.

"He's not the man who sat in my class at the university, but he might be the man I saw in the boat."

The deputy opened the door and left. Newsome had changed

his tactics to answering Tony's questions with his own questions about the right to hold him. "I have the right to travel wherever I wish and not be harassed by some local hero wearing the uniform of the government!"

"Oh, God!" said Tibby as soon as she entered the room and viewed Arnold through the mirror. Her mother held onto her arm, then slipped the sweater around her daughter's shoulders. "It's him, yes, my boyfriend. He's the one who socked me."

"Which man in the room are you identifying?" asked the deputy who had crowded into the viewing room with us.

"The one with the tee shirt, sitting at the end of the table."

"Follow me, ma'am, and we'll get the paperwork done."

In the hall, Tibby turned toward me, her black-rimmed eyes wide with terror.

"It's okay now, Tibby," I said. "Your mother will go with you. You've done the right thing."

"Suppose he comes after me again?" She hugged herself with her arms.

"Not likely. He's in a lot more trouble if Harry identifies him too."

Tibby finally nodded and allowed her mother to usher her down the hall. She stopped abruptly and turned back to me, "You'll let me know what Harry does, right?"

Harry did the same thing. "Damn bastard, that's him!" Arnold Newsome would stay in jail for a while. It was now up to sheriff's detectives to break his silence.

"We've got one other person," said the deputy, who had returned with a uniformed female. An elderly woman, her un-kempt hair shaking with terror stood between them.

"Sadie Wilburn," I said quietly, then moved just outside the viewing room. She entered, and the deputy stood the woman directly in front of the mirror. "Know anyone in there?" she asked.

Sadie took a long time, her portly back rigid and shaking at the same time. Her gray head bobbed up and down.

"All of them," she whispered.

"Name them, and point when you name," said the deputy, taking up the clip board.

"I seen the uniformed fellow and the sleepy-eyed one when they brought us in from Valdosta. Don't know their names."

"Continue."

"The dark one, he's Amado, the one who does all the bossing."

"And?"

Sadie took her time. I could hear her swallow in the silence. "The one at the end, he's paid by Mr. St. Claire. He helped us with the boat."

It was Newsome there in the boat the day I interrupted the midwives.

"The boat?"

"When we caught Theresa's baby—he took us in his boat."

"Just a minute," I said. "Was that man waiting outside in a boat the day you and your sister midwifed?"

"No, you wait a minute, Ms. Fogarty," the deputy tried to close the door, but I pushed my upper body further inside.

Sadie nodded in the semi-darkness. "His job was to get the baby away. Theresa wasn't to have it."

"He dumped it in the spring?"

Sadie began to shake her head. "I couldn't say."

"Ms. Fogarty!"

One deputy pushed on my shoulders and another escorted Sadie into the hall.

"Don't do that again," said the deputy who had shoved me around the corner. I nodded and moved from his sight.

The scenario formed in my head. If St. Claire had impregnated Theresa and he knew his tight little society wouldn't permit parenting a bastard child, much less supporting it and the mother, then he would want it eliminated.

Damn! I would have thought he'd at least be civilized enough to put it up for adoption, even give it to one of the swamp families.

Instead, he used the Wilburns and Newsome to rid himself of a nuisance. I closed my eyes.

Newsome killed the baby, then dumped it in the cave. All the other stuff—the bombing, the attack on Harry, even his terrorizing of Tibby—had been to make sure we didn't find that out.

"Are you talking to yourself?" said Tony.

I opened my eyes and realized they had left Newsome.

"There's something we need to do, Tony," I said. "You'll need Marshall on this one. Maybe you'd better call him."

Tony said nothing but leaned slightly in my direction. He looked exhausted.

"Is there any way you can test the umbilical DNA against August St. Claire's? We've got people who said they were playing bedfellows, and more than likely Sadie Wilburn can confirm this. If we could get a sample of his blood, we may have motive for murder—or the ordering of one."

Tony stood up straight. He wouldn't say "good idea" or "that's the kind of stuff I like to hear." His acknowledgement of my abilities would stay put, locked inside the head of Cuban-Southern macho that said a woman should be there only to look good.

"Loman," he spoke through the open door. "Get Marshall Long over here now! I don't care if he's on his third helping of coconut custard pie."

CHAPTER TWENTY-FIVE

"Very carefully," said Marshall who had been dragged from a delivered pizza to discuss the best way to draw a blood sample from an uncooperative suspect. "Lawyer like St. Claire will pull a sloppy police work case on us if he can."

"Court order may be the best way," said Loman.

"And the slowest. Like I said, St. Claire is going to stretch the legal system any way he can to delay the test, especially if he's the real daddy." Marshall shifted his weight on the metal folding chair someone had offered him when he arrived. "You got any idea if he gave samples in the past?"

Tony and Loman shook their heads.

"Thought not. Well, you get it and I'll test it." Marshall stood up, then turned back. "Couldn't this discussion be done on a phone?"

No one answered. I sat in Tony's cluttered office with the two men. Vernon had been sent out on a call.

"Look," Tony said, "let's get Sadie to sign a statement about St. Claire sleeping with Theresa, then search the swamp for others who may have seen something. And get a statement from Pasquin's friend who walked in on them during the actual act."

"Seems the only way, I guess," said Loman. "The man's going to fight it, saying we coerced witnesses, stuff like that."

Tony leaned back and closed his eyes. "Sometimes I get so damn tired of defending every move we're paid to make."

I said. "Can't you get a statement from Sadie tonight?"

Tony opened his eyes, and I saw the old determination there. He ordered Loman to get Sadie into a room with a court reporter and her public attorney. I, on the other hand, would wander into the swamp to roust Pasquin from his evening solitude to find his friend.

The night, black as pitch, sounded like a peaceful swamp gathering of katydids, crickets, frogs, and the occasional shrill creature who joined the song fest. The whole thing stopped when I took off down the path with a flashlight. I would walk to Pasquin's rather than risk the rarely traveled rutty road to his place. Taking the canoe would be too chancy in this darkness.

At night, under clouds that produced a ghostly gray haze, the path, barely wide enough for one person, appeared even narrower. Gum trees dispersed among a few oaks, and pines sent out their branches to snag my bare arms. Frogs, and sometimes a giant toad, refused to move off the path, their rubbery bellies pulsating in the stillness. I stepped over them, shining the light ahead to avoid what I really feared—water moccasins and rattlesnakes. Only once did I see something slither into the brush. It may have been a lizard, but I took no chances and moved quickly past the place. The incessant chirping and croaking would halt when I moved into a space, then resume behind me—the animal alarm, *Watch out!* then *All is clear!*

Cypress and pines abruptly gave way to only oak, their mossy tenants stroking me in the face as I left the path and entered Pasquin's yard. It looked much like mine, grass growing in spots, a lot of dark swamp dirt filling in the spaces. He hadn't modernized the place in thirty years and still cooled with a rattling window air conditioner. Said he didn't like the central stuff—too cold. His unit, attached to a back bedroom window, roared loudly, kind of like a dog that barked but wouldn't bare teeth.

Seeing a light in the crack between the window sill and the thick green curtain, I rapped on the edge of the screen door.

"To what do I owe this pleasure?" Pasquin appeared with his usual light-colored shirt and khaki pants, a glass of some Cajun alcoholic delight in his hand. "Come in and join the party."

I walked into a room cluttered with a lifetime of furniture and dark green curtains. "They keep the cool air in, the heat out," Pasquin once told me. Sitting in overstuffed chairs separated by a massive wooden chest were Tulia and a younger man I had never seen. In a straight-back cane chair shoved into a corner, a man with stand-up hair sipped on a can of beer. He uttered something and pointed at me, then went back to his beer.

Pasquin nodded to the man beside him.

"This here's my friend, Zeek. He's got a boat and hauls—or shall I say hauled—stuff for Mr. St. Claire." Zeek must have been in his thirties, but he was already an old creature of the woods. He slicked down his dark black hair, parted on one side. It resembled a black bathing cap. He wore jeans, neither fashionably baggy nor skin tight. A threadbare undershirt poked up in the collar area from under his short-sleeved plaid shirt. He belted the whole thing at the waist with genuine alligator skin. From the looks of the crude holes, he had made it himself.

"Zeek is the one who run in on St. Claire," Pasquin chuckled as he motioned me to another overstuffed chair. He mixed a drink on the trunk top and passed it over to me. "And this is Luanne Fogarty," he said to Zeek. "Fogarty Spring's named for her *ee—lus—turious* family."

"I know," said Zeek. He stuck out a rough hand, the nails outlined in dirt. "I learned all about the history of Fogarty Spring when I was in the fourth grade." He grinned, his yellow teeth revealing a lifetime smoker, possibly a roll-your-own aficionado.

"You're just the person I came to see," I said. "I—and the sheriff—were going to ask Pasquin to go looking for you tonight."

Zeek sat up straight on the edge of the chair, his eyes bright with importance. "You want me involved?"

"We need a statement about what you saw."

"You got it! What do I have to do?"

I explained that he would have to go to the sheriff's department. In case he might balk at the formality, I explained about all the people who would be in the room. Zeek acted the innocent, and I treated him as such. In the back of my mind, I knew better. People like him chose to live in the backwoods, but they were savvy about city ways, especially where the law was concerned. He didn't look like someone who always followed legal statutes, and with the wilderness disappearing rapidly, he must have run afoul of at least one game warden.

"I'm ready!" he said and placed his drink on the table top.

I looked at the glass. A bottle of bourbon had been emptied among the three of them. Tulia had been mute up till now, and most likely drunk. I turned toward her morass of wispy hair.

"A lady, a Miss Echols, will want to talk to you about Theresa's relationship with the midwives. She doesn't approve of them." I felt I needed to warn Tulia. The two redheads could end up ruining everything if they got into a squabble over the value of licensing.

"She better not say anything about old Miz Wilburn," said Tulia, her bleary eyes suddenly clearing. "That woman pulled six

216

healthy babies out of me and I'm still kicking." She made a fist with her free hand and spilled some of her drink on her arm.

"Then," I said, "let's count on both Zeek and Tulia's friend showing up at my house, say around ten tomorrow morning?" I wanted to give them time to sleep off a hangover.

"I'll round them up in my boat and have them at the landing," said Pasquin whose mellowed face hung in loose folds.

I took the glass from his hand and said, "Maybe you better get these people home. We need rested witnesses, if you know what I mean?"

"Zeek's got his boat," said Pasquin, not worried about his friend's glassy eyes. "And Edwin's gonna stay the night." He nodded toward the man. "You ever met Edwin?"

I shook my head, then nodded a hello. The man pushed on his hair, making it stand taller. I was reminded of Stan Laurel and expected him to scratch his scalp in bewilderment. Instead, he pointed at me and stuttered something at Pasquin.

"Yeah," said Pasquin and waved a hand at him. "Later."

"Give you a ride to your landing, Miss Fogarty?" Zeek took another sip.

"I'll walk, thanks." I left, reminding Pasquin to get Zeek and Tulia off the bourbon.

"I'm sending them home right now," he said as I flashed a light into the darkness. I heard a faint "bye" from Edwin who stood holding a battered photo album in both hands.

Back home, I sat for a minute on my screened porch. The muggy heat poked at my sweating neck and back. I sat very still, as still as the air around me. Listening to the nightly choir, I couldn't imagine living anywhere else. These critters were my city horns and sirens, my good citizens and criminals. Across the path, and through a patch of swamp, I heard the softness of river lapping against dark sand. Somewhere, far in the distance, I heard a siren—not a bird warning or even a Florida panther—but a real siren on a boat. The katydids halted their song. They heard it, too.

Inside the house, the phone rang.

"Zeek hit a cypress knee," Pasquin never yelled, but he sounded shaky and hoarse. "Can you imagine? Been motoring on that river for years, and tonight he hits a knee."

He pinpointed the direction for me, a heavily treed section of the river not far from Pasquin's place. Fortunately for Zeek and Tulia, the brigade was still out looking for suspicious people. One had heard the crunch and Tulia's hollering. He found her standing in muddy water up to her chest. Zeek was out cold, resting against a cypress root growth, the lower half of his body dangling in the water. The motor boat lay against a tree, its middle section broken into shards.

"Get me out of this stuff!" cried Tulia, her red hair now a dampened mass of strings hanging in her face. "There's gators and snakes around here!"

I had run through the woods, not caring about stepping on frog parties, and joined Pasquin at his boat. We reached the scene just as the two deputies in their own boat were rigging up a way to pull the two from the cluster of cypress knees that grew so close together not even a toy boat could wind among them. The water wasn't deep where they hit, but not far away, the bottom dropped off to unknown depths, into a spring cave with currents that neither would be able to escape.

Another boat had reached them about the same time. Nick Summers had pulled up as close to Tulia as he could without ramming into the cypress. "I tried to calm her," he said, "but she's freaked."

"We'll have to swim," said one deputy. The other one shook

his head.

"I'll do it," I cried as Pasquin cut the engine and rowed closer to the deputies. "Move the boat next to those cypress roots." I jerked off my swamp boots and handed my watch to Pasquin. Sitting on the side of the boat, I swung one leg over, then the other and slid into the river water.

"I'm coming right behind you," said Nick. I heard his splash.

In spite of its tranquil appearance, the river currents pulled at my jeans. I had entered the water in a spot that was barely over my head. When I met the abundance of cypress roots, it was waist high and muddy bottomed. I touched Zeek's neck artery.

"He's okay," I said. "Wait here for help." Nick held the man as though he would drift into the currents. "What are you doing here?" I didn't wait for an answer but swam to the panicked Tulia.

"Lordy! Miss Luanne. How did I ever get myself in this mess?" She clung to a root as if she would drown in a bottomless pit if she let go. "I can't stand this one more minute." She began to hiccup out of fear. In the glare of the deputies' boat light, she seemed a carnival freak, her redness turned to a blue-white, her pointed nose protruding dramatically underneath rounded clown eyes.

"Pull yourself around to this side," I said as I extended a hand, using the other one to maintain my balance against the root system. I could stand on the bottom, but my bare feet continued to rock in the uneven mud. I could feel it ooze between my toes, then give way. Eel grass caressed my ankles, teasing me of water snakes.

It paralyzed Tulia. Her feet wanted out but she was afraid to lift them into another spot. I grabbed her wrist and jerked. Her body, unable to fight the buoyancy of the water, drifted my way.

Using both hands, she pulled on one solid root that protruded

219

out of the murky water. This allowed her feet to rise and she floated toward me. Taking her under the chin in a lifesaving position, I pulled her toward the boat.

"Don't let your feet touch bottom," I said. "It will be easier for me if you let your body relax."

"Oh, Lord, get me out of this mess and no feet of mine will touch this bottom ever again!" But full of frantic fear, she stiffened her lower body and continued to sink.

When I finally got her to Pasquin's boat, he held her until the deputies could pull up close enough to haul her in.

"Bless be!" she said and flopped into the boat.

I headed back. Nick grabbed Zeek, still out cold, around the waist and pulled. We dragged him off the roots and into the water where I swam with him, hoping he wouldn't wake up when the water hit.

"Be careful," said one deputy. "He may have broken something when he flew out of the boat."

I reached one arm around the man's waist—thankful that he never grew the beer belly so prominent on many Southern men—and eased him into the water on his backside. He moaned a little but didn't come out of his stupor. Gripping him underneath the chin, I floated him to the boat where the deputies and Tulia pulled him in gently. I looked back. Nick swam to his own boat and climbed back in.

"You need me anymore, Ms. Fogarty?" Before I could answer, he rowed into the darkness.

One deputy shined a light in Zeek's face just as he opened his eyes.

"Damn boat wouldn't slow down," he said, then closed his eyes again.

"I don't see any blood, but could be internal injuries," said one deputy. "We're taking these two to a hospital." He turned to Pasquin who held his boat in balance as I crawled aboard. "You stay here until the investigators arrive."

My clothes plastered to my body, again revealing everything the deputies could laugh home about. With the sinkhole incident in Valdosta and the photos, somebody would eventually start the ribbing. But if these two pulled their teasing routine, I planned to let the entire department know how they sat in their boat while civilians pulled the victims out of the water.

"Scared of gators?" I asked, but they didn't hear over the sound of the motor.

I sat on a dark river with mosquitoes buzzing around my mud-soaked clothes and hair.

"Don't understand how that happened," Pasquin said, his outline barely visible in the night. "Zeek's been driving that boat for years. Never had an accident like this before."

"He was drunk perhaps?"

"Naw," he protested. "Besides, he's guided that boat in and out of here on two, three six-packs at a time."

"He said it wouldn't slow down." My mind churned with possibilities.

"Could be a malfunction of the throttle. He kept the thing in top condition, though. Just don't see how it could happen."

"Where the hell did Nick Summers come from?" It dawned on me that the young man had been out here on the river late at night. Maybe he had a job with river cleaners, but they didn't pull grass this late.

"Lots of people come out at night," said Pasquin. "Gigging frogs, fishing. Somebody phoned me about the crash. Guess it was him."

We waited another half hour, then heard a motor boat in

the distance. Vernon arrived with a uniformed man. Their halogens spotlighted the damage.

The two men placed flood lights on hooks they nailed to tree trunks, then turned them on all at once. The swamp lit up like a movie set. A thick growth of cypress trees, their ancient roots crawling about like serpent monsters, sat in dark shallow water. To the right of the growth was a deep open river lane where Zeek should have been if he had opened the boat full throttle.

"Zeek wouldn't have raced through that lane late at night," said Pasquin. "He knows how to navigate this river. He'd rev it up a bit, getting ready to open it up soon as he got around the cypress grove, but how come he got so far off?"

We both shuddered silently, especially when we could see the wreckage piled between two giant cypresses. Tulia and Zeek were lucky they didn't plunge headlong into one of the trunks on their flight out of the boat.

"I'm pulling this engine in for inspection," said Vernon. He and the deputy lifted the heavy motor, which had broken off from the boat and sat atop scraped cypress knees. Its propeller, dented into a mass of metal, nearly fell off in the process.

The deputy put some yellow tape around the trees, then he and Vernon left with the engine. Pasquin and I headed for my landing.

"I need to see about Zeek," he said as he rested in my living room. "You take a shower, get all them swamp critters off you, then drive me to Tallahassee."

It would be another sleepless night, but I didn't blame him. He would feel terrible guilt for serving the bourbon. I said a little prayer of thanks for saving their lives as I felt the warm shower water hit my face.

With wet hair, I drove to Tallahassee. We found Zeek giving

the nurses a growling fight in his hospital room.

"They say I might have a concussion in this hard old head of mine. I got to get out and see about insurance for the boat."

"Maybe you ought to wait for the police report," I said.

"Yes," added the nurse, whose sharp nose and frizzled hair made her look like Tulia's soul sister. "And let your alcohol level go down a bit."

Tulia, her feelings just the opposite, basked in a night of total relaxation like she was at a European spa. She lay back on the pillow, her few scratches covered with nothing much larger than a bandaid. She had a glass of apple juice in front of her and her legs propped up on three pillows. For her, it was as good as hotel room service.

"Old man wouldn't slow down," she said.

"He's not exactly old," I said.

"Old to me. Been on that river since he's born. Should have known where those trees were." She looked at the phone. "You can call Mama for me and tell her I won't be in to waitress tomorrow. Got a good excuse this time."

Pasquin and I stayed over an hour. I called Vernon at the office on the way home.

"Looks like something disturbed the linkage inside the throttle, Luanne. I'd say tinkering is involved here."

CHAPTER TWENTY-SIX

"This couldn't have happened without a little help," said the deputy, a man Vernon said was a mechanical expert. "See this? When the boat began to gradually pick up speed, it stuck, wouldn't slow down."

"Why wouldn't he stay on the river lane?" I asked, pushing down my near-dry hair.

"Probably got rattled when the boat wouldn't slow down. He was a little drunk, too. Could have miscalculated where he was. However, none of this would have happened if the boat had an appropriately running throttle."

"Any prints?"

"We're working on it, but it's not likely. Too many people had to touch it, not to mention the water and mud."

Vernon placed a hand on my shoulder then leaned to my ear. "Love your hair-do!" He fluffed it into disarray again.

Tony called a confab in his office. He wanted everyone involved, including Pasquin.

"Newsome is out on bail," he said as we crowded into the tiny space. Pasquin, Tony, and I got chairs. Vernon, Loman, and four deputies stood around the file folders now piled on the floor.

"He wouldn't talk about anything. Judge put a restraining order on him, set a hearing date for the battery charge, then let him go. I've got a shift keeping an eye on the woman—Tibby—and her mother, but I can't guarantee he won't go near them."

I shuddered. If Newsome got to her again, she'd get more than black eyes.

"Then there is St. Claire," continued Tony, "he isn't saying anything. If the Wilburn woman will talk and the judge accepts Zeek's statement, then maybe we'll get a DNA test. I doubt if we can hold him until the results come in. Zeek," he stared at Pasquin, "was a drunken sailor according to his blood test. St. Claire's lawyer will make a case on that alone."

"Even if you discover tampering with the throttle?" I asked.

He nodded. "That will help, of course. Depends on the judge who signs the order."

"Has Sadie Wilburn made a statement about the baby, yet?"

"Her lawyer is holding off, but we'll get it. She's scared as a cornered possum about going to jail. Now," said Tony, "we've got some info from Montana. It's from a former sheriff up there who just about can't stand these weekend warriors against so-called government interference. He retired last year, and he's got no qualms about telling us what he knows. I got it on tape, off the conference phone."

Loman, his sleepy eyes peeking beneath heavy lids, gave the appearance of a school kid who had been called on to read in front of the class. He held up a computer sheet.

"Thanks to the computer people, we were able to find the man out in wild buffalo country." He lay the paper on the desk, then pulled out a cassette tape and popped it into the player.

"Newsome is a nuisance, a hothead," began a gravely voice, "to everybody around here. Been bullying people all his life, first roaming around on private land, shooting game, setting off fire-crackers in old ladies' yards, then joining the militia. He's really

Arnold Newsome, III.

"He set some bombs near what he thought was the tax office. Stupid—he was wrong on both counts. His bombs made
little blasts that did nothing more than blacken the wall on the
outside. And the building no longer housed the tax office. To
make it worse for himself, he left his prints on one of the bomb
parts. Somebody in my own department tipped him off—not
unusual in this town. He ran." The speaker made a deep breath
rattle, like a life-long smoker inhaling through phlegm. "You fellows do what you need to do. The man has relatives up here but
don't know if they'll help you none."

Loman pushed the pause button. "Looks like he joined another militia down here," he said. "There's more." He released the
button and the graveled speech continued. "Oh, yeah, I found
out something else you wanted to know. Newsome took scuba
diving lessons at a local club." The tape went silent.

"We need evidence that can be used in court. I want surveil-
lances on the two swamp houses St. Claire now owns plus the one
he lives in here in town." Tony stood and paced the narrow con-
fines of the room.

I took Pasquin to my house. He sat a while, sipping tea.
"Man like Newsome may know how to shoot, but he won't know
the swamp so good," he said, thinking aloud.

"I still don't want to meet him alone," I added. We had opted
for the porch in spite of the humidity. Our comfort zone, the
family chat center, it surrounded us with the sounds and feels of
the forest.

"Man who's used to open prairies could get himself stuck in
a mud hole down here, bit by a snake, even fall into a dark sink

some night."

"Pasquin, what are you saying, that Newsome is stalking in these woods?"

"I figure that's what these militia men do, right? Play games with camouflage and guns, roam around woods looking for an ATF man or maybe a Papal Catholic—shoot him, even if he's imaginary."

"What brought this on?"

"Remembering, I guess." He closed his eyes for a moment, and I saw the rare frown on his brow.

"Tell me," I relaxed for one of the old man's remembrances.

"Back on the river. Don't recall the year, but it's long before your time. Probably just after war time. Some men lived over on farms east of here. They decided they belonged here but nobody else did, especially not blacks. They expanded that to Jews pretty soon, then to Catholics." He turned toward me. "Half my family was Catholic. I was christened by a priest, too. Most Cajuns go to mass."

"You were harassed by these men?" It was an event I'd never heard about, something that made my skin crawl with anger.

"More than that," he said. "They got this nasty bee up their asses and came down to the river where we loaded cargo. Tried to take our jobs. Beat up some black men pretty bad, then came after me and a few other whites they said were Friday mackerel snappers. They hollered about us being loyal to the Pope instead of the U.S. flag. Even stuck the flag in the ground next to the loading area and told us to salute it." He chuckled. "I did, too. Every time I put down a load, I stuck my hand up and saluted proudly. Clicked my heels together once."

"I suppose that just made them madder."

"Did. Pretty soon they came around at dark right before we

227

headed home. Usually, workers would head off into the forest, but we got scared and started using row boats to shuttle up and down the river."

"Were you ever hurt?"

He chuckled again. It comforted me. "Not me. They tried, but it just backfired on them." He laughed out loud. "Backfired—perfect word."

"You shot them?"

"Not exactly. They come around my house at night. I'd just moved in there. Didn't have much inside, and it still wasn't all painted and fixed up.

"I was sanding down some walls in one room when I heard sticks break outside. Heard it on both sides of the house. I figured they planned on doing something. My worst fear was they'd set the place on fire.

"I listened and guessed there were about three men out there, and they planned to come at the house from three sides. I had paint buckets ready to go and decided to make it easy for them. I opened the lids and let them rest atop the cans, then lifted the cans outside three windows. Didn't have screens up yet." He sipped his tea, the corners of his mouth sneaking upward into a smile.

"I stayed real quiet. I could hear them asking each other if they were sure this was the Catholic's house. Then one fellow did just what I suspected he'd do. He used the paint can as a step up to the window.

"Only he didn't check the thing out very well. Stepped on the loosened lid, then turned over the whole can. Spattered white paint all over his front.

"But that's not all. He carried a shot gun. When the paint hit him, he dropped it. Thing went off and blasted one of his buddies with buckshot down one side, from butt to ankle!"

He laughed, lost in the triumph of memory. "I didn't move, just stood in the corner where I could see a little of what was happening. The third fellow got scared and said they'd have to ask for help. The painted one said no. They grabbed hold of the shot man and stumbled off through the swamp.

"He whooped and hollered in pain for miles. Next day, the whole swamp buzzed about a shooting accident. Black folks had a big laugh about it."

"Did they come back?"

"Not to my place. All that stuff kind of died out about that time."

"Were they Klan members?"

"Could be, but probably just young hotheads."

"Young hotheads have done a lot of damage to this world."

"Yes, ma'am, and Newsome may be a young hothead out to do some more damage." He stopped smiling. "We better have our paint cans ready, so to speak." He picked up his hat and began to fan.

We finished the pitcher of tea and rocked in silence. Generations of Southerners have done this. Just the presence of each other on the porch is enough for comfort. The steady sing-song of the rockers on old boards and the swamp bird calls reassure us of the rhythms of life. I was thankful for Pasquin, but I didn't need to tell him. He shared my porch, my rocker, and my tea. This was enough.

"You be careful, you here?" he said as he rose and donned his hat. "Keep that deputy around here if you can."

He moved slowly down the stairs and then into the trees. I watched his back for a few yards, until he disappeared. To myself, I whispered, "And you take care, old man."

The afternoon found me restless, unable to do household

chores or look at student papers. Finally, I pulled off my clothes and donned a bathing suit. I planned to drown my anxiety in cold water currents.

Palmetto River is fed by a maze of cold underwater springs that rise through limestone caves. Constantly flowing, it comes out clear and fresh. Once you're past the muddy shore and eel grass, you can see straight down to white sand. Occasionally, foot long catfish will cruise the bottom, scavenging for bits of edible debris. The dangers are around, but alligators don't usually bother something as large as an adult human, and water moccasins stay away. If you stray into their territory—their home ground—you could threaten them into aggression. It's kind of like that with humans. Break into my space, and I'll have your hide.

Climbing down the landing ladder, I splashed into cold wetness. Within seconds I was over clear water, not quite in the fierce currents of mid-river, but in a spot that required some swimming strength to stay in place. I turned a few flips to wet my entire body, then lay still on my back. The current pulled me. I fanned the water with my arms to move backward. Then I rested again— until I heard an intrusion in the forest river sounds. Without moving from a floating position, I turned my head toward the road. A male figure moved there, his eyes facing the house. He squatted, and I lost sight of him in the bushes.

CHAPTER TWENTY-SEVEN

Like a wild animal, I angered deep down when I thought my abode would be invaded. Like a human, I panicked for a second. I was without my weapons—cell phone, pistol, friends, not even a scuba tank. Hoping it was only Vernon and knowing it couldn't be, I quietly swam to the landing and moved up the ladder. Dripping, I stood and tried to shake off the excess water. My towel lay at the front end of the landing, a spot where I might be seen from the house.

I knelt, then on hands and knees, crawled to retrieve it. As I dried off in a sitting position, I drew up a primitive thought. If I placed a stone in the middle of the towel, then made a twist around it, I could use the ends to swing at someone. *Crude, but somewhat comforting,* I thought. Finding a stone was another matter. I settled for a block of wood left over from a small repair job on the landing. It had begun to rot at the edge of the water, but it was still heavy enough to hurt, maybe to stun.

Avoiding the worn path back to the house, I skirted through the woods, my bare feet squeezing into the black mud. I stood behind a low bush where I could see the figure move to the side of the porch. He did a walk-run humped over, flattened himself against the wall, then looked into the windows one by one. From my position, I saw only legs and occasionally a back. Definitely male, he wore the tell-tale army camouflage pants with a white tee shirt.

While the man played his game with the windows, I trotted toward the car. My '84 Honda station wagon had been a faithful companion through mud puddles on dirt roads, but it couldn't unlock itself. The keys rested inside my purse on the front porch. *Dumb!* I thought. I had left the purse under a porch chair where anyone could steal it. The screen door wasn't latched, and I had left a door key over the jamb. In a world where green lizards got in anyway, keys didn't need to be hidden. A human lizard is another thing.

I watched the legs move around the house. Their next step would be to confront me in the carport. Scooting to the front, I cleared the porch steps in two jumps and landed inside where I immediately latched the screen. Ducking behind the rocker, I pulled my purse toward me where I had another house key. The heavy steps of army boots climbed the steps, and someone yanked on the screen. He would be on the porch in seconds.

In a final angry thrust of his right arm, he ripped off the screen and tossed it to the side. It landed at the bottom of the steps. He stood still for a moment, waiting for someone to respond to the noise. When no one did, he walked onto the porch, making no attempt to silence the noise of his heavy boots. I placed my purse behind a flower pot. Dropping the key into my bathing suit, I waddled around the chairs toward the door. The motion twinged pain in one leg, reminding me of the explosion.

When I neared the open space where the screen had been, I stood and leapt to the bottom step, then over the broken screen and headed into the forest. I was counting on what Pasquin had said—an outsider wouldn't know the intricacies of a Florida swamp.

"Hey!" I heard him yell, and I could hear the boots scamper over wood then hit the screen. "Damn!" I couldn't look back, but I was sure the screen had caused a fall—creating valuable time for me.

In broad daylight, I would be able to tell where to place my bare feet. Nettles and rotting logs lay all over the swamp, and I took a route with no beaten path. My plan was to run through the woods in the back of my house, then circle around to Pasquin's place from the rear. He kept a tool shed in back, a place where I could find a sharp hoe.

"Come back, bitch!" The angry voice of Arnold Newsome yelled as he took off behind me. "I got a gun, and I'll use it!"

Skirting through trees, I landed on molding leaves and dry grass. I didn't think I was leaving an easy trail. Running down a hill, I made rapid time through a dry sink that had filled in long ago then covered over with grass. The forest, full of disguised sinkholes, could be treacherous. I was counting on it.

When I mounted a small hill on one side of the dry sink, I hid in a thick grove of scrub oaks and stopped for a moment. In the distance, I heard him. He didn't know how to move quietly. Turning, I glimpsed him through the trees. His white tee shirt stood out, and his right hand grasped a rifle.

Looking around, I picked up a thick, half-rotted limb with grub worms crawling on the heavy end and waited for him to clumsily stumble down to the dry bottom then climb up again. He had no running momentum, and every move was a struggle. He bent over slightly as he made the steep climb. When he was just below me, I swung the limb into his face. It crumbled dead wood particles and white worms into his eyes and mouth. He swung at the stuff. I reached out and gave him a backward push. The gun flew, and he fell. My last sight was of him bent over

233

wearing his white tee and camouflage pants, spitting out rotten wood debris at the bottom of the bank.

My feet were raw when I caught sight of the crude shed in back of Pasquin's old house. It had an open space for a door. I scampered inside and hid behind some trash cans. Safe in the darkness, I heard my own breath for an eternity. Finally, I stood, but kept to the darker corners. Gripping an axe with both hands, I lifted it in a ready-to-chop position. I heard a rustling near the side.

"Ms. Fogarty! You in there?" The voice was young and masculine.

"What are you doing?"

Nick Summers stood before me. His huge biceps and flat pecs showed themselves above a tight bathing suit.

"I saw you running. You acted like somebody was chasing you."

I didn't know what to say, then I heard the crunch of footsteps.

"Pasquin!" I tried to whisper a scream.

"Luanne?" Pasquin peered into the darkness. He held a hoe in one hand. "What the hell?"

"Is there anyone out there?"

Pasquin looked behind him, then came into the shed. "Who's supposed to be out here?"

"Newsome. He was sneaking around my house then chased me into the swamp." I stepped from the shadows and gently lowered the axe.

"Lordy, woman!" Pasquin stared at me. "You're a sight." He stepped back, startled. "And who are you?" He raised the hoe, ready to be my Don Quixote.

My bathing suit left all my limbs exposed to swamp dirt. I

was coated in it. My shoulders and thighs tingled with scratches. I wouldn't be surprised if I woke up tomorrow morning with another case of poison ivy.

"Your foot is bleeding," Pasquin said as he stared at my stubbed toes. "Let's get inside."

"Better call Tony, and lock your doors, please." I glanced around all sides of the swamp as we moved into Pasquin's old home. Nick followed like a spooked guard dog.

"You're all right, then?" said Vernon. Tony wasn't in the office. "He threatened you, then chased you with a gun, right?" Vernon repeated parts of my story. "Then we have a cause to arrest him. You stay put."

I scrubbed down in Pasquin's bath, which consisted of a bear claw tub and a hand-held shower spray. He had some liquid soap which I used twice over my entire body, hoping any poison ivy oils would wash down the drain. I even used it on my hair. Fortunately, Pasquin was not a large man. I dressed in one of his shirts and held on a pair of his pants with a tight belt.

"I still don't have any shoes," I said as I slipped on a pair of men's argyle socks.

"You look great in anything," said Nick. He smiled from his seat on a recliner. Pasquin had given him a towel to put beneath his suit. "You okay now? I need to get back to work."

"How did you see me?" I put down the towel and stood before him, demanding an answer.

"I work with the grass puller. Sometimes I take a swim. Sometimes I sit in a deer stand and watch the woods. If the tree is close enough to the water, I can spot thick growths in the middle of the river from up high." He grinned up at me again. I could swear he flexed his stomach muscles.

"So you were up a tree, watching me running from somebody?"

"Just saw you. Guess I wasn't in a position to see who was chasing you."

After Nick left, I wrapped a towel turban around my hair. Sitting Indian style in one of the overstuffed chairs, I waited for Pasquin to put together some Cajun coffee, the strongest drink outside of pure alcohol. Even if I wanted to, I wouldn't be able to hear footsteps approach the outside. The window air conditioner kept up its engine hum from somewhere out back. It never had cooled very well, and today its streak of air ended in the hallway. The heavy green curtains, the accumulation of dark furniture, and the lack of light in general suddenly depressed me. For one manic moment, I imagined Newsome's presence lurking in the shadows behind one of the overstuffed chairs.

"He's probably at the bottom of a sink, Luanne. Man like that won't know the ins and outs of the swamp terrain." Pasquin handed me a hot cup. I sipped the liquid; it hit me in the back of the head.

"He knows the ins and outs of murder, Pasquin, and I was his target." I stopped to think for a minute. "Pretty stupid, isn't it? I mean, he knows I'm part of this investigation. If he's out on bail and he chases me, well, what did he think would happen to him?"

"Man with his arrogance doesn't much care, or at least he won't be thinking about it at the time. He's all caught up in being a *man,* somebody who doesn't think you got a right to hamper him. Could be somebody's paying him, too."

"Well, damn it! I'm going to hamper him good now!" I rose to a protective stance when a knock sounded at the front door.

The only thing I could find for a weapon was the coffee pot. At least I'd burn his pretty face.

"Luanne here?" It was Vernon's voice, a sound that eased me better than any dose of tranquilizers.

"Did you find him?" I started to snuggle close to him but stopped when I saw the uniform standing near the steps.

"Not yet. They've got the K-9 unit out there. Your house seems okay except for the screen door." He handed me the key. "Found this over the jamb. Great place to stash it. No crook is ever going to look there."

"Okay, okay, I won't do it again."

"You say he's got a gun?"

I nodded.

"Judge told him to stay away from guns and military games when he set bail. His threat to you and the gun will haul his ass back inside. I need to get on a phone about that."

While Vernon made his call, I walked outside and stood beside the uniform. "Any sign of him?"

"Not so far." He darted his eyes around the trees and kept one arm bent, ready to rip open the pistol holder at his waist. Ever once in a while, he glanced my way. I couldn't be sure, but I thought he eyed me up and down. If he had seen any photos, he was keeping quiet. I felt naked even in an old man's pants.

The afternoon drifted into evening. Vernon left the uniform standing guard at Pasquin's place. He would return to the K-9 unit, then meet Loman at the main road for the arrest warrant. The crime scene boys would take prints off my screen door. They had decided to cover all areas in this one. Clever lawyers wouldn't get Newsome off again.

I wanted to go home, to be inside my house and put on my own clothes. When Vernon returned, he gave the okay.

"They couldn't find him. Either he's at the bottom of a sink-hole or he's left the area. My guess is the second." He took my hand and led me out the door.

"The brigade has been alerted," said Pasquin and smiled his goodbye.

"That scares me," said Vernon. "Those old men out there in their boats are no match for Newsome's shotgun."

"Don't sell them short, okay?"

We took the familiar path back to my house. Twilight made shadows along the way, and I was losing Pasquin's pants as they brushed against vines and tree trunks.

"Hang on for a few more steps, and I'll take them off for you," teased Vernon.

We would have eased into that gentle bliss except it was class night. I had to drive into Tallahassee and face my students for the next to last time. School teacher guilt set in. I wondered if I had given them what they needed, assigned enough reading and research for them to really know the subject. My preoccupation with midwives and militia men left little time for Norman French invaders who did their best to obliterate English.

Vernon arranged for the campus police to meet me in the parking lot. They would also escort me back to the car at the end of class. By the time I had discussed the influence of French on English vocabulary and assigned more reading, the outside had grown pitch dark. Campus lights flickered on, but they never did the trick in this part of the world. Oak trees and moss made sure that shadows danced in strategic places. I waited at my desk until the last student left, then stood, expecting a uniformed cop to step around the door and grin at me. No one came. I sat until the building grew silent and still. The lights in my room glared, but they dimmed in the hallway. A noisy air conditioner clicked on and off, then off permanently. University custodians were shutting down for the night. I unpacked my cellular from the satchel and dialed the generic campus number.

"I'll connect you with the police," the operator said. She had listened to my plea for an escort without comment.

"We sent someone over there, Miss Fogarty," the desk cop said at the other end of the line. "I'll see what happened, then get you an escort. Stay put, okay?"

When someone finally came, it wasn't the young man who had met me earlier. "We couldn't rouse him," the new cop said. "Seems his radio doesn't work."

"Could he be in danger?"

"Naw! He came back by the station to get another radio. Said he forgot to come by here, but he'd been in the parking lot and didn't see anything. You ready to go?"

He didn't see my predicament as serious. Maybe the on-going feud between police and sheriff offices gave him cause for neglect. I planned to take this up with Tony and the dean. I didn't want to think about it, but if Newsome had hurt me while the police left me unguarded, the sheriff would have had a field day in the press.

Finally in my car, I turned off the main highway and headed down the two-lane pavement. When I reached my narrow dirt lane, I took it slowly. It needed scraping, but I hadn't had time to contact the company. An expensive task, it evened up the mud puddles and grated away the wild grass median. I bobbed up and down as the Honda took the uneven dirt like a trooper. Then, the worst happened. One hole was too deep and wide. The left front tire had nowhere to go but down. The vehicle hit hard. A crunching sound came from the front fender, and I could hear the tire whiz in open space until the motor went dead.

I sat still for a moment, then looked around me as best I could. The right side of the car was lifted at an angle so the rear-view mirror on that side showed a dim spot of taillight in the darkness. On the driver's side, I could see little outside except a wall of trees. I eased the door open. It jammed against the road but left enough space for me to squeeze out. With the flashlight I always carried, I shined a light into the hole. The sides were fresh dirt, not the muddy formation of a pothole. I followed a small mound into the grass at the side to a pile of fresh red earth. Some-one had dug the hole.

I pulled out the satchel from the back seat. Crammed full of student papers, it couldn't be closed. Retrieving the cellular from the top and standing in the car light, I dialed the sheriff's office. When they promised help, I dialed my house. Vernon would be there if he hadn't been called out again. Just as I finished the numbers, something slammed into my hands. I staggered back, turning my ankle on the edge of the hole. I could see debris flying in the headlights.

Sitting on the dirt road for a second, I glimpsed a figure in the darkness. It had turned toward the woods and was picking up something. I jumped and ran into the heavy swamp growth. This was my territory, and if he didn't shoot me, I planned to lead him into danger.

Thankful for my shoes and long pants, I fled among the trees toward the river. It would be at least three miles away at this point, but there were plenty of sinks in between. I had dived in most of them.

I still had my flashlight. Turning it off, I gripped it like a weapon. Behind me, I heard the crash of heavy boots on swamp foliage, and I could see a light waving about frantically. He didn't know exactly where I was.

Dashing down a hill, I pulled another antic with a top-dry sink. The slope wouldn't get the best of him this time. He'd keep his balance down and up the hill. My destination was the other side. When I saw the light bob up the hill, I took off for a few yards, then down another bank. Anyone unfamiliar with the terrain wouldn't notice the puddle of water covered in sediment at the bottom.

Taking the downhill at a fast run, I built up momentum to jump across the nearly five-foot wide muddy depression. I stumbled slightly on the other side and up the next hill, but I regained my balance. At the top, I stopped and hid in a clump of bushes, hoping my heavy breathing wouldn't give me away.

The light shined down the hill and part ways up it, then, whoever was holding it, took off at a run. He thought he was repeating himself—until he reached the bottom. He didn't know he should have jumped. Instead, he fell like a thrown dart into the muddy surface and sank up to his chest. I heard a scream.

Newsome flailed about in mud to keep himself above water until he begged for mercy. "Get me out, please," he said. Pitiful, his macho militia games couldn't help him now. I imagined his ankles dangling in the cold water of a bottomless sinkhole. When the sediment gave way, he'd be swimming in the stuff.

"The more you fidget, the closer you come to going down," I said. I stood above him, just out of reach of any stick he might throw. "You have a gun on you?"

"Not anymore. It fell somewhere." He looked around. His flashlight had fallen, too. It's light still shining, it rested on the side of the hill, placing Newsome at the edge of a spotlight. I had turned mine on the man's face.

"You're not much of a militia man. You keep losing your gun. Why don't you get a desk job?" I heard sirens in the distance.

"Sheriff to the rescue," I said and squatted on the side of the hill.

"I need to get out now!" He wiggled some, then stopped when the mud moved closer to his arm pits.

"Didn't they teach you to swim in that militia group?"

"Nobody swims in this stuff!"

"I hear you can scuba dive."

He stopped talking and jerked his head and shoulders backward. He tried to kick his legs up to a floating position. It wouldn't work. There was nothing underneath to push against, and the mud above acted as a barrier to momentum. He succeeded in getting a mouthful of swamp sludge.

"Nice taste, huh?"

Lights angled and flickered between trees, and I could hear Vernon's voice calling my name.

"Down this way!" I yelled back. "I've got a mudpuppy whimpering for its mama."

CHAPTER TWENTY-EIGHT

"Twice in one day. He was determined to get at you," said Tony. He stood beside the patrol car where Newsome sat handcuffed and whispering guttural oaths to himself. "Pitiful sight, isn't it?"

Vernon had been home when I called. The sudden click of the phone had spooked him. When I didn't respond to his call back to my cell phone, he came looking for me. "Scared me bald when I saw your Honda in that hole," he said, his arm gripping my waist tightly. I nuzzled against his warm shoulder, not much caring what a deputy might say.

No one could pass in or out of the road until a tow truck nudged the Honda from its prison. The halogen lights cast a space ship glare on the road and a few feet into the woods. Beyond, a sudden wall of darkness took over. Not even a tree trunk the size of the Honda was visible. I clung to Vernon's arm as I climbed into his car. He backed down the road all the way to my house, the police scene a white dot fading like a slowly dying planet.

Later, as I lay beside my snoring deputy, I felt the house wrap around me, keeping me safe in climate-controlled wonder. My body refused to be sore again, but I did occasionally feel the twinge of an ankle and brief itch on my arm. I turned and hugged Vernon's back. He grunted lightly and slid his arm over mine.

Tony had laid claim to two interview rooms by the time I arrived with Vernon. With Newsome safely in jail again, and not likely to make bail this time, tongues were wagging. Sadie Wilburn and her lawyer came out of the first room. When she saw me standing in the hall, she lowered her eyes. Her gray hair matched her mood, frazzled, like baby snakes let loose in deep space.

"Your dean called and is coming in shortly to make his statement." Loman nodded at the lawyer, but spoke to me.

"Good. I'd like to be standing right here when you take him in," I said. "And is Newsome in that room?" I pointed to the closed door.

"Not yet. We're getting it ready for St. Claire. Tony's going to arrest him today." Loman widened his eyes for a moment, his way of smiling about good things.

"On what charges?"

Loman nodded. "Anything from aiding and abetting to failing to report an assault. Let's wait and see."

"Where's Newsome?"

"In the lock-up. You want to make sure?" Loman smiled and waved for me to follow him.

We moved through the heavy outer door into a long hallway. Along one side, cells lined up like stainless steel animal cages in a laboratory. Arrested drunk drivers sat on the edges of bunks, their hangover heads in their hands. One young man, a thief caught inside a store with his hands literally inside the register, banged on the door, then the walls.

"Drug withdrawal," said Loman. "Medics'll take him for a dry-out."

We passed the last cell in the row, the one reserved for big timers and suspects most likely to cause a disturbance. The cell, like the others, wasn't barred but had a heavy door with a large window and a food slot. Special cameras on the other side of the hall focused on the inmate. Newsome didn't seem to know that. He wasn't smiling.

"His daddy's on his way here. Might be a little disappointed in his son." said Loman.

Newsome sat straight up on the edge of his bunk. His usual cockiness disappeared. For a moment, he sat pale-faced, his hand suspended in a pointing position. Then he jumped on both feet, his face reddening.

"My daddy is not coming here!" he cried from the middle of his cell. "I won't see him if he does. You got that, lawman?"

"Don't foam at the mouth, son. He's your next of kin. Don't you want any help he can give?"

"Not from him! Keep him away from me. Do you hear me?"

"Is the father really coming here?" I asked.

"So I hear."

I leaned against the wall. "Could you get Tony to let me see the meeting?"

He shrugged. "Maybe. The daddy doesn't have to come. Newsome is of age. No need to call in a parent if he's not wanted. But when I called him, the old man said, 'I'm coming down there and talk to that boy!'"

I sat in the darkness of a tiny viewing room. No bigger than a closet, it had been built for one person to observe the events in two different rooms, one on each side. The large windows, dark now because the lights in the interview rooms were off, would give anyone in my spot a span of the entire area. Squares, the same color as the walls, at the top of each mirror, gave the appearance of being air vents. They were speakers.

I leaned back in the chair and closed my eyes. Somewhere I had read that men who joined militias, who played child-like war games, had come from angry, inadequate backgrounds.

I wanted to see how Newsome would react when his father heard he had dropped a newborn baby inside a river cave, then tried to blow up two divers.

"Luanne," Loman whispered through the door, "it's your dean. He's coming in to make a statement."

I sat up. A shadow appeared across one mirror as someone opened the door of the interview room and light from the hallway shone across the table. Suddenly, the entire room went bright. Loman placed a tape in the recorder, then he flipped on a switch near the mirror. He waved like a little child as he did. I waved back, knowing he couldn't see me.

Loman stood at the mirror end of the room as Tony and the dean moved inside and sat at the long table. Tony turned on the recorder and announced the date, time, subject, and people in the room.

"You're sure you don't want a lawyer with you?" He said it for the tape. "For the record, the subject is shaking his head no."

Loman took his seat and opened his little pad. His pencil hovering over the pages, he became more intimidating than the recorder.

Tony said, "Start at the beginning—I mean how you knew all the participants in these war games."

Dean Boseman's hands moved together, then apart, then landed flat on the table. He took a deep breath and spoke to the recorder.

"It's a gathering of men who like to—well, to challenge themselves in the swamps—only on weekends, of course."

"Would you call this a militia of sorts?"

"No, oh no," the dean held up a hand and shook his head, "not a militia that opposes government or anything like that. It's just for fun, you see."

Tony's dark eyes rested on the man. "Do any of you have any business deals together?"

The dean shifted in his chair, looking from Tony to Loman and back again.

"Some might," he said. "I think there are some joint land purchases. Something like that."

"Where?"

"Where? Oh, you mean where is the land. Near some springs, I think. Swampy area. I couldn't see what they wanted with it."

"Couldn't you?"

"Well, no, but some of them said something about developing a resort—I think. But I don't have those kinds of funds." He held up a palm as though warding off the evil eye.

"And they let you stay in the militia anyway?"

"Of course. I helped in other ways, I guess. And I played the war games. They were great fun."

"Yeah, I'll bet they were," said Tony who momentarily looked at Loman. Robot-like, he continued. "Tell me about the time Newsome joined your group."

"Just one day, St. Claire showed up with him."

"And you all embraced this guy, Newsome?"

"I wouldn't say embraced, but we accepted him, yes. You see, being a little younger and stronger than the rest of us, he did a lot of the muscle work, like setting up camp. And, I think St. Claire arranged for him to watch over the camp during the week."

Tony said, "Ms Fogarty was nearly killed by this Newsome."

The dean nodded. "Yes, yes, I was alarmed to hear about that."

"Did you hear about it at the camp?"

The man shook his head. "Newspaper."

"What about a Ms. Brennan, a real estate agent. Did you see her around the camp?"

The dean rubbed his hands together, then pushed them down to his knees. "Some woman came to the camp once in a while to speak to St. Claire about the deals. Nobody ever introduced her to me."

"And Miss Grassfield?"

"I didn't know her, didn't realize the dead woman was the same one who helped around the camp until I saw the photo in the paper." The dean swallowed hard.

"Helped around the camp? How?"

"Cleaned up after meals. Stuff like that."

"Did either of these women carry on intimately with anyone at the camp?"

The dean's pain increased, and he squeezed shut both eyes. "I don't know. There were rumors that Miss Grassfield was somewhat loose." He shook his head. "I really couldn't say."

Tony asked, "Did anyone ever say anything about a baby being born?"

The dean looked bewildered. Shaking his head, he said, "One or two of the fellows mentioned adopted babies, but nothing about one being born."

Tony ended the interview, then told the dean to stay in town and be available for questioning. The three men left the room. I could hear the dean's footsteps as he hurried toward the exit.

"For an academic, he sure didn't know a lot of stuff," Loman said.

"I hear you want to listen to the elder Newsome," said Tony as he entered the viewing room. Light streamed in from the hallway. "Just stay out of the way. I've got to arrest a prominent lawyer."

CHAPTER TWENTY-NINE

I shut the door and flipped a lever. It seemed flimsy for a sheriff's office. I could feel Vernon behind me.

"Sometimes you make me do things I shouldn't," he whispered, caressing my hair with one hand, my waist and hip with the other.

"Such a naughty boy," I said and turned to face him.

There's something about the danger of it all, the off limits quality, that makes sex all the more exciting when people are just outside the door. If any of his fellow deputies could have peeked in, they would have glimpsed a woman whose bra had been unhooked and lifted to her chin, her blouse unbuttoned and her slacks on the back of the metal chair. Her lover's shirt and tie were still there, but his uniform pants and jock shorts lay on the floor. The woman's bare butt brushed against a neat stack of files, all of which went flying, as he bent her over the desk. The passion would be spent in minutes, and the two would lie still on the gray surface, their pleasure overcoming the discomfort of pen cups and loose papers.

The phone rang. Without moving, Vernon reached to pick up the receiver. He spoke with my legs still wound around his back, his own bare butt mooning the door.

"Mr. Newsome is flying down here tonight. I'm supposed

to meet him at the airport at ten tomorrow morning." He replaced the receiver and looked down at me. "Let's do this again, sometime."

"Just tell me when to lock the door."

He pulled himself away and sat down in the metal chair, jumping slightly at the cold on bare skin. I pushed off the desk and sat in a chair. I was on the last blouse button when the door pushed open. Tony stood open-mouthed. Vernon's jock shorts rested on top of one wingtip shoe.

"Damn, shit, and hell!" Tony's olive skin turned green. "Can't the two of you ever learn? What if the sheriff or Loman had walked back here with me?" He looked at Vernon. "Get your britches on and get out of here."

He looked at me, the fire burning behind his black eyes. "And you get out and stay out. This department is off limits for you until we get to the bottom of this case."

"The bottom?" Vernon asked, his eyes laughing.

Tony glared at him, then slammed the door. The flimsy lock dropped to the floor.

Local television went big city that night. A VIP had been arrested, charged with aiding a capital crime. Cuffed and shackled, August St. Claire teetered between Tony and the sheriff as they led him to the booking area. His lawyer followed behind, wearing his uniform of gray suit and briefcase. They had located St. Claire on a tennis court. Besides the hardware, he had to parade before the cameras in white shorts, his thick hair disheveled. Once, he tried to answer a reporter's inquiry, but his lawyer shut him up and moved between the two.

"They'll never prove these charges," he said as he twisted

his wrists in the cuffs.

"Say no more," said the lawyer in a monotone. He didn't look at his client.

"Okay, here it comes," I said as I scooted close to the television set. "When the three of them come out the door, the deputies move in with Josie Wilburn. See!" I had recorded the newscast for Vernon. The whole thing had been planned. St. Claire would come face to face with Josie, and detectives would watch the reactions. It worked. St. Claire's face froze and his head turned slightly as his gaze followed the woman's move into the sheriff's station. She did likewise, her face jerking upward with a slight sneer before looking away.

"I see what you mean," said Vernon. "Tony had better keep them apart."

"It's not going to be easy. St. Claire is most likely in cahoots with her lawyer. Damn! I wish I could hear these interviews. And I'd like to hear the midwifery report."

"Meaning Patricia Echols?"

I nodded. "They'll give Josie a chance to talk before pressing information out of her sister."

"Guess we kind of ruined your privileges at the office, huh?" Vernon pulled my hair. He knew where we stood with Tony, but he seemed to know it would blow over.

"I could swear you have something on Detective Amado." He didn't answer me.

A midsummer squall hit the county that night. Outside, I heard tree limbs crack then crash against the house, and I prayed they would miss the windows. The lightning never stopped. It flashed, then glowed, then banged like a cherry bomb. Once in a particularly loud strike, it hit something near the river. That's when I remembered Charlene Brennan going into the sinkhole. It stormed that day, too, and in a crack of a gunshot, she had suddenly veered into the park and plowed into the sink. No one had noticed another car, and certainly not a Hummer vehicle, on the road. "But, a motorcycle," I thought, "would it be possible to pull alongside a car and fire through the window?" I held tight to Vernon's back and lay awake for hours feeling Charlene's fear as the motorcycle raced after her. Drifting off finally, I thought, "Must have been terrified…why else would she have been traveling so fast?"

"She probably slammed her foot on the gas, a reaction to the shot," I said aloud while I brewed the morning coffee.

"Who?" said Vernon. He munched on a piece of toast, holding it away from his clean uniform. "Make it a short answer. I got to run."

"Just talking to myself," I said. "No coffee?"

"I'll get it at the office." He kissed me on the forehead, then squeezed my butt. "I'll go out to the airport about nine-thirty to meet Newsome. Tony said to put him up at the W-A." That meant Wally's At-home, a motel not far from the sheriff's station. Cheap but clean, its owner-manager played at detecting and cooperated with the law by keeping an eye on anyone housed there.

I took my time with breakfast. Outside, broken limbs and storm debris cluttered the road, and I crossed my fingers that Vernon would make it to the main highway.

I fidgeted around the house, my head full of how Charlene might have been shot and who could have done it. I longed to be at the department to hear the interviews, but Tony would have none of it. "Get your info from Vernon, between screws," he had said when I tried to convince him to let me in. "You blew it this time."

I drifted to the porch. The storm had left the air brisk and rather dry for a Florida summer. I rocked for a while, trying to plan for the last class lesson, but my brain couldn't be bothered. I grabbed the cell phone and took off down the road instead. Walking in the car ruts, I looked for places that needed repair. I had stooped to push aside a rotted limb when someone dropped out of a tree and landed in front of me.

"Ms. Fogarty!" Nick Summers stood straddling the grassy medium between the ruts. He wore tight jeans and no shirt. A woman half my age and addle-brained might have swooned at the sight. His deep brown eyes and heavy brows stood out below the newly shaved head. His skin had an even tan wherever visible. "I was watching to see if you were okay."

I stood up. "Nick, what the hell are you doing up that tree? Don't you have work to do on the grass pulling boat?"

"I get breaks." He grinned again, like the same little boy prepared to get a happy face stamped on his forehead.

"Well, I'm just fine, thanks." I nodded, not knowing how to handle what I was beginning to see as a crush.

He moved closer. I could smell body oil. He reached toward my arm but drew back before touching me.

"Nick. Maybe you better go for a cold swim."

He nodded. I felt his presence, close and tight.

"Would you go with me?" He moved toward me; I stepped backward into a tree. "We don't really need suits."

I tried to look about the woods, nervous under his gaze. I shook my head.

"Somebody took pictures of you one night," his voice nearly

254

a whisper.

"You?" Anger hit me in the gut.

"No, not me. I saw somebody out there with a flash one night. Then I saw you come out." He smiled. "You had nothing on."

"Nick, you need to leave now." I pulled away from him.

"I'm attracted to you, Ms. Fogarty. You must know that by now." He pulled me against his chest.

"I'm old enough to be your mother, Nick." I gripped the cell phone. Suddenly it rang, vibrating against his bare back.

Nick stood straight and a light of realization flickered in his eyes. He backed away, nearly tripping over a downed tree limb. In a flash he disappeared into the swamp.

"Cycle wasn't there," Tony was saying something about tire tracks. "Guys brought in the camper and a Hummer, but no cycle. They said some suspicious-looking tracks went toward the water."

I grunted something, stumbling down the dirt road to the safety of my house.

"You got your tank filled with air, Luanne?" Tony asked.

CHAPTER THIRTY

The only added danger to diving in a sinkhole at night is the glare from the topside halogens. Underwater, it's no darker than normal—which is pitch black. I donned my head light, then eased into the cold water, Vernon behind me.

From a history of the area, we knew this sink had several offshoots that went nowhere, one that connected to the slough and another that connected with the transition to the Palmetto Springs area. A few feet from the top the water felt stagnant, the grime and debris from weekend campers hanging in vine traps around the sides. The slight wake I made brushed away beer cans and drink cups as I descended. I didn't dare touch the walls. At this point, they were dirt-colored which meant debris would flake off and scatter, blurring my vision.

Suddenly, the ledges stopped and I felt the colder water of a deep cavern. Currents shot up from deep holes, blasting frigid water like a fire hose into a sink. Vernon had gone off the other side. As we descended we had flashed our headlights around the walls, looking for signs of a motorcycle. Reaching the cold water meant we would have to search the wide depths, maybe even go into the transition tunnel.

I watched Vernon's light grow larger as he swam toward me. He had to raise his hand into the glow to signal the direction we would take. He would go around one way. I would swim the other, then we'd meet on the opposite side. If the cycle were not resting on a ledge somewhere, we would have to search the slant that served as a bottom. As a last resort, we'd see if the current had carried it through the transition where it was bound to get stuck. If not there, we'd give it up to the deep—if it was here at all.

The darkness, nearly impenetrable, forced me to move slowly. Every once in a while a surprise cold current slapped at my fins or pushed down on my back. I braced myself. Beginning under the ledge, I moved downward, flashing my light onto scurrying schools of small catfish. Occasionally, a huge one would travel beneath me, the light not fazing his right and left slow glide that propelled him into the cold depths, his long whiskers searching for bits of edible debris. The hole's walls revealed nothing but loose dirt. In the distance, I could see the pinpoint of Vernon's light.

The sinkhole wall suddenly opened up into a rushing current where the transition tunnel began. I had to swim hard to avoid being sucked through it. Turning downward to get away from the swift water, I spied the tires. After that, I could see something like a handlebar. Signaling Vernon, I swam close to the slanting floor of the hole. The motorcycle had been swept close to the tunnel, but its weight had slammed it into the soft dirt. I brushed some dirt aside. It immediately filled the light around the cycle, and I dared not brush it anymore.

"It's down there," I said to Tony as I dragged myself against the steep bank. "Get the crane ready, and a couple of ropes for us." Vernon joined me. We removed our tanks and drank from giant plastic cola bottles.

When the crane pulled out the bike, it was nearly dawn. A crowd had gathered from somewhere. Loman decided they were lovers who, finding their lane occupied, got out of their cars to see why bright lights focused on the sink. He said they didn't look like militia types. "Made love, not war, last night."

"The seat has a cover on it," said Marshall as he stooped near the dripping, shiny black machine. "Could find some prints under it." He walked around, squinting in the bright halogen, even holding his hand up to deflect the glare. "Something scratched here," he said as he bent toward the neck near the handle bars. "Could be initials."

It looked like the one I had seen in the camper.

"Seems like a dumb dude to toss it in the water like that," Tony said.

"Another reason to suspect it was Newsome," I said.

Weary from a night of swimming and no sleep, Vernon and I followed Tony back to the sheriff's office. He had no time to lose. If he didn't charge the people he had in custody, he would have to let them go.

"Newsome's father is due in this morning," Tony said. "We're going to put him face to face with his son."

I had managed to dry off the sinkhole water from my body, and put on jeans and a tee shirt. But, my hair hung in hard, damp clumps around my ears. In the ladies room inside the jail, I pushed my head under the tap and rinsed it as much as I could without splashing water over my clothes. Using a towel lent to me from jail supplies, I rolled up my flecked dark-brown locks and squeezed the water hard. The room had one of those hand blowers; I stuck my head under it. Nearly dry, my hair frizzled in all directions. I almost had it tamed when a female sergeant opened the door.

"Lieutenant Drake said to tell you he left for the airport." She had sneaked me into the jail side of the sheriff's department.

Tony would be in the interview rooms.

"Get him to call me as soon as he can," I said. "On the cell phone."

CHAPTER THIRTY-ONE

"Stinking, rotten kid," said the elder Newsome as he pushed himself out of Vernon's car. The man wiped thorny hands on his khaki pants and limped toward the door.

Vernon shot me a glance, then muttered as we entered the door, "It's been like this all the way from the airport. He despises his son. Probably beat him down for years."

"We're going to walk him past the door to let Arnold get a glimpse of his father," said Loman.

Vernon's hand brushed mine. "Stay in the viewing room," he whispered. "Tony said for you to stay out of his way. It'll be okay if you don't interfere."

I walked in front of Vernon and his Montana guest, darting into an open door to let them pass. As soon as they disappeared, Arnold came into the hall, a deputy at his elbow, uttering a few swear words under his breath as he entered the interview room. I raced through the door that would let me view the proceedings without irritating Tony. I didn't close the door, but peeked out to watch the hallway drama unfold.

"This way, sir," Vernon's voice sounded closer. "Just past that open door."

A uniform deputy passed the door first; Mr. Newsome followed with Vernon at the far side. The old man's face glanced inside, then jerked back. His body stiffened.

"What the hell, boy!" His gravel voice rocked the empty hallway.

"Daddy!" Arnold didn't move. His hands gripped the table. Staring up, he didn't blink. This full grown kid was terrified of his old man.

"Don't you whimper at me…" The old man raised a fist and made a movement toward the room. Vernon grabbed his arm, and the deputy stepped in the doorway.

"Sorry, sir. You can speak to your son later. Just come down here with us."

"Why is he here?" said a shaken Arnold, when the officers had gathered in his room. I had closed my door and sat down to watch through the mirror.

"You want to talk to us about your involvement with Theresa Grassfield, the Wilburn sisters, Mr. St. Claire—and Charlene Brennan?" Tony asked.

"Who's that?" Newsome leaned back in his chair.

"Charlene Brennan, a real estate agent."

"Never heard of her." He lowered his eyes. His clinched fist turned white at the knuckles.

Tony breathed deeply. "Okay, Mr. Newsome, are you ready?"

"I want a lawyer." he said. His lips trembled slightly, and a few drops of sweat appeared on his forehead.

The men, except Newsome, left the room. In the hall, Vernon said, "He's nervous as hell right now. His father's appearance had a greater effect than I expected."

"These militia types think they have a beef with the government. Beefs with each other is more like it," said Loman. "And a good old child-beating daddy tops them all."

I scooted back into the viewing area when Loman and the

others joined the elder Newsome in the second interview room. Despite his annoyance, the man looked nervous, his eyes darting from his gnarled hands to our faces. "We need some background right now, sir," Tony said. Loman pulled his notebook from his pocket.

"You want to know about that boy's troubles in Montana?" Newsome smiled then appeared to relax a little. "Arnold came to be a sore spot. He thought he'd be a hero and harass the law. All it did was bring it down on our heads fast and furious. The group finally got a stomach full and suggested he leave. I went along with that even if he was my son." He stopped and shook his head. "Don't surprise me none that he's in trouble down here."

"Will your group in Montana take on his cause?"

"Hell, no! They'll be tickled that he's far away and can't come back." Newsome looked away. "Dumb kid," he mumbled.

"Where did he learn to scuba dive?" Vernon asked.

"Got lessons at a local boys' club. Don't know if he done it much after he growed up." He frowned.

Tony continued. "Would he know how to make a bomb?"

The old man shrugged. "Guess so. It ain't no genius job to do."

A light tap sounded at the door, and a uniform looked inside. "Newsome's lawyer is here."

Tony leaned forward. "Mr. Newsome, do you want to speak to your son alone? He may not agree to do that, and he doesn't have to. He also may want his lawyer present."

The man, his thick facial skin bunched up in time-weary lines, stared, unblinking. "Yeah, I want to talk to him."

Loman sat quietly for a moment, then nodded and stood up. "Then let's see if he'll talk to you. Wait here."

In the short time they had been talking to the father, the lawyer had convinced the son that not only did they want to face the father, they wanted a deputy in the room with them.

A uniform deputy sat in a middle seat, young Newsome and his lawyer at one end, old Newsome at the other. Arnold began to sweat and tremble. The men and I crowded ourselves in the closet-size room behind the mirror.

"You bomb somebody, boy?" Old Newsome's voice over-powered the room.

Arnold fidgeted, his eyes darting from the table to his lawyer, but never at his father. "You always said cops will…"

"Don't you tell me what I said!" Newsome's eyes fixed on his son's face. "I know what I said, and I ain't never told you to bomb nobody!"

"But that's the message I got," Arnold tried to show some defiance, but his voice dropped and he looked away.

"Why would you do something like that? What was the cops about to find out?"

"They…" Arnold squirmed, then leaned to his lawyer and spoke into his ear. The lawyer whispered back, and Arnold put his head down and talked. "They knew about a birth and were looking for the baby. It belonged to a militia member here, some-body who didn't want it found." He breathed outward in a heavy puff, then sat up and continued. "I did what the man paid me to do—got the kid for him."

Silence like a circling buzzard hovered in the room. When the elder Newsome finally spoke, he seemed in a rage. The temples on the sides of his leathery face bulged and throbbed. "Did you kill a baby?"

Arnold began to shake his head faster and faster. "Nothing

like that. He wanted the kid, said to bring it to him, but…"

"Who's this fellow that paid you to do that?"

The lawyer pressed his hand on Arnold's arm. "I'll take care of that information, sir." He turned away from his client and faced the father. "Mr. Newsome, you certainly don't have to be a witness for your son. However, I will need a statement from you as to his background—birth and upbringing and all that—before you leave town. Where are you staying?" He positioned a pen to write down the address on a legal pad.

"Oh, I'll tell you about this kid all right!" Newsome was nearly yelling now. "I'll give you some clues about one surly brat!"

"Just what I need," said the lawyer, a smile on his lips. He turned to the deputy. "Now, sir, I'd like a few moments alone with my client."

The lawyer was smart enough to take the elder man's statement out of our hearing. By the time he turned over his interview to the district attorney, he would have his defense case mapped out—child abuse followed by acting out rage.

"Something is not right," I said. "He told his father he took the baby to him—meaning St. Claire, I guess. I'm going to see Marshall Long."

"Stay out of this, Luanne," Tony's voice sounded a warning.

I glanced at the other men. They took it in stride, Tony's usual chastising. No one gave a hint they knew anything.

Marshall's lumpy body spread over his chair as he stared into a glaring computer screen. His puffy index finger moved down the glass surface, and I imagined a streak of fried onion ring grease followed.

"Got to find this report," he said, refusing to look up at me as I entered the room with a security escort. "Did it too late last night. I can't be sure how accurate it is." He squinted his already tiny eyes as though that would help him locate the file name. "Hell! I wish I could remember what I labeled the thing."

"Try the name of the victim," I said.

"What do you want, Luanne? I ain't got time for you right now."

"The umbilical we found in the towel in the cave—you think it came from the drowned baby?"

"That's what I said. Would bet my grannie's lemon pie on it." He ran his finger back and forth across the monitor the way people used to do in those speed reading courses. "Not too many newborns hanging around old swamp cabins that I know of, and since we can't find a body, it's likely traveling the River Styx about now."

"Newsome says he was taking the kid to somebody. But, if he really dropped it in the cave, then he drowned it, right?"

"Somebody else could have done it."

"How?"

Marshall placed his hands on his heavy thighs and leaned back in his squeaking chair. "Look, Luanne, I can't say if he was drowned far from shore, near the shore, or in a tub filled with that water. If he drowned at all, and..."

"In the birthing pan!" I said. "I'll bet one of the Wilburn sisters drowned it in a pan of river water, then handed it over to Newsome. He wasn't taking it to anyone, except to Old Man River!"

Marshall frowned. "I never knew a midwife to drown a live baby. Abort one, yeah, but not kill it after it was born." He shrugged and leaned forward to his monitor once again. "There it is!" He used the highlight key.

"What was it under?"

Marshall nodded silently for a moment. "The victim's name," he said to the computer.

CHAPTER THIRTY-TWO

"Looks like two sisters got the hell out of town." Tony paced his office. "And St. Claire's lawyer got him out on recognizance."

Vernon, Loman, two uniforms, and I crammed through the doorway to listen to the latest crisis.

"St. Claire's maid said he packed a bag and left four hours ago. Josie Wilburn's lawyer got her out on bail, and now she's not at her swamp house, nor at the Valdosta house. She may even be dead for all we know."

"What about St. Claire's wife?" I asked.

"She moved out two days ago, went to her sister's in Atlanta."

"No scandal up there." Loman made a big check in his book.

"She's old money like he is," added Tony. "But I guess she couldn't stand the bastard baby news and all."

"Neither could he," I said. "That's why he wanted the kid done away with. Making public nookie with poor white trash, then having to support their kid just won't cut it in his circles."

Loman's sleepy eyes opened wide a moment, then he mumbled, "That's a man's comment."

"Yes, it is. I just thought I'd say what you were thinking."

"We've got plenty of motive. St. Claire wanted that baby out of sight, out of mind." Tony stared at the wall as though the answer would appear Biblically before him.

"How do you know he didn't just say 'abort it, and here's the money'?" I said.

"No," said Tony, "Theresa probably insisted on carrying it to term. That would guarantee St. Claire's full-time support."

"Okay, let's say he hired the Wilburn sisters to do an abortion, tell Theresa it was a stillbirth, and give the body to Newsome."

"But," said Vernon, "the baby aborted alive?"

We all stood in silence.

"The question is," said Vernon, "which one of the people here actually killed the baby."

"Marshall Long said he's heard of women who do births and abortions, but never of one who killed a baby that was born alive."

"Maybe it's time to hear a little more of what Sadie has to say," Tony said.

Sadie had refused to return to the swamp house she had lived in most of her life. She said it belonged to Mr. St. Claire now, though he hadn't paid them yet, and she didn't feel right there. I suspected she had some fear of meeting her older sister on a creaky stair landing. She had given Tony an address, one with no phone and maybe no running water. She said the cabin belonged to a woman who had used the Wilburns in most of her birthings—twelve live born babies in thirteen years. I guess the woman felt she owed them one.

"It's far down an offshoot of the river. No better way to reach it than by boat. Do you want Pasquin?"

Tony paced the floor. He put his hands in and out of his pockets and ground his teeth. "Yeah," he finally said. "Get hold of him."

I spoke to Pasquin on the cell phone outside the sheriff's office. I felt uneasy. Tony's usual reluctance to use me on the case was made worse by the missing photos and sexual games with Vernon; he seemed jumpy as a flea. To make things worse, the afternoon had turned sultry. Rain was on its way.

"Pasquin says he knows the place and will meet us at my landing." I spoke to Vernon and Tony in the lobby. "Will you call her lawyer?"

"Have to." Tony reached for my phone. "Don't think he's going to like fighting mosquitoes and gators."

Nothing happened until the summer afternoon rain ceased. With a blanket of steam attempting to smother everyone, we loaded onto Pasquin's motor boat. Sadie's lawyer, his shirt and suit jacket soaked through with sweat, stumbled as Vernon helped him aboard. Patricia Echols, again decked out in a safari suit—pale yellow this time—moved so gracefully that the edge of the boat barely swayed under her weight. She came along in the capacity of the agent in charge of midwifery incidents, Tony said. I suspected they had a date, and she had no intention of letting him call it off over some swamp venture.

The gentle putt-putt of the motor seemed labored with six people stuffed together. Pasquin slowed at every bend.

"Mustn't dump anyone to the gators," he said. "Besides, twilight ain't the best time to go river boating."

The humid mist began to lower as the sun set. The river and its swampy background took on a dark green hue with the massive cypress trees nearly black. Only someone as familiar with the river as Pasquin could guide the motor around the protruding knees, some rising several feet away from the bulging bottoms. We moved from open river to a deep narrow stream lined by oak trees that dipped their moss over the water. Pasquin noted the spot where he had let me off to walk to the Wilburn house. I could barely see the opening between the trees now, and just a few feet beyond lay total darkness. Without a light, heavy boots, and maybe a gun, that would be no path to take on a summer night.

"Got a ways to go, then we turn off kind of chancy like," said Pasquin, his weather hardened face and straw hat only vaguely visible in the dying light. "Won't be no moon tonight." He took a flashlight and shined it into the water. "Gator eyes there." He followed the two shiny balls a few feet until the gator dipped under the surface.

By the time Pasquin slowed to a near stop, the sky had turned solid black. Tony and Vernon held police flashlights, shining them along the grassy edge. Only once did we see a family of turtles move underwater as the boat approached. Using the boat light, Pasquin turned into a narrow water lane, an offshoot of another offshoot. With its lack of distinct shore, it told us the water here was also deep. We wouldn't drag on a muddy bottom.

"When we pass under the oaks in a few minutes, I got to cut the motor. Too much grass. You," he nodded toward Vernon who sat at the opposite end of the boat, "gon' have to give up that light and take an oar. I'll take the other one and guide us over to the landing."

Pasquin turned off the outboard motor, then pulled it from the water until it rested on the boat behind him. I held Vernon's flashlight, shining it toward a muddy patch cut through the river grass. The water became shallow here. When the boat softly scraped the bank, the two men held it steady with the oars.

"You folks will have to get your feet muddy, but you'll find a footpath just beyond the mud. Follow it on up that little hill. Under some trees, you'll see the house. That's where you want to be. I'll just wait here with the skeeters."

"Mud is deep here," said Vernon as he turned to help each of us from the boat.

"Damn it!" The lawyer's wing tip shoes sunk into the mire, his pants legs following. His foot made a suction sound when he pulled it out and attempted to step wide across the mud. The action threw him off balance, and he fell to his knees. "Shit!"

"Mr. St. Claire pay you enough for this?" said Tony.

"He hasn't paid me a dime, sir. What makes you ask that?"

Tony didn't answer.

I held tight to Vernon as I disembarked. I felt my shoes sink only slightly over the soles. When it was Patricia's turn, Tony handed his light to Pasquin and lifted her from the boat. She landed past the worst of the mud.

Tony led the way, his light shining just ahead of us on the lane. Patricia kept pace behind him, occasionally touching the back of his shirt or belt. Maybe she did it for balance, but the effect it had on Tony couldn't have been a far second. Sadie's lawyer stumbled in front of me, then Vernon took up the rear with another light. More than once Patricia let out a little squeal when a frog leapt clear of her foot.

"Look," said the lawyer as he stopped abruptly, "let's get something straight before we reach the house. I am court-appointed. For some reason, everyone thinks I'm being paid by St. Claire, but it isn't so."

Tony turned around, his light focusing on the man's face. "Do you plan to let her talk or have we come out here to listen to a lot of advice about keeping silent?"

"Whatever she needs to say to get the deal we discussed."

Everyone stood silent for a moment as Tony hesitated. "Good." For a moment I thought he'd call off the trek, but he turned around and began walking the lane again.

I let myself drop back. As best I could, I stepped beside Vernon and held his hand.

The marshy terrain gave way to harder ground. Suddenly we were pushing away long strands of moss that hung from a grove of oaks. When the flashlights hit the gray mass, they reflected a spidery weave backed by total darkness. A few more feet of this and we saw the light.

"Pasquin said they use kerosene lamps." Tony spoke in a whisper.

The cabin looked like the one where Theresa had given birth, only its roof didn't sag and there were curtains and screens on the windows. Flickering lights burned in two rooms.

I heard the buzzing first, then felt the bites. Before I could smash the mosquito, Patricia did a little dance.

"Let's get out of here. These mosquitoes will eat me raw," she said.

I heard Tony say under his breath, "lucky mosquitoes."

We stood on the wooden porch, its gray boards nailed solidly in place. All except Vernon, who waded through uncut grass to the back. Tony pulled his gun and held it by his side.

"There's certainly no need for that!" said the lawyer in a loud whisper.

"Mister, we don't know who else is inside this house. Now, stand back." Tony lifted his hand toward the man who took his advice.

We all moved to the shadows while Tony knocked on the screen door. The wooden door wasn't closed on this hot night, but the absence of any light inside the entrance made us cautious. When Tony knocked harder the second time, footsteps sounded on the wooden floor. Slowly, a lamp made its way to the door.

"I figured you'd be coming here," said Sadie as she unlatched the screen. "Stay here. I'll get some more light."

There is nothing like sitting in a thin-boarded, unair-conditioned swamp house in the middle of a Florida summer night. I guess I got used to it when I was a kid. No one had air conditioning then, and we didn't know it was hot. Tonight, the person who knew it best was Patricia Echols who swatted moths and mosquitoes in the air, then wiped her face and neck with a package of cellophane-wrapped tissues until she had used every one of them.

"You don't have to answer anything, Miss Wilburn," said the lawyer who had taken a seat beside the woman on a worn sofa. He draped his sweat-soaked jacket across the arm and jerked loose his tie.

"I'll say what I need to say," said Sadie. "Ask your questions."

"Tell us about Theresa Grassfield." Tony pulled a hand-held recorder from his pocket and placed it on the wide arm of his wooden picnic chair. Its seat slanted downward in the back. Tony's knees appeared to raise up and block his view. Patricia and I sat in two plastic chairs pulled from the porch.

"I been promised something if I talk. Right, Mr. Amado?"

"I said I would speak to the prosecutor on your behalf."

"You gonna keep him to his word?" she asked her lawyer.

"Yes, but you'll have to give testimony in open court—maybe against your sister."

Sadie breathed deeply, her body swaying slightly on the stiff sofa as though she wanted to rock.

"I been helping birth babies all my life," she said, her head

273

nodding to affirm herself. "Started when I wasn't more than six. My mama was known all over the place, from the Georgia line down to Perry and across to Port St. Joe. Women couldn't get to a hospital back then, didn't have money to pay a doctor. They'd call her out at all times of the night and day. Me and Josie would go along soon as we were big enough to carry the pans." She looked at us and chuckled. "Didn't phase us much. We done seen calves and pigs and cats being born. Didn't see why humans should be any different."

Sadie sat still and quiet for a moment. She sighed, closed her eyes until we thought she might have drifted off. When she opened them, she looked at the ceiling.

"I'm tired of this running. I'm gonna tell what I know. Don't go to church much, but the ladies down at the Baptist say I need to tell the truth, to wash myself clean."

"Good idea these ladies have," said Patricia who nodded her head up and down.

Sadie rocked in silence, then whispered. "Selling babies is not right."

"I'm going to run a tape," said Tony. He clicked on the hand-held machine when no one said a word. "You can begin now."

Sadie reached behind the sofa top and pulled out a paper fan, the kind furnished by churches to the congregation years ago.

"Theresa showed up a year ago or thereabouts. She looked poorly. Done spent all the money she had saved from a waitressing job. She needed a place to stay; we took her in. She was to do some chores around the place. Wasn't too good at it, though." Sadie went silent. Still fanning, she seemed to be contemplating something.

"She didn't have no home really. Never married nobody, but

lived with some men off and on. I think she'd just left one when she came here. Some no-count drunk." Sadie stopped fanning and stared at me. "She hadn't got no sense when it came to men. Just fire between her legs."

I squirmed and glanced at Tony. His raised knees blocked his face.

Sadie glanced down at her fan. "But she just couldn't leave it alone. Just had to do it again."

"She met someone here?" I added.

"Met Mr. St. Claire when he came looking at property. He came round to our house with that fancy real estate woman. She dressed so pretty—kind of like you do." Sadie nodded toward Patricia who was now rubbing her neck and upper chest with her bare hand. "Theresa wanted all that, and she thought she knew how to get it."

"Theresa must have been a little old to lure men," said Patricia, who immediately glanced toward me.

"No older than that real estate woman." Sadie rocked gently.

I darted a mean eye to Patricia.

"Go on, Miss Wilburn," said Tony. "Theresa, you say, seduced St. Claire?"

"Nothing like that. She just made herself available. Took him food over to that other house he was rebuilding. Fed him real nice when he came to offer us money for our place." She made a sound like a little laugh. "Even babysat his grandkid."

"Theresa said she was cooking for the men who met at Calley's. Said they was paying her. And she did start buying clothes and stuff. Looked a little better for a while."

"Did she ever say who the other men were at this camp?" I asked.

"Just mentioned St. Claire all the time. He's the one that paid her. She'd say there were rich men down there who liked to get all dressed up in army clothes and play games in the woods. She'd laugh about it most of the time."

"How long did all this last?" asked Tony.

"Till he realized she was carrying his child. One day, I see her in this kind of jersey dress she bought, and her front is sticking out a little too far. I been around too many pregnant women not to know what that meant. Right away, me and Josie offered to abort it, but she wouldn't have nothing to do with that. Said she had a hold on the man if she kept the kid."

"St. Claire panicked?"

"Now that's a curious thing. He had this idea, see." Sadie looked up, her eyes suddenly terrified. "He said he had clients in Miami. Said he represented somebody who might pay for a nice white baby. Then he offered us more money than we'd see in two lifetimes. But we also had to sell him the house in the bargain."

Silence hit the cabin. Above my head, I heard the constant buzz of a mosquito, reminding me it was the female who bit and sucked blood to nourish her eggs.

"Being midwives and knowing what to do, you took him up on his deal?" Patricia's voice reflected her anger. Tony shot her a warning glance.

"Josie said we could do it." Sadie lowered her face to her sleeve and wiped away the perspiration. "See, I thought—and Josie said—that the baby would be better off in a rich home down in Miami." She breathed deep as though coming up from an exhausting swim. "And with the money, we'd never have to birth another one."

"What led you to the cabin?" asked Tony.

"Theresa didn't know about his offer, and he didn't know

276

she planned to soak him for support after the birth." Sadie took another deep breath as though the humid air was drowning her lungs. "We had to keep Theresa from having the baby in town or giving birth at the house. She had to think it was stillborn. That's when Josie got her concoction ready." The woman darted her eyes toward Patricia.

"The oleander?" I said.

Sadie nodded. "It's dangerous. We used it a few times before for abortions. A little adjustment and it can induce labor. It ain't pretty. Gives the woman convulsions, but the baby comes out."

"Go on," I urged when Sadie stopped to fidget with the fan.

"She put it in some orange juice. When Theresa started to get sick, Josie said we'd best take her to the doctor. It was a trick, you see, to get Theresa to come with us. We never took nobody to a doctor before, but she didn't know that. We put her in this old boat we used for fishing, took along some birthing pans and towels and headed for the cabin. Theresa didn't know much about the water routes. She couldn't tell where we were headed."

"But why the cabin?" Patricia asked. "Couldn't you have done this in your own house?"

"Oh, no," said Sadie, shaking her head, "we couldn't be sure of the oleander, and we didn't want to bury anybody on our land."

"Oh, my God!" moaned her lawyer who pushed his face into his hands. "Don't say another word."

"Too late," said Tony. "We've all heard her. Continue, Miss Wilburn."

"By the time we reached the cabin, Theresa was heaving something awful. She held onto her big belly like she was trying to keep that kid inside. By the time we got her on the bed, she started screaming. The kid came fast."

"The oleander worked?" Patricia asked.

Sadie bowed her head and whispered, "The kid was a healthy bastard. He came out wiggling like, then he gave a little cry."

Silence hung in the room like a death pall.

Sadie lifted her head. In the dim light, her eyes watered. "I forgot to tell you about that man in the boat with us—the one sent from Mr. St. Claire."

CHAPTER THIRTY-THREE

"Josie said this young man would help us out, that Mr. St. Claire had paid him. He'd been hanging around, watching the house on St. Claire's orders. When we went to take Theresa out, he was already in the boat. At the cabin, he said he'd wait right around the bend under a grove of trees."

Patricia had given up drying her face and melted like a plastic doll.

"And he was there when I arrived?" I asked.

Sadie shook her head. "He must have seen you coming. When we got out the back door with the baby, he was half way down the river in the boat. He waved at us to hurry up. We just hurried too much, I guess. Not easy to run through marsh grass."

"Meaning?" Tony leaned forward, his voice a near whisper.

"That fellow was too careless, scared out of his mind. He stood up in the boat and tried to balance it by holding onto a tree limb. I got in first with the pans and nearly dumped the whole business when I sat down. Josie got in with the baby, but the stupid man wouldn't wait till she balanced herself. He just grabbed an oar and took off for deep water."

Sadie stopped, looked at the ceiling and wiped tears and sweat from her cheek. "Josie hadn't sat all the way down yet, and her foot caught on the bag of pans. The boat rocked hard, and the man was standing up. He lost his balance and fell against the side of the boat. I heard Josie scream, and when I looked at her, she was gripping the boat and staring into the current. The baby had slipped away from her."

"And drowned in deep water," I said.

Sadie nodded and rocked in unison, her mind seeming to reside in madness for the moment.

"That man swam around looking for the baby for a while but finally said it was gone, pulled down by the currents. He said he needed his scuba gear to go after it, but it was too late for that." Sadie breathed hard, her chest rattling with pent-up tears. "He made us get out and walk. Said he was going to dump the boat where it couldn't be found."

We sat silent in the steaming room. When Tony clicked off the recorder, we jumped as though it were a gunshot. I looked around the old walls that had been placed there by hands from another era, by people who knew the ways of the swamp and how to ward off creeping death. Like decaying boards, the people couldn't stand it forever. Eventually, the whole natural force caught up with them, rotting them like trampled layers of marsh grass. The silence closed in.

"I'm going around back," I said softly.

A kerosene light flickered in the back room. Outside, it was so dark, I had to grope against the old boards. The steps were at the back, but Vernon wasn't. I moved into the grass a little and whispered his name. He appeared behind me, taking my elbow when I jumped.

"Sh! There's somebody inside that room. I've heard some movement, but no voice."

"If it's Josie, you'd better tell her that Sadie just told us what happened to the baby."

Vernon handed me his flashlight, then pulled out his revolver. "Don't turn that on until I tell you to." He edged toward the back steps.

Pressing each one with his toe before placing his weight on it, he climbed the crude steps and walked slowly across the back porch to the rusted screen door. When he pulled on it, the hinges complained with a distinctive scraping. I followed, even though he waved me back with his free hand.

Standing beside the screen, I saw him turn at the door where the light shined brighter. He pointed the gun, using both hands in the traditional police stance for arresting a dangerous criminal. For a moment there was silence, then a voice spoke.

"Come in, deputy. I ain't got the means to shoot you."

The sisters had run to the end of the earth, which had turned out to be a primitive cabin in the far reaches of Palmetto Swamp. With nowhere left to go, and St. Claire on his own run, they stopped. Josie, sullen and resentful, nevertheless went quietly alongside Sadie. Tony insisted on cuffing the two women.

"Before you go," I said, "tell me what happened to your dogs."

Josie, startled for a moment, tossed her head in the air. "We'd been feeding them strays scraps from the table. Then St. Claire came along and said they was bothering his work crews, scaring his grandbaby. Sent that young man to make us poison them. He said we had to."

"Newsome? He made you poison them?"

Josie looked startled for a moment but said nothing. Her gray hair, white under the flashlight beam, bobbed up and down as she trampled to the muddy shoreline.

"Look," Tony said after a short silence, "there's not much room in Pasquin's boat. Vernon, you and Luanne and Patricia stay here and wait for a sheriff's boat."

"Those idiots will be lost in no time in this river maze," said Vernon.

"Get Pasquin to either come back for us or send one of the river brigade," I said.

Before they moved away from us, Josie suddenly turned to me and said like a venom spitting viper, "Those two fools deserved everything they got!"

"I can't stay here," whined Patricia as she knocked at mosquitoes buzzing around her coiffured hair.

"Okay," said Tony. "Here, take my hand." He helped her down the rickety front steps.

"I don't believe this," I said to Vernon as I watched their light fade on the trail down to the boat. "Tony Amado gave in to a woman with no argument."

"It's hormonal," was his only comment.

When the light finally dimmed to nothing on the trail, Vernon and I turned back to the house. The quiet hung like the night mist over the darkness. Inside, the kerosene lamps still burned, their yellow glow reminding me of lightning bugs. Around us, screech owls sounded alerts, and in the distant waters, frogs took up the alto part. The ever present dampness remained, covering us in itchy sweat.

"Wonder who this place really belongs to," said Vernon as he headed back inside.

"A friend, they said. Wonder where the friend is." I followed him into the living room where the air loomed close and heavy. A couple of mosquitoes had invaded the territory, and in the silence, their buzzing sounded like a distant chainsaw.

"St. Claire wants to develop most of this area," I said. "I wonder how far he's got with the deals."

"Shouldn't be too hard to find out through county records."

"I wonder," I said as I stared into the flickering kerosene lamp, "if he sold a lot of babies."

"Not a pretty thought, is it?" said Vernon as he moved down the shotgun hallway, opening doors as he went. "Not much here except in that back bedroom, the living room, and the kitchen area. You know, we never found any money in the Wilburn account. These sisters seem to have been hard put for a decent place to live."

I went to the kitchen, a room bordering the back porch. Filled with old board shelves, a pump sink, a table and three rickety chairs, it felt like a ghost from the far past. A new kerosene camp stove sat on the floor. "I think the sisters moved themselves in here. There's no sign of anyone else." I spied a few jars on one of the shelves. Taking a whiff of the red jelly, I held it in front of the flashlight. It was transparent, except for tiny particles of what could be grape peels. "Homemade. Think it's got oleander in it?" I smiled, but not for long. Bits of crushed pink flowers might look just like grape skins.

"Bag it," said Vernon. "Here, wrap it in this dish towel."

We ended up wrapping three bottles in the cloth.

I wandered through the rest of the house. One small room, completely bare, adjoined the one where the sisters had a few clothes, a box of papers, and two old iron bedsteads.

"Shouldn't we take that box of papers with us?"

Vernon nodded. I followed him to the back porch. The only thing there was a large plastic garbage bag. "We'd better look,"

283

said Vernon.

A take-out fried chicken bucket sat at the bottom of a clutter of paper plates, bones, and plastic utensils. More paper plates with streaks of fried egg rested atop them. A few empty water bottles and soft drink cans were stuffed around the edges.

"They either had someone get this for them, or they snuck into town themselves," said Vernon. "And look at this." He held up smaller containers. "They even had biscuits and cole slaw."

"And jelly to go on the biscuits," I added. Taking a pen from Vernon's shirt pocket, I lifted the paper plates by the edges. "There are three used plates here. If I had to, I'd guess somebody else ate with them—three at the table for one meal."

"Let's wrap up this stuff and take it with us," said Vernon.

We heard a loud, "Whooowheee!" in the distance.

"Brigade's here," I said and let out an equally loud holler. My voice echoed over the swamp, quiet now as terrified critters maintained silence.

Dragging the trash bag, I trudged behind Vernon to the river. He carried the box of papers under one arm and the wrapped jellies under the other, while focusing the flashlight on the trail.

"You folks got a load there," said Tulia, her red hair flaring like the aurora borealis in the boat light. "Pasquin said to get on down here for you." She and Edwin steadied the boat as we piled on the evidence.

"You know this place?" I asked as Tulia pushed off with an oar.

"I know all the places on this river, yes, ma'am. I was born here, remember?"

"So was I, but I couldn't find all the cabins."

"You went off to college. Got yourself out of the swamp circle. This cabin belonged to an old lady who died about a month ago in the hospital up in Tallahassee. Somebody bought up the cabin and land just about that time, too. Don't like all this selling going on." She shook her head.

By the time we reached my landing, it was after two in the morning. We loaded the contents of the cabin into Vernon's patrol car and headed for the sheriff's office. The city lights seemed a century apart from the dark cabin we had left.

"Good thinking," said Tony as he pushed the bag, box, and jelly jars into a corner of his office. "Now go home and sleep. At ten tomorrow morning, Newsome is going to sing for us. His lawyer has promised to bring him in, and has advised him to come clean. And," he added, "he's still saying he killed no one."

"And if he did, it was because Newsome was abused as a child."

Vernon and I lay exhausted in my bed, our energy spent from a long day with midwives and swamp bugs. The cool air blew across our bodies, sending hints of scented soap into the air.

"Vernon," I said. "Tony blew up at me twice, but he hasn't carried through with his threat to ban me from the office."

Vernon grunted but didn't answer.

"And you don't seem too concerned about it."

"If anybody else had caught us, or if they'd come in during the actual deed," he laughed, "I'd have been concerned."

"But you aren't, and Tony is your supervisor."

Vernon grunted again.

"What do you have on him, Vernon?"

He didn't answer. I turned and began to tickle his side.

"Stop!" He pinned me to the bed and leaned over my face. I could feel his warm breath as he bit my ear. "There are things you don't want to know."

"Yes, I do! I want to know it all."

Vernon pulled away from me and lay back on the bed. "I gave my word, Luanne. Long before I met you. Something happened then, something that wouldn't look too good for Tony." He turned his face to me. "Nothing terribly bad. I mean…" He turned away again. "Only I know about it, and I gave my word. As much as I trust you, I need to keep my promise."

I rested quietly. Visions of Tony doing all sorts of illegal things, even sexy things, danced in my head. "Are there any nude photos or office sex events in Tony's background?"

Vernon grunted again.

"Vernon, do you think those photos are going to surface now that St. Claire will be arrested?"

"Got to find him before we arrest him."

"And the photos have to be found."

I let Vernon drift into sleep. For a long time I thought about my secret questions about my mother and Pasquin, wondering if he could be my biological father. Was I the product of a war-time fling? But it was something I had squelched, ancient history that had no bearing on my life now.

And, I had no right to force a secret from Vernon.

CHAPTER THIRTY-FOUR

"I'm telling you, I never shot nobody!" Arnold rose off the chair before his lawyer pulled him back down and whispered in his ear.

"Until you tell us the truth, Mr. Newsome," said Tony, "we plan to charge you with shooting Charlene Brennan. We've got the tire tracks, your motorcycle, and some men who said only you rode it."

"Well, that could be a lie, now couldn't it?" His face reddened as he tried to stare down Tony. "Somebody else could have ridden it."

"Did they?" Tony's black eyes revealed nothing as he returned the man's stare.

Newsome couldn't keep up the threat.

"Okay," he sighed and leaned back in the chair. "I rode after the woman that day, but I didn't shoot her. I got behind her on the road from the camp and then on the paved road. She tried to outrun me, but her big car couldn't maneuver like the bike. About the time she got to the sink turn-off, the weather broke loose. Wind and rain hit me in the face. Then the lightning started. Scared the shit out of me. I ran the bike off the rode and nearly fell over. By the time I looked up, her car was bouncing down that road to the sink." He picked up a ballpoint pen and wound it between his fingers. His lawyer pulled it away. "I didn't even know she'd been shot until I heard the news."

"Mr. Newsome," he said, "why were you running after Miss Brennan in the first place?"

"You know that." He lifted his head and looked toward the mirror as though he knew I watched him.

"Answer him," said the lawyer.

"That woman had been doing St. Claire's dirty work. You know, drumming up sales of swamp property for him. Then she got wind of how he was raising the money. He said she got a conscience all of a sudden. Something about adoptions and stuff. She threatened to go to the county board about it. He said she couldn't be trusted anymore, that she'd break up the whole militia unit out there."

"Militia unit?"

"Yeah, the guys who camp there on the weekends."

"The ones who play little boy war games?" Loman said.

Newsome glared at the sleepy-eyed man.

"They weren't games."

"Especially when they involved real bullets," Tony said.

Newsome squirmed. "I told you. I never shot anybody."

"But you would have, wouldn't you? If St. Claire had commanded you to, paid you for your services."

Newsome's face winced. He looked as though he'd cry.

"Did St. Claire ask you, that day, to chase Miss Brennan down the road?"

"He left before she came by looking for him. When he didn't show, she got touchy and said to tell him she'd see him in court. I figured that was my cue. I tailed her."

"Tell me, Arnold," Loman said, "what would you have done if you had caught her?"

Newsome's forehead twisted. He blinked his eyes a few times and remained silent.

"You have no idea, do you? Chase her into a sinkhole, beat her up, shoot her with your shotgun? My guess is, Mr. Newsome, the woman would have outsmarted you in a minute. She knew the terrain. You didn't. It was still a little boy game to you, wasn't it?" Loman's face grew serious. He stared at Newsome.

"Other people had guns besides me." Newsome gulped like a child standing before the principal.

Newsome's lawyer stopped the conversation. Tony changed the subject, leading him to the birth scene, then on to chasing me through the swamp. Each time, he said he had been ordered—and paid—by St. Claire. He refused to confess to killing anyone.

Outside, after Newsome shuffled back to his cell, Tony spoke to Vernon and me. "He's probably right. Marshall said the bullet came from a side angle. Unless he pulled alongside her and aimed into the passenger window, he couldn't have shot her. From the skid marks, it seems he never got that far."

"Then someone was standing in the trees beside the road." I shuddered. I had walked into those trees alone.

"We've got crime scene techs out there now. By this time, the bullet casing may be gone, but we're looking anyway."

"Any word on St. Claire?" I said.

"None. Loman contacted the cops in Atlanta. Mrs. St. Claire has no idea where her husband—soon to be ex—is and doesn't want to know. Talk about the breakup of royalty."

I envisioned a figure hiding in the palmettos at the side of the road. He would have known Charlene's expensive car. If he'd had a gun—and what self-respecting militia man didn't—he could have hit her from a few yards away.

"Tony, does St. Claire have a gun?"

"Probably lots of them."

They say that when the frog grows quiet, his heart beats faster than normal, that he knows danger lurks and prepares to hide or jump in a flash. I lay on my bed like a swamp frog. Silence smothered me, and I couldn't sleep. I wanted to leap somewhere safe. My heart pounded.

I stared up at my neatly painted ceiling. Outside, the heat pump ran its engine to cool the house. I turned and sat up Buddha-like on the bed. Leaning over, I lifted the edge of the curtain and peered onto my back yard—or what served as one. The house backed up against thick swamp. A few steps of wild grass gave way to oaks, pines, and the underbrush that could hide the thousands of creatures who preyed upon each other on the food chain. Sometime, years ago, my father had planted three oleander bushes to make the place look more civilized. Untended like those at the Wilburn house, they grew out of control and, except for the bouncing pink flowers, blended in with the swamp foliage. Their light green spear-like leaves moved softly in the breeze that indicated an approaching afternoon rain.

Oleander in great bunches had caused problems in areas where fires broke out. Firefighters had to wear masks to keep from breathing the lethal fumes. A careless twig broken off for a green camper's toothpick would be fatal. A few crushed flower petals in grape jelly would leave a human helpless, and dead, in a short time.

They deserved what they got.

I let the curtain drop back over the window. Picking up the phone, I dialed Marshall Long's office.

"We just got the bottles, Luanne. How do I know what's in

290

them?"

"Can you see if all three have been opened?"

"Just hold on," he said, then yelled through the receiver, "you owe me for this. I'm up to my belly button in tissue stuff here."

"I'll buy you an oyster dinner at Panacea," I said.

After several moments of silence, he came back on the line. "Looks to me like they are all home canned, and two jars haven't been opened. One has been and some jelly has been taken out of it. Is that all you want to know?"

"No chance you could fish around in there while on the phone?"

"Not hardly, but just on first sight and smell, I'd say it's made from scuppernong grapes. Darkish red stuff."

"If somebody mashed up oleander flowers in it, you wouldn't notice?"

"Not without the microscope and tests. Taste might tell, but then you'd be in no position to report it, would you?"

"Call me when you know, okay?"

"Call me when you're ready to hit Panacea, okay?"

I couldn't wait for the tedious forensic tests. I called Pasquin. "Meet me at the landing."

"In the boat?"

"Of course, in the boat. Did you think I wanted you to swim?"

"Well, I have walked through the swamp a time or two."

Pulling on boots that reached my knees, I dialed the sheriff's office and told the switchboard where I was headed. Tugging a long-sleeved tee shirt over my head, I reached into the bed table drawer and pulled out my pistol. It would rest in my bag along with the cell phone. Almost as a second thought, I stashed the camera in there, too.

By the time I reached the landing, a few feet across the road, I felt the sweat in back of my knees dripping down my calves. In the distance, I heard Pasquin's slow motor approaching.

"Don't think you ought to go back to that place all by yourself," he said.

"I'm not. I've got you with me."

"I'm just the boat man, ma'am. Can't do much saving if you get into trouble."

"All the troublemakers, except one, are in custody, and I have a hunch that one is in no condition to harm me."

I sat at the front of the boat where the breezes would rush my face as Pasquin guided from the rear. We passed fishermen in straw hats, sleeping more than fishing. On the shores, gators took advantage of the last rays of sun before the clouds built up to drench the already soaked air. In the distance, thunder rumbled.

"Now don't go telling me to turn back just because of a little thunder," said Pasquin.

"Just get us to that cabin before lightning starts, okay?"

We pulled into the deep river lane and found the muddy ramp just as black clouds threatened to split open their bowels to the earth.

"You better tie up and come inside," I said.

We trudged up the embankment, then under the oaks, and finally to the porch where Josie and Sadie had sought temporary solace. A jolt of lightning slammed across the sky. At the same time, torrents of rain poured through the pock-holed porch roof.

"Damn! This ain't no place for keeping dry," said Pasquin.

"The rain cleans all the floors, even inside." I stepped into the living room where drops began to fall on two spots in a corner. Walking down the hall, the same thing happened, and in the small empty room, a near gusher swept one wall.

The leaks in the kitchen were over the pump sink. Otherwise, the room was dry. I knelt and ran my hand over the wooden slats.

"What are you looking for?"

"A damp spot or where it was damp recently."

"Ma'am, that could be anywhere in this house."

"More like a scrubbed place. Like this," I said as I bent over a space that appeared clean, like bleach had been recently used on the boards.

"It's on the table, too," said Pasquin as he ran his hand over the end and down one leg, then smelled his fingers. "How do you suppose that happened?"

I sat back on the floor. "Pasquin, if you ate oleander accidentally, what would be the first thing that happened to you?"

"Well, I know the last thing would be death, and not in too much time, either."

"Yeah, but what would be the first thing?"

"Bad stomachache. Puking all over the place, I suppose."

"And somebody would have to clean that up—after you died, right?"

He scratched his face and fanned himself with his straw hat. The rain nearly drowned out his voice. "Wouldn't want vomit hanging around in this weather. Smell would get to you in no time."

I smiled. "Let's sit here and enjoy the rain. It will be over shortly."

The cabin produced a profound humidity in the rain storm. My long-sleeved shirt clung to my skin.

"Why do you wear that thing?" said Pasquin as he pinched some damp cloth between two fingers.

"Mosquitoes, I've had enough of them. And these," I held up a booted foot, "are for snakes."

"You don't need them on the trail."

"I don't plan to walk on a trail." I pulled the pistol from my leather bag and placed it on the table beside me.

"Young lady, did you bring me in harm's way?" Pasquin donned his straw hat and placed both hands firmly on his hips.

"You'll be fine right here. Just wait for me."

The rain slacked off, then let up altogether. The inevitable swamp mist hovered for as far as I could see out the back of the cabin. I walked a few paces across some mud and stepped into waist-high marsh grass. My boot immediately sank a half-inch into the soaked earth.

"You be careful out there. Water lane curves around back here. Gators sunbathing all over the place," said Pasquin. He had dragged one of the kitchen chairs to the porch where he fanned himself with his hat. "I'll be right here when you get back."

"There's a cell phone in my bag. Use it if you need to." I didn't want to say if I didn't come back. I had walked through grass like this hundreds of times and lived to over forty.

I stood still, circled my gaze around my feet, and looked for trampled grass, a muddy place where people could have passed through a few nights before. The rain had pelted the area. The grass bent over in at least four places. In one, the grass not only bent over, it was broken. I placed my feet there and walked. Listening for rattles and the swoosh of a gator tail, I moved slowly, keeping my eyes on the path. Once, I smelled something dead, only to find an armadillo, his bloated belly armor bursting from death gasses. I stopped when I saw the thick hide of a gator slide into the water just beyond the reeds.

Further down the trail, I stretched my neck and focused on

the sky. That's when I saw them—buzzards, two black vultures circling the air a few yards ahead. I headed in their direction.

The putrid sweet smell hit me with a vengeance, and I raised one arm across my nose. A pair of magnificent brown-black wings took off suddenly, stirring the air directly in front of me, as a frightened buzzard joined his buddies in the sky. I stood at the water edge where green lily pads floated, their flat tops bobbing like rafts in the gentle wash of the river lane.

Pasquin said gators liked the spot, but they didn't like this offering. It was half out of the water. What the birds hadn't eaten from the face, the humidity took away. Both hands were nearly skeletal. From waist down, he moved in rhythm with the river wash. No one would ever identify the features on this corpse. But vultures didn't take the hair. The full dark strands with graying temples lay in the mud, the top part shampooed in the recent rain. All that was left of August St. Claire's seductive good looks was his good hair.

CHAPTER THIRTY-FIVE

"You and Josie fed him jelly laced with oleander, didn't you?" I stood before Sadie Wilburn.

"No, not me," said Sadie, her head turned downward. "Josie said the man never paid us for the land like he promised. We nearly starved. Had to stay in old run-down places. He kept saying we lost the money when we lost the baby. He met us at the cabin to talk about a new deal, one where he'd have the money in a few days. Josie said she didn't believe him." Sadie lifted her head, her eyes glaring. "Then she fed him chicken and biscuits—with jelly."

"How did he get outside?"

"He had convulsions in the kitchen, but he died pretty quick after that—on the trail outside, I think."

"You got him to walk outside?"

"We dragged him most of the way. He was near gone by that time. We tried to get him into the river, but we got tired. We rolled him down to where a gator basked in the sun. I didn't look after that, but I heard the gator grunt. I ran back inside. When Josie came, she was laughing. Said that old gator would have vittles for a week."

"Dear God," I said and left the room.

"We found a casing," said Vernon as he came toward me.

"Looks like the shooter was standing across the road where you thought."

"St. Claire?"

"You're one smart cookie." Vernon squeezed my chin between his fingers. "We probably can't prove it, but one of the campers said August went walking through the swamp on that side of the road that day, even in the storm. He said he wanted to buy up that lot, too. Funny thing is, that land is owned by the state. Nobody is ever going to buy it."

I stared up at the man who could send thrills up my spine with a boyish grin. "August? You're on a first name basis now?"

He shrugged. "Dead men got no class, lady."

Two weeks later, the papers blew the case out into collective public curiosity. Mrs. St. Claire, who must have hoped for a quiet, tasteful divorce, ended up in front of the cameras at her husband's private, closed-casket funeral, then again as she ordered moving vans around her driveway. Josie would be charged with murder, with Sadie as a reluctant witness. Newsome got slapped with assault and a few other felonies, not to mention what the feds had waiting in the wings for him. He may have hated the government, but he would be a guest in its house for a long time. In spite of all his bravado, he managed to never kill anyone. Like Vernon said, "the man had the intent but lacked the talent."

"Why aren't you out with Miss Patricia?" I asked Tony. "And what's all this?" I surveyed the cluttered desk, files in chairs, and evidence strewed around the floor, more like the old Tony.

"I got tired of tidiness, I guess. I'm working late. Get Vernon and get out of here."

Ascending the deep cool spring water, I felt the currents cascade over my skin. I burst through the surface and rested my arms on the wooden landing. From where I basked in the Palmetto River, I could see part of my front porch. It shined in the sunny swamp, my sanctuary from creatures of prey. Peace crept into my soul. Theresa's little baby had been avenged, and the swamp freed from encroaching carpet baggers who would turn it into a plastic wonderland, ever on the verge of dying with no hope of rebirth. "Not this year," I whispered to a minnow that swam around a rusted nail.

The umbilical had matched Theresa's DNA. The baby had to be floating around the watery bowels of a north Florida cave. We'd never find it, couldn't even get into that system right now. In no time, the underground currents had made a new opening. It was too small to squeeze through. Besides the walls were still brittle, likely to come down with a slight shove.   Something in the water direction had been changed in the explosion. Near shore, bubbles popped up on schedule. Tulia started the rumor that it was the baby's gurgles. She said at night around there, you could hear little cries in the palmetto bushes, like a baby crying for its mama. Already the legend had spread through the river brigade. Baby Cave, they dubbed it, was haunted. And it haunted my sleep on nights when Vernon wasn't in my bed. If I had only chased the sisters and managed to save the baby. As it happened, both mother and baby died.

I heard a car motor pull in front of the house. Someone beeped a horn. I pulled myself out of the water and walked to the drive. Kendall rested against his veterinary wagon. He smiled.

"Looks like Pukey knows where home is." He nodded toward the porch steps. On the top, the light brown dog, his coat filled in and shiny, sat with his tongue hanging out in a smile. His tail slowly wagged, then picked up speed as I came round to stand in front of him.

This was a swamp survivor, I thought. He'd had sense enough not to eat the poison and outlived his fellow dogs. It was that sense that made all the difference in the world.

"Pukey isn't such a good name," I said. "Let's try Plato."

The next day Harry's Volkswagen pulled into my yard. He sat on the passenger side, and a familiar face grinned at me from the driver's seat.

"I think you know Nick Summers," said Harry. "He's a pretty good river man, and a diver. He's going to help out at the dive camp."

Nick grinned at me, shoving his tee shirt sleeve over his shoulder as he gripped the wheel. He jerked his eyes back and forth from me to his rippling muscle where a fresh tattoo of a mermaid danced in jerks. *LuLu* was written just below the fish tail.

"You two know each other, right?" asked Harry after a long silence.

I nodded. "We'll talk, Harry. Later."

I rocked in the darkness on my front porch, allowing the night humidity to shower me in sweat. The steady click-clack of the chair reflected my irritation. This stupid, muscle-bound kid had found a way to stay around, and I was going to have to fend him off or quit the entire diving job. I squeezed my eyes shut and imagined a steady teaching schedule in the fall semester. About to swear aloud, I heard a rap at the screen door.

"You got time to talk to two old men?" said Pasquin. "Maybe even serve us a little tea?"

I opened the door, happy to be distracted from the Nick Summers dilemma.

"You remember Edwin." said Pasquin, pointing to the little man who peeked at me with a lowered face.

"Do you want to sit out here or in the living room?" I asked.

Pasquin and Edwin sat in rockers on the porch while I poured leftover iced tea and cut some pound cake. They would sip and eat in the semi-darkness, opting for their fellow swamp creatures over the dry, cool absence of life inside the house.

"Edwin's got something to give you," said Pasquin as he took a bite of the cake wedge. He nodded to his friend.

Edwin shoved thick fingers through his stand-up hair. He reached into a large pocket of his fisherman's pants and pulled out a white packet.

"Sorry," he said so softly I hardly heard him.

I opened the cardboard package. Spilling the contents onto the small table, I found three photos and an envelope of negatives. If I hadn't recognized the porch, I wouldn't have been able to tell who owned the two bodies of bare naked flesh.

"Edwin got a little out of order with his brigade duties," said Pasquin. "Didn't realize this was where you lived until later." The old man chuckled low in his throat. "Got you bare butt naked, ma'am."

The swamp creatures followed Pasquin's lead and turned up the volume on their chirps and grunts. From deep inside, I felt a laugh grow, and soon all three of us roared into the night. Edwin placed both hands atop his stand-up hair and squirmed around in chattering hee-haws. Pasquin's lined face bunched up and poured sweat until he had to use his hat and fan away at his laughter.

"And all the while I thought dirty-minded deputies were playing darts with these!" I held my middle as the belly laugh ached. In the darkness, I hoped the sound would reach all the way to Baby Cave, that Theresa's little boy would gurgle a little louder tonight.

Acknowledgements:
Many thanks to Ken McDonald and Larry Clark for diving,
law enforcement, and all round swamp survival advice,
and to Dianne for starting the midwife debate.

Other Memento Mori Mysteries

The first Luanne Fogarty mystery by Glynn Marsh Alam
DIVE DEEP and DEADLY

Matty Madrid mysteries by P.J. Grady
MAXIMUM INSECURITY
DEADLY SIN

A Dr. Rebecca Temple mystery by Sylvia Maultash Warsh
TO DIE IN SPRING

AN UNCERTAIN CURRENCY
Clyde Lynwood Sawyer, Jr.
Frances Witlin